Kenrickey
Book 3 of the
Luna Chronicle

by

S. C. Dane

Published by
Melange Books, LLC
White Bear Lake, MN 55110
www.melange-books.com

Cover Art by Caroline Andrus

Kenrickey
S. C. Dane

In the northern Maine woods, a wolf pack unlike any other reigns the landscape. With the ability to shift into human shape, they are the supreme rulers of their territory. Until the real humans threaten their secret realm…

Ken Rickey is one of those humans. Until he's entrusted with the secret of the wolf-people, an honor he'll do anything to uphold. For among the wolf-people, Ken has found loyal friends in Armand and Eaen, two of the younger wolves in Luna's pack who share his sense of adventure. Welcoming them to his human world and keeping them safe isn't going to be easy, especially when there are those who suspect the truth.
An intuitive woman, **Naomi Foss** is quick to unearth the mystery of Ken's two friends. Human they may seem, but there is a wildness about them which is fast consuming Ken, altering him in extraordinary ways. But the acceptance of Naomi plunges Ken and his wolf friends into dangerous territory, where the exposure of Luna's pack becomes a lethal reality. Can these young lovers and friends stand against the threat while keeping their secret from those who hunt them?

A tribute to my small pack of women,
who are giants of wisdom.
I am little without you.

Chapter One

I lay on the cool ground, peering out from between the balmy arms that embraced me, and didn't dare move a single hair on my body. Not that I was in any kind of hurry to relocate. I mean, how often does a guy get cuddled by a wolf-woman? I sure as hell wasn't going to disturb her, and I sure as hell wasn't about to piss her off. Or piss off her mate, for that matter. Who, by the way, was curled up on the forest floor with us.

I'd already seen what that wolf-guy was capable of, and if he wanted to, he really could snap my neck like a twig. On his own, he had killed three mature wolves with his bare hands, or paws, whatever. He looked all innocent sleeping beside us, but when he had attacked those wolves to protect his mate and me, *Christ,* he really could tear someone's head off to shit down their neck.

So, I was not going to disturb them, and was going to stay snuggled in until *they* stirred. The sun hadn't peeked up over the trees yet. It was still pretty dark out, but I could tell it was morning because I could see the tops of the trees against the lightening sky. And if it wasn't for the heat that she-wolf radiated out of her as if she was some kind of portable oven, I'd be freezing my balls off, because it's always coldest before the dawn, or something like that.

Our cozy little nest got even cozier because Grane, as if aware I was awake, unfolded himself from his wolf form and sat up as a human being. No shit. My head felt like it would pop off my shoulders whenever I witnessed the miracle of it. I mean, bodies were *shifting* in front of me. Crumpling, and growing hair, and tails and ears and *teeth.* Holy Lord, but these wolf-people had big freakin' teeth. Sharp, strong and long. The wolf, who was now a man, rolled onto his side to muzzle

1

his face into his mate's neck.

When I say muzzle, that's exactly what I mean. That wolf-man might have looked human, but he definitely wasn't. He exuded wild animal. Predator wild animal, too, not some little bunny rabbit that goes hopping through the forest. But pure he-could-turn-me-into-carrion kind of predator.

His mate pulled her arms from around me to reposition herself right into his waiting embrace, as if he was the safest place on earth. Instantly, the cold morning air wrapped around my naked body to chill it. I sat up, hugging myself to keep warm.

Grane pierced me with those hypnotic yellow eyes of his, and I plastered myself to the forest floor, then sure as hell made sure I stared off into the forest. *No direct eye contact.*

"Good morning, Porcupine," he whispered gruffly.

I swallowed, then cleared my throat before I answered him. Christ, he was un-nerving, and I tried like hell to always remember to move freakin' slow and keep my head low. And absolutely not disrespect his mate, Suma.

"Morning, Grane." My chest tightened as the memory of his attack on me the night before rushed back like a hundred horses trampling me. He had not physically harmed me, just scared the literal piss out of me again. Good Lord, he could strip me down to a blathering two year old in a nanosecond.

"I am truly sorry I scared you so badly yesterday."

But then he could restore my ego by gobbling a healthy dose of humble pie.

He was beyond remarkable.

I was with wolf-people for jumped-up-criminy's-sake, beings that could morph from human to wolf, or wolf to human, and they were letting me hang out with them as if they liked me. My heart thumped so hard in my chest I had to gulp for air with the sheer miracle of it.

And the thing is, I liked them right back. In spite of the fact that just being around them kept me teetering on the lip of sanity, I was drawn to them. Yeah, they were living marvels of nature, but my attraction went beyond that. These wolf-people were nice. Suma had cradled me all night long as if I was a baby, for God's sake. She even sang me a lullaby to comfort me after Grane had caused me to piss my pants. Well, I didn't technically piss my pants the night before because I wasn't wearing any. I was as naked as they were, which by the way, I had done to comfort them. Nuts, huh?

But I'm rambling in my head and Grane definitely doesn't like babbling. What was it he was saying? Oh right. He'd apologized for scaring the crap out of me. I ran my hand through my hair and took a wicked deep breath before I answered him.

"It's okay. I mean, you had to know if I was telling the truth or not, right? I mean, I see where you guys—" I clamped my jaw shut because those freakin' yellow eyes *leveled*. I was rambling.

The white haired wolf-woman turned in her mate's arms so that they were both facing me. She smiled softly, and man, she was gorgeous looking all dreamy like that. She had these deep brown eyes that reminded me of puddles that hadn't been disturbed. There were layers in her irises that just stilled me.

A low, nearly imperceptible rumble rubbed across my skin, and the hair on my entire body prickled. I averted my eyes to the tree line again and felt the blood rush to my head. Grane had caught me staring at his mate.

"Holy, I'm sorry."

He didn't say anything more because he didn't have to. These wolf-people communicated like nothing I'd ever seen before, except in the nature programs I grew up watching as a kid. There was no mistaking what their intentions were, and my body reacted. Instinctively.

Suma's giggle trilled like little birds and I nearly looked straight at her again because of it. I remembered at the last second to lower my eyes. "Grane, the human is fine," she sang.

Her mate lowered his dark, gray head when she admonished him. Loving hell, the guy had scars covering his body like tattoos, yet he yielded to the woman in his arms as if she had all the power. Like I said, Grane was beyond remarkable.

"Kenrickey, you slept all right?" Suma's lovely voice warbled again as she directed her question at me.

"Yes," I practically stammered, the wolf-man's yellow eyes boring into me no distant memory. "I slept great, thanks." I nodded, and kept

3

my eyes focused on the ground. By this time, I didn't think that either one would hurt me much, or kill me, even. But I sure as hell didn't want to upset them. I was not exaggerating in any way when I said they had *teeth.*

My two bunkmates rose together, and like some kind of synchronized dance they stiffened and turned their faces away from the rising sun. Suma hopped up and down on her toes, and Grane's muscular body tensed and vibrated. They both thrust their noses into the air to assess their surroundings.

My goosebumps crawled back with a vengeance. They smelled something, or heard something coming, and if it was more of those wolves like Grane had fought and killed, then *holy fuck.* I didn't get up, but I definitely got my feet under me.

Suddenly, Suma dashed toward the tree line, and I couldn't get my mouth closed before I gasped. The gray wolf-man turned to me and grinned.

"It is our pack leaders, Kenrickey. Stay low," he advised. I dropped my back to the earth as if it sucked me there, and I sure as hell did not ask him to repeat his command. Around these guys, you didn't act like some stupid human being who asked questions for the sake of conversation.

But I did look to where my new friends were focusing their attention. A red wolf and a brown one glided out of the trees to the west of us. *Sweet Jesus.* These two were not the ones I'd met a couple of nights before. Aside from the obvious difference in physicality, there was no fun and loose skinned jocularity in this pair. These two wolves were lethal. And the brown one, the big one, was focusing his attention on our little group.

I swallowed the bile in my throat before it spewed into my mouth, because his golden eyes ate a hole in me. Freakin' right I was taking my protector's advice. I shoved my back into that cold dirt just so I could make myself invisible.

The gray wolf-man jogged toward the newcomers, too, and I stole a peek from under my lowered lids to watch how Suma and Grane greeted them. In spite of having human bodies, they dropped to their hands and knees and pressed their faces under the chins of their pack leaders. The

4

battle-scarred wolf-man peeled his shoulders back and exposed his entire stomach, chest, and neck so that he was completely vulnerable to both wolves.

The red and brown wolves' tails swung in circles like the blades of a helicopter as they sniffed Grane and Suma all over, and then the four of them rubbed their bodies together as if they were reclaiming their closeness.

Incredible. I was watching a reunion of creatures who loved each other and were glad they were reunited. There was no doubt in my mind about that.

Grane smiled as if he sat on the front porch of heaven.

That lasted for about a second because that big-ass brown wolf refocused his attention back onto me. His massive, furry body stiffened as his lips curled away from his long, sharp fangs.

Ho-ly. Shit.

I barely heard Grane introduce me through the pounding of my heart in my head, and my thoughts vanished in my panic. I tried my ass off not to even breathe, but I was gasping, and I clutched my genitals and squished my eyes shut. Dear God, I could hear the brown wolf getting closer. His snarling alerted every single strand of hair on my body and they stood to attention like a squadron of nervous little soldiers. He was going to kill me, and it was going to hurt.

A mewl squeezed past my constricted throat. I couldn't help it. Then a woman yelped, so help me God, she *yelped* the name Alec. My attacker bounced against his rigid front legs and stopped dead in his tracks. I know because his hot freakin' breath huffed across my bare, sweating body, he was *that* close.

"Alec, he will not harm you," stressed a woman's voice I had never heard before. I slid an eyeball in the direction of that voice, and watched a pair of naked legs stride to the side of the brown wolf. They bent, and a red-headed siren knelt down beside him and draped her arm over his back then buried her face into his thick coat. The wolf-woman was beautiful. And hot—in the sense that heat blasted from around her in waves.

"Brown wolf, he has submitted," she purred.

Oh yeah, I had submitted all right. To the fact I was going to die a gruesome death.

"Grane would not have let him live if he could harm us," she whispered without lifting her face from that sleek fur.

My would-be killer turned his wide head toward the scarred wolf-man, who had not budged from the spot where the reunion had taken place. My thoughts steamrolled back into my brain. Grane was a subordinate to the brown wolf and couldn't interfere to save my life. I was at the mercy of his pack leaders—the brown wolf and this red-headed wonder.

Ah fuck. Please oh please let this woman talk some sense into him.

I crushed my back further into the dirt of the forest floor, pulled my shaking hands from my genitals, and splayed my entire body for the brown wolf to do as he would. It was the only hope I had of surviving this encounter.

Suma's voice warbled from behind the pack leaders. "Brother, the human helped us with great risk to his future. He deserves our mercy."

A snarl curled from the deep chest of the brown wolf, but the woman who held him whispered steadily. "We will need this one, Husband," she breathed, again without lifting her face from his flank.

The brown wolf whined.

Frustration? Was it possible he might decide to let me live? I panted with the sudden rush of the possibility, but absolutely did not move any other muscles. He could still kill me, and I was not about to offer him a single reason to do so. Christ, just my being here was reason enough for him.

Finally, Grane came near and spoke on my behalf, but not before he squatted with his head hung low between his muscled shoulders. "He freed me, Alec. I had been collared, and he freed me." The wolf-man's voice thickened with shame as he explained.

"I'm so sorry, Grane," I squeaked before I even realized it. I'd had no idea I'd tranquilized and collared a wolf-man, let alone one as noble as Grane, and my stomach shriveled in sympathy for him. I was learning pretty quick just how amazing he was. I mean, after what I had witnessed, he could probably physically dominate his pack leader, yet he didn't. The gray wolf showed only love and affection for his pack. It was a fucking wonder he hadn't killed me himself given what we'd done to him. I felt like a piece of crap, yet here was this awesome guy acting like he was to be blamed for something.

The red-head was quick to rebuff him, thank God. "Gray wolf," she corrected as she slipped away from her mate. "Give me your hand."

Grane's eyes watered as he breathed, *"Luna."*

What power did this woman have that could make Grane shiver like that?

Her voice flowed like cream. "Give me your hand, gray wolf," she repeated as she knelt down in front of him. That muscle-ripped man trembled like a puppy, but he placed his long hand in hers as if he trusted her with every inch of his scarred skin.

"I see, mate of my sister," she murmured, "and our pack will benefit from your great sacrifice. My heart glows in your wisdom, and we anxiously await the gift of your offspring, the gift of your blood with ours."

Grane snapped his head up to look at the wolf-woman before him, and she smiled like an angel. I couldn't take my own eyes from her, until the brown wolf's warning growl sent my attention scurrying back to the tree line. But I had seen the look on Grane's face, too, and his tears of gratitude spilled unchecked.

I stole another glance. I couldn't help it, especially since the brown wolf left his post beside me to join his mate and Grane, and then Suma completed the group. They knotted and hugged and kissed and no one wasn't crying. Hell, even I started to.

When they finished celebrating the gift of a union, and a new life growing in Suma's taut belly, they turned their attention back to me. I remembered everything about subordinate displays, and lay back down with my face and throat exposed to the brightening sky. The sun was now over the tips of the trees, and the heat from it caressed my goose-flesh. Hope swelled in my heart in spite of the danger I was in.

The woman Grane had called Luna approached, straddled me, and curled her long fingers around my throat in one graceful motion. Fire girdled my waist and throat, and I struggled to keep my eyes focused away from her even as her clutch shut off my wind.

"Brown wolf, *try,"* she coaxed with a voice that reminded me of ancient trees.

Try *what?* I squirmed, but waited only seconds before I found out. The pack leader minced closer with his head lowered menacingly, and a growl wormed through the physical barrier of my skin. Then the wolf yawned, exposing his lethal teeth all the way to his bone crushing molars. He spread his four iron legs and shook his gargantuan frame as if he'd been swimming. Then with a roar, he ignited into a bonfire while, *so help me Jesus,* those furred legs stretched and bared into human limbs. He lasered his golden eyes on me and glared with the human face that was Death. The fringes of my world blackened and blurred as I lost consciousness.

My eyes opened right up on the red-headed woman, who was kneeling in the grass with her human-shaped mate wrapped around her back. Jesus, even in his human form he was threatening, intense. I snapped my eyes to the ground like a good puppy.

"Kenrickey, sit up."

Negative, Ghost Rider. If I moved wrong, or looked in the wrong spot, I was going to die in an unpleasant way. I shook my head.

"Porcupine." Grane's smile warmed his voice, settling my nerves. A little. "Sit up."

Suma's lilt came from directly behind her mate, only higher up. "Kenrickey, it is all right. Alec will not harm you. Please, join us."

I slowly lifted my chin with her reassurances caressing my nerve endings, while the four wolf-people waited patiently for me to scrape up a little courage.

A voice I hadn't heard before spoke. "You are right, Grane. He is..." He trailed the final word as a deep growl I knew in my blood. "...an odd human."

The brown wolf. Who hadn't offered to take my skin and check it. Okay, so maybe Grane and Suma were telling the truth about my safety. I rolled onto my side, and unfurled my torso into an upright position, as if I was a plant in a time-release video. Then I dared to look up at the foursome.

Grane smiled reassuringly.

"Porcupine, these are our pack leaders Beth and Alec."

He was introducing me? What the hell was I supposed to do now, get on all fours, and rub all over them? Lick their chins? My hand wended itself through my hair, and a gruff laugh reverberated in the morning air.

"You were right about that, too, Brother. He *is* a porcupine."

Giggles bubbled forth, and I couldn't help myself. I grinned, too, even though I was surely the butt of their joke. Laughter was good, and as long as my death still lurked in the perimeter, these four could chuckle *and* point if they wanted.

"Kenrickey?"

I turned my attention to the female pack leader and bowed my head.

"Is your name Ken, with your last name being Rickey?" she prodded gently.

My head bobbed in the affirmative.

Her soft smile was a gift of the angels. "You came with the biologists? To track wolves?"

I didn't pick up the danger of her questions. "Yeah, back at school we'd heard rumors, and one of my professors wanted to check it out. He was pretty excited about it. I mean, no one has seen wolves in this state for years."

As soon as the words streamed out of my mouth, I knew I had effed up. Big time. The sun was suddenly blocked out by a looming shadow, but the heat intensified as if I was only feet from its burning orb. *Sweet Jesus.* The guy was too tall, too muscular, and too damned rigid to do anything nice.

I fell back to the ground and willed my body not to curl up into the fetal position.

The pack leader's voice breathed across my skin.

"They have not been sighted, *human,*" he snarled, "because your kind has wiped them from the earth."

As I was about to be.

My head nodded in agreement. "Yeah," I squeaked. I wasn't exactly the personification of bravery here. "It's bad, I know, and I'm wicked sorry, but we're trying to fix that so that woo-o..." I swallowed past the thickening of my throat, and licked my frozen lips. "...so that wolves can come back. I mean, *you're* here already, but—" I clamped my mouth shut because I was being the Rambling Man again.

"Ken, we have been spotted?" Anxiety pitched the tone of Beth's

S. C. Dane

question.

I didn't know what to say. This was definitely shaky ground here, and pardon me if I didn't want to end up scattered across it.

"Kenrickey, our pack leader asks you a question."

I shot a withered stare at Grane, who was trying to navigate me through this. Which was, surprisingly, a bit encouraging. I actually dared to look toward the woman who had asked the question.

"Yeah, sort of. Not really, I guess. Some guy thought he had a wolf, but by the time we checked it out, it had escaped or something. And then there was the one they thought they'd found on the coast, but the State couldn't get anything conclusive on that one."

Three wolf-people exchanged worried glances, and it was Grane's turn to be out of the loop. Not exactly a comforting development.

"What is it, Luna?" Concern dripped from his voice.

The pack leader ignored his question. "Was there any evidence to back up these claims?" She pressed her body tight against her mate, and then my ears started *buzzing*.

Alec, her mate, coiled his long hands around the woman's elbows so tight his knuckles turned white, and he burrowed his face into her nape. He was whispering, cooing into her long, red hair, and I swear to all that's holy her irises roiled like the ocean at Thunder Gulch. And then they stilled. Flattened, leveled off, and her mate's knuckles resumed a healthy pink. Plus, the buzzing stopped and my head suddenly felt its absence, like the pressure of a vacuum.

"…anything out?"

I turned my head toward the sound. "Huh?"

"Did you and your teachers ever find anything out?" Grane bristled toward me, and I blurted out *No* before he could body-check me as he had the night before.

"No," I repeated, anxiously searching the faces around me. "No, we didn't. They were just rumors, and the guy who'd bragged about having a wolf didn't really have much to offer. He only blabbered about werewo—ooolves…" I shut my eyes and rolled them into my skull. *"Aaahh shit."*

A sizzle crackled in my head until it weighed like a cast-iron skillet. I shot a quick glance at the redhead again to witness the breaking of an ocean in a hurricane. I slapped my hands to my ears and dropped as the buzz in my head zipped down my spine, jellying everything from my waist down. Pissing myself again was but a vague notion that shriveled in my crippled brain.

A bee droned lazily around my head, and I swatted at it once I'd pinpointed its location by listening for it. It dipped and bobbed away, and I cracked an eyelid to watch its departure. But saw four curious faces peering down at me instead.

"That was interesting," remarked the tall guy, who still held his mate in his long hands. His face was lit up with an impressed grin, but his mate didn't look quite so fascinated. In fact, she looked rather alarmed, and blinked as if to snap the lid back onto something that had gotten loose.

"Luna," Grane whispered with adoration.

Suma just stared, and looked as though her thoughts were speeding down the Autobahn.

"I didn't—What the *hell* was that?" Beth's shaking voice ran a lasso around our little group, and the four wolf-people stepped in to fill the spaces between them.

"Luna-Beth, you are amazing." Her mate's grin stretched across his face to reveal a straight row of luminous teeth. "Do it again," he urged.

"No!" The redhead and I both protested in unison. She looked as stricken as I felt. God no, please don't do that buzz thing. I looked down to see if I had pissed myself. *Nope.* No idea why I hadn't, but I wasn't looking that gift horse in the mouth.

"Are you all right?" The question was aimed at me, and it came from Beth, or Luna, or whatever her name was.

I nodded then shook my head.

Grane reached his hot hand out and rested it on my thigh. I practically vacated my skin, but he didn't remove his hand. "Porcupine?"

"What the—?" I wheezed, and my words spilled out of my mouth in a panicked rush. "If you guys are gonna kill me—I mean—electric shock?—How the hell? Holy shit, I need air." I puked the bile from my empty stomach.

Suma immediately wrapped herself around my back, and her heat engulfed me like a comforting quilt.

Alec backed away, as did the rest of them, to give us some room, and a twinge of gratitude pressed on my heart. They were not going to kill me. If anything, their emotions were as much in question as my own, and they sure as hell seemed as confused as I was. Then, like the glowing presence of the sun after a rain shower, I realized that I was not in danger here. I was the danger. These creatures were fragile, and in jeopardy, and my presence here only made their precarious situation worse.

Because I was not the only human being in these woods.

And I would not be the only human being to stumble upon them.

"You guys hafta get out of here." I pulled away from Suma's warm embrace, wiped my mouth, and stood on legs that were quickly tensing up.

My audience braced in reaction to my sudden alarm. I lowered my head and softened my shoulders to ease them, but planted my feet to the forest floor. If the wolf-people objected, I was ready for a face-off. I mean, their lives were at stake here, and I sure as hell didn't want to endanger them more than I already had.

Alec's brain was a steel trap. "How long before the others come looking for you?"

Desperate not to offend him, I raised my gaze to his, but dropped my arms to my sides. "It won't be long. They saw me take off with two wolves, so they're probably already searching." Their vulnerability stripped me, even though I knew for a fact what they were physically capable of. Hell, if Grane wanted to, he could kill all three of the humans who threatened his family, and we'd fend off his attack like new-born kittens. And Beth? Who the eff knew what hoo-doo she could unleash.

Except that we were expected to return to civilization and would be missed if we didn't. Then there would be no stopping the insurgence of people, cops, wardens, dogs, planes. The wolf-people would be found.

And dissected or shot on site.

My empty stomach rolled.

"Can you keep them away from us?" Alec's face hardened.

"I don't know," I admitted. There wasn't any point in glossing things over because they'd see through the lie like a pane of glass. Plus, I had no desire to get crushed under Grane's bulk with his fangs an inch from my face, or hear that god-awful buzzing in my head.

To be frank, I didn't know what kind of excuse I was going to give my professors. I had taken off with only the thought of helping Grane out of the mess for which I was responsible. My fingers raked my hair, and I exhaled the fear creeping up my backside.

"Guys, I don't know what to say to them. I want to help, but I don't know what to do."

"Grane, did they follow you far?" Alec squared his shoulders and straightened his spine. Jesus, he must have been about six foot four. At least.

"No," the gray wolf-man responded. "We outran them easily, even with the porcupine. They should not find us for a while yet, especially now that I am not wearing a collar." He added the last bit to reassure his pack leader, but I cringed under the weight of his words, and shot a regretful look in Grane's direction.

Alec visibly bristled, and then shivered to relax his muscles. Oh, yeah. I was definitely the dangerous element here.

"Ah, 'scuse me?" I poked an unsteady hand into the air. "Um, you'd all be safer if I just left, you know. I'll come up with something, some story to tell the others." I couldn't deny I hated the idea, and that my heart actually squeezed at the thought of leaving these wolf-people.

Of all of them it was Alec who shook his head. "No, Kenrickey. Not yet."

Relief flooded through my veins. Boy, how quickly things had turned. Was it only a few days ago that I was as much Grane's captive as he was mine? But, here I was hoping I could stay in the woods forever. The image of the other two wolves, the ones who were my age, took form in my head. Yeah, I would love to stay and get to know those two better.

Three sets of eyes narrowed as they assessed me, and Alec grinned as if he'd just heard a good joke.

"Yes," he purred, if wolves could do that. "The boys would like that, too."

Grane stiffened like a muscled statue, as if the next words uttered would disintegrate him.

"Alec," he breathed. "You mean to send the boys with the

porcupine."

"They could learn the ways of the humans and watch over us from the enemy's side," he uttered his plan with conviction, but turned a soft eye to his subordinate. "My brother, I know the pain—"

Grane cut him off. "They will do it with my blessing," he gruffed, bowing his head to his pack leader, his approval pregnant with meaning. Suma draped her arm around her mate and gazed at him with pride.

A thousand questions swirled in my head. The first one was if I'd heard them right. Eaen and Armand coming with me? No way. How cool would that be? My heart fluttered in my chest, and anticipation heated my face.

Beth interrupted my internal reverie like a pin on a bubble. "Our boys are innocents, and unlearned of human ways. Of *all* human ways," she stressed, and planed out my emotions with those marine eyes of hers that clotted the blood in my veins.

"I wouldn't hurt them," I swore, my eyes bulging.

The redheaded woman dropped her lids and lifted them. A low-grade hum reverberated softly throughout my entire body. "You would not," she said. "But humans will. They must be protected at all cost. *You* must protect them at all cost."

I was beginning to grasp the full scope of her meaning. Going into a foreign world—scratch that. Going into an *alien* world would be the most dangerous thing they could do. They literally risked their lives and the lives of these wondrous people crouched before me, and the world that I was from was so full of unforeseen trouble that something as benign as an unintentional bump of bodies on a sidewalk could be a disastrous trap.

Was I really up for that level of responsibility?

The humming in my head expanded and fizzed down my neck. *Oooh.* My mouth shaped itself around the sound that seeped from my throat, and my muscles ticked involuntarily. The hum rippled into waves of vibration, and then the image of two dead wolves, strung up by long sticks slicing perpendicular through the tendons of their hind legs, eddied into focus. Their soft muzzles, caked with the burgundy of their dried blood, hovered inches from the desecration of a rifle butt and a pair of boots, the faceless murderer posing with his trophies. My stomach lurched violently as the primal urge to kill swelled from within and suffocated reason.

The hum crescendoed like a jubilant choir and rocked my body to the earth. Then it cut off abruptly, as if sliced off with a conductor's wand, and the ensuing silence left my bones hollow. One word tapped at my skull like drops of water from a leaky faucet.

Protect.

Protect.

Protect.

Hell, yeah. I would protect. With a ferocity I didn't know I possessed until two seconds ago, though it seemed as if it were an essential part of me, as if the need to keep my loved ones safe was as elemental to my being as my heart.

I peeled my eyelids upward to assess the mess I probably was. No way did I lose that kind of control and keep things under wraps.

"Ken Rickey." The red witch called my name, stressing the *n* with a full pause before the capital *R*. The pronunciation was mesmerizing, and I responded without hesitation, turning my face for her viewing.

"You are up to the challenge," she announced to all, even though she addressed me, and a collective sigh swirled around us. The trust the others placed on this wolf-woman humbled me to the ground. She was a queen in this pristine forest, and the sooner I took the contamination of my teachers out of here, the sooner I could shed the growing sense of shame rapidly filling my stomach.

"Then the human leaves now and takes the biologists with him." Alec's decree rumbled in the clearing like the deep bass of an electric guitar. All heads nodded, including my own.

Chapter Two

The winter snow didn't melt soon enough, and my classes stretched tediously. Since the autumn trip into the northern Maine woods, I simply couldn't look at my biology classes in the same way again. Darwin had it unbelievably freakin' right. Shit *evolved.* I understood that as crucially as I knew blood coursed through my veins to keep me alive.

The lie I'd concocted for my professors when I returned from my flight into the forest went disproved, since the evidence of all the data had taken an accidental tumble into the lake we'd flown over during our departure. The proof sank like the stone I'd cached in the center of the bag it was stored in.

I still couldn't believe that ball-sy move. But it proved I was willing to do anything to ensure the survival of a species. I felt damned proud of myself, and it felt good to have my loyalty tested and proven.

My professor, Mark Hersey, was not so impressed. In fact, he placed me on academic probation for my little stunt. All throughout the winter semester, I was forced to keep my head low and my grades up. Which wasn't difficult since I had a renewed passion for research, and spent so many hours trying to figure out where the wolf-people fit into Nature's scheme I'd forgotten I actually had a life off campus.

Except for the times I let my mind drift back to the north woods. As far as I knew, Eaen and Armand, the two young wolves I'd met through Suma and Grane, had spent the winter getting prepped for their debut to the human stage, and curtain time was drawing near.

I clicked the lid shut on my laptop and stood up to look out my kitchen window. The Machias River snaked through frozen mud, snow-flattened grasses, and gray, leafless sticks of alders. The only sign of spring was the absence of snow. Ice floes were still wedged to the steeper walls of the riverbank where the sun couldn't penetrate. But, at least it had become filthy, old, and rotten; it wasn't fresh. As the days lengthened, the ice would disappear completely and then my new life would begin.

I spent time preparing for the rendezvous, as well. I'd rented a different house, chosen specifically for its remote location. Eaen and Armand would need privacy as they acclimated, and this was the best I could do on my parents' allowance. Explaining to my folks I didn't want a roommate to help defray some of the costs sounded petty even to my ears, but they were generous parents, and eventually eased up and forked over the extra cash to my checking account. I owed them big time for that, and was more than a little pleased that at least my GPA would show I'd been studying, and not partying my ass off like the rest of the student body seemed to do.

I'd also started running again. That little quest through the forest with Grane and Suma while they searched for their two brothers was a slap to the face, a real wake-up call. We humans were soft and lazy slaves to comforts and indulgences, and my ass had suffered and sloshed as I'd tried to keep up with them. If I was going to hang out with two wolves, I'd need to be a hell of a lot sharper than I was last fall.

The click of the furnace turning on echoed in the sparsely furnished cottage, and then its muffled roar filled the emptiness as it spewed hot air to warm the place. I sighed as if I starred in a soap opera, and flaked back out onto the old sofa with my laptop. I had a thesis to finish, and the humming of the furnace only reminded me of the red wolf and the fact it wasn't fully spring yet.

I put my head down and concentrated on the keys.

* * * *

It was the cooing of the doves in the mornings that clinched my belief it was finally spring. Plus the fact the temperature at night didn't dip below freezing, so the ground was thawing twenty-four hours a day.

My skin itched with anticipation. Classes weren't done yet, but I didn't give a shit. I'd been studying hard enough I could afford to miss a few, even if Professor Hersey got his panties in a wad. I had much better things to do than listen to his tight-ass lectures.

I had lives to save and a species to preserve. The whole thing was straight out of some science nerd's comic book. Except this was freakin' real, even if I suffered moments of doubt any of it had ever happened.

Those times were tough. Professor Crandall, who'd also been on the trip with us, hadn't actually seen the wolves I'd run off with, but she stuck close to her colleague, supporting his accusations. And every hairy eyeball, every academic jab and block I got from Hersey, whose research I'd sunk, reminded me that last fall's adventure wasn't some fantasy I'd made up.

All that shit I'd been swallowing for a full semester had been worth it. The time had come to pick up Eaen and Armand, the two younger wolf-men I'd met during my adventure last fall. I took one last look at my car, and hoped the road where we were supposed to meet up wouldn't be too muddy.

The miring glop ran deep in Maine, which was why nine out of ten people owned a Subaru. Myself included. It was a shitbox, but the thing drove like a freakin' snowmobile in the worst weather. It was a tough little bastard, and if something was going to get me down those back roads and out again, it was going to be that car.

I folded myself into the driver's seat, cranked the door shut, and set my map on the empty seat beside me. I had a long drive ahead, and wondered for the thousandth time how in hell I was going to return with two wolf-men in the vehicle. What if they changed and people saw?

I could only hope I'd be driving fast enough that anybody who thought they'd seen something would question it. But I threw in some extra blankets to hang in the windows if I had to. Just in case. I wasn't taking any chances. There was no room for error, and the morbid landscape Beth had conjured just for my personal viewing pleasure, of the wolves hanging dead by their hind legs, sent my heart into an unhealthy rapping.

Nope. Not taking chances. I pressed my foot on the accelerator and steered the Subaru north.

* * * *

Kenrickey

The moon sat fat in the night sky, dulling the usual brilliant sheen of the stars. But it lit up the woods and the old logging road I was on, and as long as I kept the Subaru lined up with the fissure of the tree line against the night sky, I kept skidding and jerking forward without getting stuck.

This was the first full moon after the Spring Equinox, exactly when Alec had instructed me to meet them. I just hoped I had the right place, since my sense of direction was about as keen as an autumn leaf in the wind. Aside from the time I'd snuck up on Grane. Then, I'd had the advantage of GPS, and it had almost gotten me killed. My stomach cramped as the memory of it floated in front of my mind's eye. He'd been holding a snarling white wolf in his arms, and all I'd been able to look at was the same radio collar, which Hersey and I had fastened to a wolf, around the *human's* neck. I'd stood there staring at Grane as my brain leapt to make connections, but splatted like Wile E. Coyote instead.

Funny how things worked out.

I parked the car once I got it turned around, after doing what seemed like a thirty point turn. Talk about tight. I took out one of the blankets from the back seat and spread it out on the warm hood, shed my clothes, then got as comfortable as I could under the circumstances. Hard telling how long I'd be in the woods waiting for Armand and Eaen to show. Would they even come after all of this time? Would they want to? Christ knows, leaving the relative safety of the forest was a huge step, and if the shoes were reversed? I sure as hell wouldn't do it.

But then, they didn't have much of a choice, did they?

I inhaled and let my breath out in a plume of steam, studying it as it baffled into a ball, then evaporated. *Damn it was cold.* I wrapped the blanket around myself to keep warm, then closed my eyes so I could hear better.

With the closing of my lids, the forest expanded, swallowing me within its enormity so I felt super small and insignificant. I loved it, really. Feeling like that reminded me of my place in the world, that I was just some fragile organism with an undetermined life-span.

Psst. Kenrickey.

I sat up when a pinecone bounced off my forehead, and swiveled my head around like an owl. I saw no one, but my goose-bumps weren't just

19

from the cold. I'd heard something. I left the blanket where it was as I slid off the car.

"Eaen? Armand?" I whispered, uncertain—like pinecones fell horizontally all the time. But the night woods were vast, and I had to admit, *scary*. Another pinecone hit me between my shoulder blades. I spun around, and found myself staring up into a face sporting one hell of a row of moon-lit teeth.

Then I was staring up at the top of the trees with a band of fire around my throat and a set of dark eyes boring a new hole into the side of my face.

"Hi, Eaen," I croaked, but sure as shit didn't look at him. Uh-uh. I kept my face averted, and my arms and legs flopped out onto the cold, wet ground. The creature looming over me was twitchy enough without me pulling his trigger.

"You are alone, Kenrickey?" His voice sighed like a whisper in spite of the force he exerted on my bare body.

I rubbed the back of my head into the dirt with an answering nod. Eaen relaxed his grip. A little.

"Where's your brother? Where's Armand?" For a brief second I panicked, unsure of Armand's presence. Was he dead? Had some accident happened over the winter? The long fingers encircling my neck cut off my wind. I flipped my eyes back to the shadow of the tree line like a good boy.

"He is close, Kenrickey."

I caught the warning. They weren't stupid enough to trust humans, even if it was just me. I choked out a sigh of relief anyway. Armand was with us and he was okay.

In my peripheral vision, I could see Eaen cock his head, as if my response wasn't what he'd expected. He eased his grip, and slid his warm hands down to my chest to rest his weight on me.

"Armand, come out and see the porcupine I caught." His smile eased the worry from his face and helped to settle the romping rabbit of my heart. These guys were scared, too. Armand had stayed in the woods in case I had some sneaky human trick up my sleeve. Pretty effing clever, really.

When his brother approached, the taller wolf-man stepped away so

20

we could greet each other. I remembered my lessons from last fall, and stayed on my knees with my head down. Armand trotted near, his bare feet practically silent on the carpet of dead pine needles.

"Porcupine," he bellowed good-naturedly. "Get off your knees and give me a greeting that is fitting." He swooped in close and lifted me by my armpits, then hugged me in a tight embrace. His body was like lying on the beach sand in the height of summer. Freakin' *hot*. I didn't even notice I hugged him like I was eight and he was my missing teddy. Then Eaen wrapped his arms around the both of us, pulling us even snugger for a group hug.

A few seconds later, Armand pulled back to get a better look. "Kenrickey, it is good to see you," he complimented as he took a deep breath through his nose. "You smell healthy. The winter has been easy for you?"

I grinned like a sap as my heart squeezed tight. I'd missed the wolf-people, had missed the way they never spoke with contractions, but pronounced every word with precision, like they had respect for the language.

Christ. Teach them something? These two should be on a lecture circuit across the country espousing the joy of living.

I answered before they would think I was a simpleton. "Yeah, but it was long," I admitted, then grinned again at my new friends. "Man, it's really good to see you guys. I wasn't sure if you'd make it." I hugged them close again, and they didn't even resist. If those had been human guys I did that to, they would have knocked my front teeth out and called me Nancy.

"We would not have missed the chance for such an adventure," the tall wolf-man said as an eager smile crept across his face.

"Excellent." God, I was happy to see them. "I've got all sorts of things planned to show you. This is going to be so much fun." I stopped rubbing my hands together as if I was Frankenstein's Igor, and took a deep breath. Shit, but I still couldn't believe how effing incredible this whole meeting was.

Armand's words helped to settle me down.

"We are here to learn, too, Porcupine. Beth says you must teach us to write now that she has taught us our letters." Yellow eyes, stirring with hopeful anxiety, assessed my reaction to his pack leader's orders.

"Write?" Of course, they needed to learn how to write. What kind of a freakin' idiot was I? They lived in the forest, far from civilization. I was stunned they could even *read,* for God's sake.

They were both now staring at me as if I possessed a single brain cell.

"Yeah, of course," I blurted. Man, was I smooth.

"Hey, I've got clo—" I started to say as I took off for the car.

The wolf-men flinched like I'd shot a gun, and then the skyline swept across my field of vision, and I was gaping at the stars with a band of hot fingers clamped around my throat, and their likeness clutched around my ankles. *Jesus,* but I was forgetting how nervous they were.

"Guys," I croaked through my crushed vocal chords. "I forgot. I'm sorry." My eyes bulged as if to take in more of the lunar view.

"Move slow, remember, Kenrickey?" Armand's face hovered, his fangs unsheathed.

Yowza. Again, I scraped the back of my head into the dirt as I nodded, and then my eyes shrunk to their normal size as the wolf-man loosened his grip. Sweet oxygen slid into my starved lungs. They were right, of course. I'd made a sudden move on a chess board that for them was no game. Their lives were the ones on the black squares, and I'd forgotten that.

Armand uncurled his roasting body to its upright position and offered me a hand. I clutched it in my own, grateful not just for the leg up, but also for the camaraderie it extended.

Sorry, Porcupine, but we are scared.

I imagined the wolf-men saying that, complete without the contraction. The funny thing was, when I looked up at Eaen, he smiled apologetically—his expression an exact mirror of the thought.

I apologized again for good measure, and then told them about the clothes I'd brought, without running toward the Subaru this time.

"They're in the car," I hitched my thumb over my shoulder. "I'll go get 'em."

I walked off, brushing pine needles from my bare ass, and ignored Armand's pursed lips. Yep. These guys were nervous all right, and I suspected the introduction of the clothing and the car ride were going to tilt their self-control. Good thing I'd kept my nose to the books all semester. The ride home might take longer than I'd thought.

I fished in the duffel bag I retrieved from the back seat, and handed a pair of sweats to Armand. He peered down at them as if I was offering him a snowball in August.

"They're pants, Armand. You put your legs in them." I shoved them gently toward his chest. He took them and shook them out, pinching them between his tapered fingers.

"They stink." He wrinkled his nose.

"I just washed—" I dropped my protest as reason dawned. Of course, the clothing would stink. I hadn't given it any thought as I'd poured the detergent into the washer. Those clothes reeked of everything he wasn't accustomed to, *everything human.*

"You'll get used to it." Yet, there was a part of me that hoped he didn't, and the word *tamed* whispered like a ghost at the back of my mind. Somehow, I'd have to find the balance between teaching them about the human world without letting it corrupt them. Was this part of Beth's warning, too?

My mind got corralled back to the present as I watched the spectacle of Armand trying to dress. He struck a leg into the tube of fabric, hopped twice to regain his balance, then fell on his butt.

I was too mortified to laugh, but Eaen's burst of laughter resounded through the cold, night air.

"You try it if you think it is so easy," Armand growled at his upright brother, but he managed to grin past his scowl. I let out my breath.

"Watch and learn," Eaen crowed at his brother's good-natured challenge as he sat down, then thrust both of his long legs into the pants. He hitched them up around his waist while bouncing to his feet, his grin victorious.

I tossed him a t-shirt to wear, and saved the button-down for Armand. If Eaen had no trouble dressing, then he could manage slipping into the shirt.

He poked his head through and yanked at the neck. "I feel like I'm wearing Grane's collar," he griped, his humor dashed.

Mine went with it as the memory of Grane trying to tear the collar from his neck sprang up uninvited before I could lock it down. He'd wrestled with that damned thing until blood had run down his shoulders, and I was the one to blame for it.

Shit.

Armand and Eaen swiveled their heads as if synchronized. Their twin looks of curiosity skittered like squirrel feet across my nerves.

"What?"

Eaen shook his head. "Nothing, Kenrickey," he dismissed and changed tack. "Now, about your auto-mobile..."

Hey, if he didn't want to talk about what I'd done to Grane then that was peachy with me. I jumped on the change of subject like it was the last bus home.

"Get in when you're ready." I stepped toward the car alone and turned.

"Are you two ready?"

They were frozen in their tracks. Armand's lips were pressed so tight together his nostrils flared, and Eaen worked his white-knuckled fists. They were nervous as hell about the car and it didn't take animal instincts to see it.

By some subtle cue, the two wolf-men separated and circled the vehicle, sniffing and snuffling as they narrowed the distance between themselves and the human contraption.

Suddenly, they leapt through the open door of the back seat and hunkered down, their faces drifting and pressing to the scents that teased them.

Game time.

I shut the rear door, settled myself into the driver's seat, and cranked the ignition.

Eaen exploded in a flurry of activity behind me, grappling in a panic for the door handle. Armand sat like a boulder and sweated as the heat from their bodies swelled to fill the interior of the car. I pushed the control for the back window, and Eaen thrust his head out before it was half-way down. His ribs expanded against his t-shirt as he inhaled life-giving oxygen like a man who'd just escaped drowning.

I pressed the gas pedal and crept forward. Eaen's torso, wrapped in my Metallica t-shirt, filled my side-view mirror as he stretched his entire upper body out the back window. Christ, he looked just like one of those wiry hard-metal fans you didn't want to fuck with unless you were female. His wide, sharp grin stretched across his face as he punched his nose into the scenery as we drove by. The guy was enjoying the ride, and my heart swelled for him. If he could accept novelty this easily, then our road to civilization wasn't going to be very bumpy at all.

"Kenrickey stop," he shouted, and tucked himself back into the car.

I slammed on the brakes and felt him fall against my seat, but he rebounded instantly to hover over his brother.

"Armand is sick," he whined as he stretched across the back seat to open his brother's door so he could let him out.

I smashed the car into park and ran around to help. Poor Armand was green and spitting as he rolled onto the ground in a sweltering heap.

"The car slides…slippery," he moaned.

That was a pretty accurate description. I shot a worried look at Eaen, who had his strong arm draped across his brother's back.

"It is all right, Arms. Breathe deep," he coaxed gently, while my chest squeezed too tight. Seeing a powerful young man offering such gentle comfort to another? Well, it shouldn't have been so rare and beautiful, but it was. That's our society for you.

Armand's broad shoulders strained against the cotton of his button-down with every gulp of fresh air he inhaled, and a V of sweat darkened the back.

"Sometimes, riding in the front helps if you get car sick," I offered.

The vomiting wolf-man rolled a tortured look my way, as if the thought of getting back into that moving cage was beyond his endurance.

How in hell did you convince a hundred and seventy pound wolf to get in your car?

Alex, I'll take Great Riddles for $200, please.

Suddenly, Armand's body shivered violently as he gripped his head in his long hands so hard his fingers turned white. His body trembled as if with a great fever, then with a stifled roar the man before me slid, buckled, and contorted. He stretched his long body to rid itself of the kinks, and shook the tension from himself as if it was water weighing his fur.

I gaped at a blonde wolf, and my knees wobbled.

Jesus effing Christ, I will never get used to that.

S. C. Dane

I sucked in a lungful of night air, too, while Armand the wolf stepped out of his rumpled clothing and sneezed so hard it thrust his face toward the ground. Ah but, he looked up with his yellow eyes sparkling and his tongue lolling in a soft pant.

Armand had recovered from his car ride, and I had the solution to getting us home before daylight. He could ride passenger as wolf so long as he stayed low or watched for other vehicles. It wasn't perfect, but hell, I had a feeling this wasn't going to be the first time we'd have to find different ways to skin a dead cat.

"Let's go, guys," I swung my arm toward the backseat like a movie usher, shut all the doors, slid the Subaru into drive, and sped into the night with the greatest of treasures beside me: two new friends who trusted me with their lives.

There was no way I was going to screw this up.

* * * *

I pulled the car into my driveway just as the eastern sky spread like a smashed rose on the horizon. We'd made it home before it got too light out. I stretched as I lifted myself from the driver's seat and yawned, then opened the rear door for Armand and Eaen.

They were curled up on the backseat, butt to butt with their long legs folded beneath them. The drive through Bangor, even though it was late and there was little city traffic, had been too much for Eaen and he'd succumbed, like his brother, to his most natural form. The wolves had ridden in sleepy silence for the rest of the trip.

Eaen still had his wide, black head supported on the armrest, but Armand raised his when the door squeaked open. I wasn't too tired to notice that when he yawned he revealed a long, sharp row of daggers designed to crush the marrow from bone.

I raked my hand through my hair and yawned sympathetically to Armand's wide-mouthed stretch, as if I couldn't remove myself from the chain reaction.

"We're here, guys. Home sweet home."

Eaen's triangular ears flopped at half-mast when he lifted his head. Then his tongue unfurled like a party favor, and he spread his toes as he arched his back in a luxurious stretch.

26

"You up, sleepy head? We're here." I had to admit the sight of them all drowsy like that made me feel ridiculously warm and fuzzy. Like I was their big uncle or something, even though the stark truth was if they had the mind to, they could rip my throat out and eat my innards.

Worry as small as a wren flittered across my skin for a mere second and flew away. I peeked in at my passengers. No, they were cool. And as long as I didn't do anything stupid, they would honor their mission to keep their pack safe. I was part of that equation, and the truth of that tripped a bee in my head.

The buzzing. *Jee-sus.*

That didn't flit like a songbird, and the sight of the black and blonde wolves strung up... *fuck*. It simply wasn't going to happen. Not on my watch, anyway. I scrubbed my hand through my hair and took a deep breath, which triggered another yawn.

God, I was tired, and my brain was saturated.

"I'm heading in, guys. You set, or do you want to follow me into the house?"

They tumbled out of the car, then stretched and shook their great frames. Christ, they were huge, and didn't look particular innocent anymore, either. They were effing *wolves*. My blood sizzled with a dose of adrenaline.

"Ah...guys?" I glanced around as the details in the landscape sharpened with the rising of the sun.

Eaen and Armand quit sniffing the ground to look up, their shining wolf eyes boring into me expectantly.

"It's pretty private here, what with the river out back and the Nature Conservancy and all. If you want, go ahead and scope it out. Just don't go toward the main road and you'll be fine."

I headed for the front door as they swept around the property with their noses skimming the dewy ground and their bushy tails erect. Their paws barely touched the earth before their sinewy legs sprung their strides forward in robust glides. I stopped in my tracks to watch them.

Grace.

That's what I witnessed in the morning sunshine. Lethal grace. And damned if the buzzing wasn't making a comeback. I shut my eyes against a rising thought—it was the essence of their powerful elegance that would be their undoing. And I was going to have to figure out how to camouflage *that?*

I rubbed my hand through my hair, an absent-minded habit. *Later.* I would worry about our next step later. Right then, all I needed was my bed, and to sleep away the rest of the day. I took one last look at the wolves scoping out the dooryard and headed for the house.

* * * *

It was pitch black in the house when I finally woke up, my bladder so full it hurt. I stumbled to the bathroom without even bothering to wipe the crust from my eyelids and straddled the toilet.

"Good evening, Kenrickey."

"Jesus!" I tripped sideways, slamming my hip into the sink as I fumbled for the light. "What the—?"

Eaen was stretched out in the bathtub, soaking up to his armpits in steaming water, and grinning like the Cheshire Cat. "You never mentioned that water flows into your home. It is hot, too," he drawled as he sank lower into the water.

"Yeah, ah…I get both hot and cold." What else was I going to say? I finished my business, and swiped the steam off the mirror. "Where's Armand?" I looked past my reflection to the tall wolf-man who filled the tub. His hair, curled in soaked spikes, was so black to be almost blue.

"Asleep in your room," he answered lazily, his eyes closed.

"I didn't see him." My blood pressure surged. If Armand went missing? On his first day?

"Under you," he explained without lifting his lids.

"Under me?" I actually looked at my feet.

Eaen nodded, his chin dipping into the water, but kept his eyes shut as he inhaled the steam from his bath.

"Under my bed, you mean? He's asleep under my bed?" That was absurd, wasn't it?

"He felt safer."

"Oh." Well, that was kind of neat, really. That protective feeling swelled in my chest again, like I was the big uncle. I headed for the door to go check on Armand myself while I wondered if he'd changed into his human form since the ride in the Subaru. If he'd kept his fur all night and

28

day, then he wasn't feeling too secure about our situation and we'd have to figure something out. Hopefully, the guy just needed some time. If not? It was a scenario I preferred not to entertain, especially since I wasn't ready to part with my new friends so early in the game.

I tapped on the door of my room as I entered. Now that I knew I had a wolf-man under my bed I moved more cautiously. No point in startling him to action.

"Armand? You awake?"

A thick arm grasped the edge of the mattress, and the muscles flexed as it pulled the body out from its hiding place. Armand grinned, all heavy-eyed with sleep. "Hello, Porcupine." He stretched to his feet and yawned.

I grinned. I couldn't help it. The whole idea of some guy, wolf or not, sleeping under my bed struck me as silly. And touching. "Sleep well?" I was pleased to see him on two feet.

He nodded and rubbed his belly, then stuck his nose in the air, sniffing from side to side. "Where's Eaen?"

"Taking a bath," I tossed my chin in the direction of the bathroom. Just then, I felt a very warm body approach from behind. I could hear the water dripping on the floor, and was certain he didn't have a towel. I turned to see if I was right. Yep. And got a full frontal soaking to prove it.

Eaen shook his body as if he was covered in fur, and still managed to soak everything in a five foot radius, including me.

He grinned wickedly, fully aware of what he'd done. I lunged for him, his wet skin slipping from my grasp. He bolted for the living room and perched on top of the couch. I leapt and tackled him anyway, and we crashed to the floor. In an instant, I was muckled in a headlock with Eaen's laughter rumbling in my ears.

Armand joined the fray by latching on to Eaen's ankles and rolling him to his back like he was nothing more than a log. Eaen had no choice but to release me, unless he wanted his brother to tie him into a human pretzel.

"Enough, I give," he cried, his laughter jangling as he eased his grip so I could slip loose.

I sat upright, my chest heaving. Christ, Eaen was strong. And

Armand had gotten the upper hand? I needed a few lessons from Bruce Lee, even if he was dead, if I was going to wrestle these guys. I looked at the young men tangled up on the living room floor with me, their chests heaving, too, from our fun. The three of us struggled to suppress idiotic smiles.

What a motley crew, I thought. We were like a litter of pups, for God's sake. If Alec and Beth had seen us just then, I sincerely doubt they'd think we took our mission very seriously.

But then Armand threw his face to the ceiling and howled all the air in his lungs, letting off so much steam it had to feel good.

Oh yeah, *freakin' awesome!* I cast a quick glance at my two friends whose eyes and teeth shimmered in the moonlit room, and felt nothing but absolute acceptance. I raised my own face to the rafters and whooped, and was instantly joined by raucous howls that not only sprung the fine hairs from my skin, but tingled my guts, *and* filled me with pride. We'd have put any heavy-metal band into the dirt.

So what if we'd wrestled ourselves to the floor. At least it helped to relieve the pressure we'd been under since meeting up. God knew we needed it, and would most likely need it many times again before this campaign to help the wolf-people was over.

* * * *

"What is that smell, Kenrickey?"

Eaen looked up from his spot over on the couch. I was standing in the kitchen with the fridge handle in my grip, the open floor space of the conjoined rooms stretching between us.

I glanced up from rummaging in the fridge to look way over at the wolf-man stretched on the sofa. "What smell?"

"Apples?" Eaen sat up, putting his bare feet on the floor.

"You smell that?"

He nodded.

Jesus, he was twenty feet away, at least. I reached into the crisper and pulled out an apple, bouncing it on my palm as I turned to Eaen. "You smelled this? From way over there?" I shot him a look of disbelief, challenging his keen sense of smell.

The dark-headed wolf-man unfurled himself and stood up. His

30

clothes were a little small on him, making him look even bigger than he actually was. His hair, still damp from his bath, jiggled as he nodded.

I gave the coveted fruit one more flip in my palm, then torpedoed it at him. He snatched it like I'd lobbed it underhanded. Not only could the wiry bastard wrestle, but he could have played pro ball if he'd wanted to. Armand, I was sure, had the same physical aptitude.

Shit. I was so out of my league.

Armand emerged from my bedroom with a book in his long hand, just as Eaen snapped his sharp teeth into the flesh of the Granny Smith.

"Is that an apple?" The shorter wolf-man pushed his nose in the air and frowned, as if not trusting his senses. "How is that possible? It is Spring." He followed the scented path of the tossed fruit, and then veered to the fridge. "They are in that," his tapered finger pointed at the icebox.

He was a goddamned bloodhound.

"Yeah, in the crisper. Want one?" I bent back into the fridge to get Armand the treasure his nose had uncovered, and handed him the fruit. He chomped on it with gusto, sending the sticky juices flying so even I could smell the apple.

"I love apples," he said around his crammed cheeks.

Obviously. I smiled, and glanced down at his other hand, the one not dripping with sticky juice.

"You've got a book there, huh?"

Armand nodded while he handed me the book. I flipped it over to read the cover. Mary Shelley's *Frankenstein*. A story I'd had to read for my Humanities class when I was a freshman. I was surprised I still had it after four years and a hundred scientific textbooks later.

I remembered it as a great tale, but not much else stuck with me, except that the monster had been misunderstood because he couldn't communicate his feelings. Plus, he was butt-ass ugly.

"It's kind of a sad story, Armand. You know, man makes monster, man tries to kill monster, blah, blah, blah."

"It sounds very interesting, Porcupine. Teach me to read it. *Please.*" He rested his warm hand on my shoulder and peered straight at me since we were about the same height.

"Sure." If Armand wanted to learn how to read with Shelley's *Frankenstein,* then so be it. I mean, he wasn't a small boy learning the alphabet here. He was quite capable of grasping complex issues. Christ, he wasn't— I caught myself thinking *raised by wolves* and stopped short with a snort. "Yeah, you'll enjoy it."

I unfolded the book to the first page. "Letter One. To Mrs. Saville, England…"

I shut the book and rolled a tortured look to my friend. "Are you sure? I mean, there are so many other books to read." It had practically killed me to read it when I was forced to, now I was volunteering?

Armand nodded, and Eaen joined his brother in wanting to read *Frankenstein*, too.

Oh, hell. "All right," I conceded. "You know the alphabet and how to put letters together, right?"

"Yes, Kenrickey. Beth taught us and we can read, we have just never done so with *this.*" Armand tapped Exhibit A with his tapered finger. "We do not have these in the forest."

Christ, I was an idiot. Of course, they didn't have books in the forest. I groaned, and Armand winked good-naturedly. He wasn't offended, thank God, and a wave of gratitude washed through me. I cleared my throat. "Okay. Letter One…"

The three of us lay siege to the couch, making ourselves comfortable for the rest of the evening while I droned on through the pages. Occasionally, one of the wolf-men would interrupt with a question about a word spelling or punctuation, but their grasp on vocabulary was astounding.

So was their ability to glean subtle meaning from an entire scene, even if their reading dragged a bit slow when they first attempted it. My English professor would have been salivating, and I was reminded of just one more reason their species was superior to ours. Humans, for the most part, were dolts compared to these two.

I was certain the parallel of the story and their lives was not lost on the two wolf-men

* * * *

I skipped class the next day, too, just to make sure Eaen and Armand had settled in and could be safely left on their own for a few hours.

We were outside. I was spread across the porch steps enjoying the last of the warmth from the spring sun, and my new friends were standing at my feet, looking up at me.

"You want *me* to go hunting?"

The two wolves circled, fanned their bushy tails, and stared up longingly. I stayed put on the porch with my boots planted on the top step. The evening sun hovered fat on the horizon, all set to get punctured by the pointed spruce so it could deflate and rest.

Eaen and Armand had been with me for nearly two days and hadn't eaten anything except the fruit in my refrigerator. They must have been starving, yet they wanted some bumbling human out with them to blow their chances at a good meal?

"No way." I balked. "You guys need to eat. Besides, I'm a vegetarian, I don't hunt."

The blonde wolf dashed up the stairs and pushed his broad head into my back, lifting my ass cheeks off the porch.

"Cut that out." I swatted as effectively as a baby bird, and with one more nudge from Armand, found myself on the ground in front of Eaen.

"You guys are killing me, you know that?"

Their tongues lolled, and I swear to Mary, the mother of Jesus, they were laughing.

Until headlights slashed across the trees at the edge of the lawn and both wolves froze.

"Holy shit. Hide! Get in the house!"

The black wolf bolted past me like he'd been fired from a sling-shot, and his brother spun in beside him.

"Fuck, the door!" It was shut and they couldn't get in. The thumbs they had as humans were useless dew claws on their lower legs. The car crunched up the gravel driveway, its headlights bobbing in the dusk as it neared.

How I leapt from the ground to the porch, I have no clue, but as soon as I twisted the knob the blonde wolf shoved himself against the door and hustled inside. His brother clung tight like a burr.

"Go to the bedroom. And for God sake, no matter what, don't come out."

My heart pounded in my forehead, my lungs, my legs. Holy Christ, I hope they weren't seen. And how in hell did we let the car sneak up on us like that? I shot another look at the wolves who stood rigid in the center of the room, their triangular ears swiveling as their eyes burned holes through the path to the living room.

"Stay put."

I backed out and shut the bedroom door. Dear lord, I hoped they stayed there.

The knock on the front door resounded like a gunshot and I flinched. *Jesus, Ken, get an effing grip.*

I took a deep breath, and strode to the front of the house, but before I got there, Jeff stepped through the front door and into the living room with the beautiful Naomi in tow.

"Hey, bro. What's up?"

Jeff. A classmate, the boyfriend of a classmate, and a royal fucking asshole. What a package.

"Hey, Jeff. Naomi." My voice trembled queerly, and I cleared my throat as my hand shot up to rake a swath through my hair. I also gulped a lungful of oxygen before I spoke again.

"What are you guys doing here?"

Jeff lumbered into the kitchen to set his six pack on the counter. The bottles rattled as he pulled an unopened beer from the carton. His hand, which always made me think of a bear paw, practically eclipsed the bottle it held. Plus, the rest of the effing guy was enormous. He probably stood six foot three and had the body of a freakin' linebacker. His shoulders were as broad as the stuffed chair in my living room. I knew that, because every time the guy sat down in it he had to shoe-horn his way into the damned thing to get comfortable.

"You weren't in class Friday, Ken. Where were you?" The voice lilting such sweet sentences caressed itself across my skin.

Aah, Naomi. Sweet Naomi. One of the smartest women in our class, and quite possibly the most naive. She was Jeff's girlfriend, after all. My stomach twisted into its familiar knot whenever I let myself reminisce about the Almost. How I almost got the nerve up to ask Naomi on a date, how I almost challenged Jeff the human bear for her when he muscled in, almost....

I swept my wits into a solid pile and snagged one of Jeff's beers, then offered one to Nae, who declined it after a brief glance at her control-freak boyfriend.

Yeah, right. She didn't do anything without consulting him first, which wasn't the Naomi I remembered. She used to be quite the shit. Full of sass, tossing her long blonde hair along with shots of tequila. That girl could drink a sailor under the table, and remember jokes like nobody's business. Which, I realized then, her long hair was shorn clear to her shoulders.

"Nae, your hair." She'd cut her sleek, blonde hair, for Christ's sake. The long tresses I'd watch bob in dainty curls just above the curve of her slender waist were gone, no longer there to beckon my stare like come-hither fingers.

She palmed the stub ends of her new cut, which now hugged the curve of her jaw, accentuating the pink blushing up into her cheeks. "I needed a change. Besides, it kept getting in the way, and Jeff said—" She dropped her sentence, and combed her slender fingers through her honey hair, avoiding my stunned gaze altogether while she studied the arm of the chair she sat on.

So, Jeff made her cut her hair because it bugged him. I could blacken his eyes for it, the asshole. I averted looking at the two of them before I followed through on the urge. God knew, there were too many times already I'd wanted to nail that bastard. He treated Nae like shit, and the reason he tolerated me, Nae's only friend, was because we helped the dumb-ass pass his classes.

For some reason, she stayed with him, so I put up with it. Because I wouldn't risk not being able to see Nae again, which would happen if Jeff and I didn't get along. And me and Nae had been friends since our freshman year. Having the same classes meant we got to spend a lot of time together that first semester, even though I'd always wondered why she tagged along even after classes were over.

Shit, I was a punk fresh out of high school, and she was pretty. Smart. And wanted to hang out with me instead of her girlfriends? She said she was a tom-boy, grew up with brothers and trees and trucks.

Her telling me that was like someone pulling the plug out of my big toe, and all my hopes for having her as a girlfriend spilled out onto the ground, leaving me as empty as a glass gumball machine. Nae saw me as a *brother*. Of course. I mean, she wouldn't have been sexually attracted to a guy who took his microscope to the frog pond, even if said guy wore hearts in his eyes for her.

But she stuck, and after a couple of semesters of being lab partners and just friends, I'd finally worked up enough courage to pull The Move. You know, plant a kiss on her rosebud lips, present my heart on a silver platter, fondle those tantalizingly perky breasts.

Then she met Jeff, who had just transferred in, and the Naomi I knew got swallowed by the Swamp Thing, which is why I ultimately decided I would rather keep her close even if we were just going to be friends. Losing her wasn't an option then either, and I knew I would if I spilled my guts because A: Jeff would take her away, and B: she probably still thought of me as a brother, and then The Thing would know how I felt, take her away *and* she would go willingly.

I dragged a good pull of beer down my throat and cocked an ear to the bedroom so I could get my effing mind off Naomi.

Silence.

We chatted about small stuff while one half of my brain stood by my bedroom door, and the other half got used to watching Nae's short hair caress her slender jawbone. Eventually, it grew dark outside so we could no longer see out the windows with the lights on inside the house.

"Yo, you missed a pop quiz in Hersey's class, bro. Not a big one," he shrugged, "but you still missed it." Jeff didn't just deliver the news, his attitude was meant to goad me. He knew how much it would bother me to miss one of Hersey's quizzes. The Bear crunched his frame around in the chair to get more comfortable, more smarmy.

As if the sight of that jackass getting cozy wasn't bad enough, I'd also missed a pop quiz. Of course, Hersey popped a surprise test on the class. Ever since I'd plumbed his data to the bottom of Lake Too-Effing-Bad, he'd had it in for me, and my first absence was a good chance to hit me where it hurt. Coincidence, my ass.

"Whatever," I dodged Jeff's insinuation even though it was true. I hated agreeing with him, like doing so would mean Nae would like him more. As if that were possible.

I watched her as she dug through her purse, imagining myself caressing away the crease that always appeared between her feathery brows when she concentrated. I swallowed the drool filling my mouth as she slid out a folded wad of notebook paper with her pale hand. One of her delicate fingers sported an intricately knotted silver ring. Her mother's, I knew, given to her before she'd passed away.

"Notes from Friday, even though you missed the quiz." She still sat on the arm of the stuffed chair with Jeff, and her short hair whispered across her shoulders as she handed me the notes. Her sympathetic smile softened the golden flecks and greens in her hazel eyes.

"Thanks, Nae." Christ, I missed her, even though I saw her nearly every day in class. Trouble was, Jeff rarely let her out of his sight, so we wound up being a threesome. Couldn't the guy have had a different major, at least?

"Well, we gotta go." Jeff prized himself out of the chair and stood up. He left his empty on the floor and ambled to the kitchen to snag another for the road.

"See you in class tomorrow?" Naomi's voice warmed the air in the room.

"Yeah, sure. I'll be there"

Jeff's paw clapped itself to my shoulder. "See ya tomorrow, bro." He brushed by me, filling the door frame as he slid out, and then he and Naomi were in his car, heading down the drive to the main road.

I stood in the doorway until the taillights disappeared, then dashed to the bedroom.

Yellow light flooded the empty room, and the night air flowing in through the open window carried the melody of courting frogs.

Eaen and Armand had gone hunting without me.

Chapter Three

"She smelled like snow," Eaen smiled, revealing his sparkling, strong teeth.

"She smelled human," Armand growled from the stuffed chair. He'd finally sat in it after he'd sniffed it all over, finding it safe since Jeff had been in it. If it had been outside, I swear the guy would have pissed on the piece of furniture to reclaim it. The blonde wolf had not been happy about our unexpected visitors.

"Is she pretty, Porcupine?" Eaen ignored his brother with a wave of his hand.

"She is human," Armand gouged in despite being ignored, squashing the edges of *Frankenstein* in his fingers. He was so not impressed by our unexpected visitors.

Defeated, Eaen shrugged and flopped against the back of the couch, and then the three of us settled into a quiet circle reading, instead of addressing the albatross of a dilemma.

Armand and Eaen were going to have to figure out how to interact with more people besides me. The arrival of Jeff and Naomi brought that problem to the forefront. Perhaps Nae could be the one to start with, *if* we could get her away from Sasquatch.

"At some point, though," I began, not with a little trepidation, "you guys are going to have to get introduced to the public. You know, as part of…" I dropped the last of my sentence under Armand's cloudy glare.

His jaw muscles popped as he clenched his teeth together. "I know."

"The first human you face, Arms, will not be Jeff," Eaen warned. He, too, could see the storm brewing within his blonde brother. Jeff's

38

presence in the house rattled us all, and Armand seemed particularly pissed about it. I hadn't a clue why, but I sure as hell wasn't going to ask him. If he wanted to talk about it, fine. I wasn't going to pry.

Eaen's next words sent my heart on a mini-vacation. "We should meet Naomi," he suggested, and raised his eyebrows in a hopeful expression.

"She is with The Bear, remember." Armand raised only his yellow eyes from his book.

What could we say to that? Armand was right. The two were inseparable, thanks to Jeff's possessiveness, his jealousy.

"They don't have all the same classes. I could probably get her alone for a bit." I looked for approval from both of the wolf-men.

"That would be good, but let us practice a little first?" Eaen's hopeful expression turned pensive.

"Of course. I wouldn't just bring her over here without getting us ready," I assured him. "We'll head to town tomorrow night to see just how close you guys can get to people. We'll go from there, okay?" I rested my hand on his knee. His heat radiated through the cloth of his sweats.

"That is a very good plan, Porcupine," Armand complimented, and then put his nose back into his book.

"Great, we have a plan. Now I will let us get back to our studies." Eaen winked, delighted, and relished in his grin as he pulled my Zoology book back onto this lap. He had been drawn to the Sciences as irresistibly as Armand had been drawn to Classical fiction.

I took the two figures in before shifting my attention back to my notes. The wolf-men blew my mind, really, and seeing them poring over their books served only to strike me with how utterly wild they were. Even reposed their bodies exuded a latent threat. If it was the constant heat, or the way their muscles flexed, or the sagacity in their eyes, I just didn't know. But, what I did know was these two straddled the poles between being dangerous to others, and suffering under the whims of a merciless race.

My mind drifted to Armand and his volatile reaction to Jeff. Who would strike first if given the chance?

* * * *

The following morning, I left the two wolf-men to their books to make the drive to campus, where Naomi and Jeff greeted me in the parking lot. She was wrapped up in a thick wool sweater with only tights covering her slender legs. The nip in the morning air rouged her cheeks to a shimmering pink. Naomi, as usual, was completely unaware of how striking she was.

She hopped her shivering self over to my car and offered me a breathless *Good morning.*

Christ, my heart snagged, yet I managed the practiced routine of delivering a nonchalant *Morning, Nae* back at her. Of course, Jeff was on her heels like mold. I gave him my practiced greeting, too.

"Cold enough to freeze a witch's tit," he complained as he blew his hot air into his cupped paws, then rubbed them together.

Only five more weeks of this shit. I slid my bag off the passenger side seat of the Subaru and slung it over my shoulder. Five more weeks until graduation, and then this forced friendship would be over. I wouldn't have to put up with Jeff's ignorant puss and Naomi...well, she was getting what she wanted, right?

As I slammed the car door shut, my eyes caught the sight of someone familiar, but not. Odd that I'd care, given I was on campus and that sort of thing happened all the time. But the guy sitting behind the wheel of the Range Rover plucked at my conscience, like I ought to know him from somewhere.

He flipped an unfolded newspaper up to read, shielding himself from view, and that was the end of my wondering.

I trudged to class with Jeff and Naomi falling in beside me, the man in the SUV forgotten as we headed into the Science building. We took our regular seats toward the back of the room, where Jeff preferred to sit because of the big table. He didn't want to squeeze his Yeti ass into one of the chair/desk combinations that lined the room. Of course, Naomi went with him and since she asked, I went too.

God, I was getting sick of it, following her like some love starved puppy while Jeff got the real feast. I slumped into my chair and arranged my books and papers for Hersey's lecture. I just loved my Monday mornings, where I got the double shot of asshole first thing.

Hersey finally came in and took his sweet old time arranging his material. Then he went to the chalkboard and scratched a date at the upper left-hand corner in yellow chalk.

6-3-12.

What the eff was this about? This class of seniors would be long gone by then. I looked to Naomi, but she shrugged her shoulders. No answers from her, so I turned my attention back to the front of the class. Hersey yakked about the quiz and then, staring right at me, announced there was no making it up. Whoever missed it would get a zero.

Nobody groaned at the unfairness of it. Hersey was a hard-ass, and apparently, no one else missed Friday's class except me. I glanced up in time to catch his full smirk. Nice. Who was the professional here?

I doodled around the date I'd copied onto my notes. 6-3-12. My pen swirled around while the professor did a quick recap of the quiz and lit into those who hadn't done well. He was such a charming guy if you got on his bad side, I'd discovered. I let my mind wander as my pen continued to trace curly-ques. The drone of a bee meandered and bobbed, and my pen stilled upon the page. I scratched the base of my skull with my free hand as the buzzing intensified to the point where I had to concentrate to hear what Hersey was mouthing off about.

"...tagging and documenting wolves on this date, come see me in my office by the end of the week."

My head snapped up, and Hersey met my stare, like he'd been watching me the whole time he'd been addressing the class.

The *fucking* asshole. He was going back to the north woods to prove what he'd found, and he was rubbing my nose in it. Sweat prickled the back of my shoulders and my underarms as the nib of my pen pressed a blue hole into the paper. The image of Armand and Eaen lounging safe and comfortable in my living room with their books rose in my mind as bile crept up my throat. The buzzing exploded in a brilliant flash of light.

The next thing I knew, Hersey's gaze was level with mine because I was on my feet. The surge of hatred for that man rolled through me like a semi-truck, and my emotions shifted through the gears. I was on a high-speed collision course with no brakes.

And wading toward Hersey through a sea of desks.

Time slowed down, and that smug look on his face fell away as his eyes widened in shock, and I watched, disjointed, as his mouth opened with an impotent reprimand.

The screech of metal desk legs across the tile floor brayed from far away, dulled by space. The distance between me and the man who threatened all that was pure and beautiful in this shit-heap world dwindled, and my eyes zeroed in on the noose of his tie he'd meticulously knotted that morning.

My shoulder muscles bunched as I raised my arms to throttle that neat throat, and then my wind was smacked from my lungs as The Bear's bulk crushed me from behind and yanked me toward the door. I struggled against him like a rabbit, but he was huge, and even my anger couldn't overpower Jeff.

"Hersey, you cocksucker! You're a shit-for-brains lo—"

Naomi slammed the door, effectively cutting off my tirade to Hersey, and Jeff threw me down onto the hallway floor.

"What the fuck, Rickey?" His wide chest heaved under his university sweatshirt.

I leapt to my feet and charged for the door. I wanted that guy's neck in my hands so bad I couldn't see straight. Jeff blocked my way like a wall.

"Are you fucking nuts? He's a teacher, for Chrissakes. You'll get your ass kicked out of school." He jabbed a stubby finger into my sternum.

"I don't care!" I shouted at the mountain in front of me. "Didn't you hear? He's going back."

Jeff's confused look was a sharp slap back to reality. My anger hovered like water on the lip of a glass, as the part of my brain that manages rational thought finally started playing catch up.

"Who cares, for fuck's sake? It's not worth your future."

"Not worth—?" I swallowed my impotent rage, took a deep breath, and stared long and hard at the ape in front of me. He didn't know, of course. I looked over my shoulder at Nae, who stood with her hands over her mouth. Neither of them knew. This was my burden. I'd volunteered to help Armand and Eaen and their pack in the north woods and *this*— this infuriating mess was part of what I'd signed on to do.

I swallowed another deep breath and ripped at the hair on my scalp. A frustrated scream built in my lungs, and I bent over and yelled at the tiled floor instead. When I straightened up, both Jeff and Naomi were eyeballing me like I'd just purchased a one-way ticket for the funny farm. No passing *Go* or collecting $200 dollars.

Okay, so I was totally blowing this like the weak idiot I was. I needed to settle down and act like none of Hersey's shit made a difference. I didn't need him to be at the ready for anything rash I might pull. We didn't need him on his guard. That wasn't going to help anyone.

I headed back to the classroom, but found my path blocked by the guy who'd just saved my ass. Great, now I owed him one. I stopped to glare up at him.

"I'm fine," I lied. "I'm just going back to class to get my stuff." When I ducked my head to shove past the Hulk, he side-stepped to block my way again.

I snapped my head up. "What?"

"I'll go get it," he offered, then pointed his beefy finger at me again. "You stay."

He's an effing cave man.

My head nodded anyway. It was probably best.

Jeff headed back into the room we'd left in a bit of rush, and I looked askance at Naomi, who, I figured, would be wearing a look of pity on her face.

Surprise, surprise. She was smirking wickedly, her defiant beam illuminating the Naomi I remembered from our early days.

The corner of my mouth lifted in a conspiratorial grin. "Yeah." I cleared my throat. "That went well."

Her laughter was a slip of silk tugging on my belly. "You were great. The bastard had it coming after how he's treated you all year."

My grin took over my entire face. "Yeah, I guess he did," I allowed as I rubbed my hands across my scalp and sighed. "Except now I'm fucked."

Nae stepped in close to reach up as if to adjust a thatch of my hair, then her hand dropped as she stiffened, and she stepped brusquely around me. "Hey, Jeff, you got it."

I watched her stride over to her boyfriend and take my bag from him. *Am I going crazy, or did Nae and I just have a moment?*

No, that was the adrenaline sharpening my nerves to a fine edge.

She only had eyes for Jeff, and I was imagining things. But, if I wasn't?

The girl of my dreams strode over with my bag extended in her graceful arm. "Here," she winked slyly. "Go home. I'll get your notes from the other classes."

When I grabbed my bag, she held it for a brief second longer than was necessary.

"Thanks, Nae," I made sure to catch her hazel eyes, to indicate my sincere gratitude, the longing, the— I dropped my lids before I revealed anything else. *She thinks of you as a brother, jerk.*

"I'll see you guys later." I turned on feet that barely carried my shaking legs, and did my damnedest not to wobble back to the car.

Holy sweet loving fuck—what a morning.

Once in the driver's seat, I grasped and twisted the steering wheel to get a grip on my emotions, which were more tangled than the traffic circles in Augusta. Somehow, Vegetarian-Boy had turned into Robo-cop to protect the innocent, and Naomi had shined her smile on me just like she used to do in the days before The Bear. Hell, yeah, it was an effed-up day, bad news included. I couldn't wait to get home and share the latest developments with my friends.

* * * *

Eaen and Armand were as dismayed as I was about my righteous outburst in the classroom.

"We are proud you stood up to him, Porcupine, but that was not the place." Armand held his yellow eyes on my face just to make sure I got his meaning.

I dropped my gaze to the floor. The shame I'd been feeling flamed under their cool scrutiny and doubt chilled my bones. What in the hell had they been thinking when they'd asked for my help? They needed someone else. They needed a human who could at least use his brain. After my thoughtless attack on my professor, it was crystal clear I was not their candidate, and with frustration tightening my voice, I admitted it to the wolf-men who sat with me.

"No, Porcupine," Eaen muttered softly, "you are the one we need."

"But I messed up, Eaen. I shouldn't have let Hersey get to me like that," I protested, even as the wrath I'd felt earlier came surging back.

My hand raked through my hair, and I got up and paced the room. Two pairs of keen eyes followed my seesawing.

"We all succumb to our instincts." Eaen's quiet voice was a meditative stream. "It is who we are, and the elemental must be acknowledged."

I stopped pounding the floor. The wolf-man's words carried the weight of acceptance, not reproach, and my self-pity was assuaged in an instant. As was the anger. I plunked back down in my vacant chair, and looked back and forth between my friends.

"So, now what?"

"Now," Armand replied, "we wait with our eyes and ears open." Eaen nodded his agreement, but I could only offer a bewildered stare.

"Come hunting with us, Kenrickey, and you will see what I mean." The blonde wolf-man's smile spread across his face, revealing four dagger-like fangs.

My breath stuck in my throat. Christ, he was lethal.

I didn't argue with him this time about the hunting. I would go whether I ate meat or not, and felt the queerest itch of anticipation scurry up my spine. Was I actually going to enjoy hunting, especially since uncovering some violent tendencies of my own? Eaen's sage words floated through my brain—*We all succumb to our instincts.*

"Sure, I'll go," I conceded as a sly grin tugged at the corners of my mouth.

The expression was not lost on my cunning friends.

"Good," said Armand, whose grin returned to be a mirror to my own. "We go at dusk. Then you will learn one of the most valuable skills a wolf can possess. *Patience."*

I couldn't freakin' wait.

* * * *

True to their word, at dusk Eaen and Armand led our little hunting party through the tangle of grasses and budding alders that bordered the river. Once we arrived at the edge of the woods, they doffed their clothing, draped it neatly across a fallen witch-wood-berry tree, and then effortlessly contorted into wolves.

My breath caught in my throat as my heart skittered inside my ribcage. "Jesus, guys, I don't think I'm ever going to get used to that." I had known their change was coming, and I still wasn't prepared for the shock of it.

Eaen shook his heavy frame and fanned his bushy tail back and forth across his back. Apparently, he thought my reaction was very funny.

Armand was all business. He stuck his nose to the ground and padded nimbly along a muddy path skirting the riverbed. Eaen and I followed at a trot. I was glad I'd spent the winter running to get in shape because we didn't stop until the sun was completely gone and the first stars popped out onto the canvas of night sky.

The blonde wolf halted us at the edge of a beaver dam. In the dark, it was difficult to see the details, but its mass formed a black outline against the small marsh that surrounded it. The stench in the air was undeniably beaver.

And I knew beaver, since I'd worked around dams before, when I pulled a stint as a working student to help pay my tuition. As a Biology major, I got first dibs on joining up even though I wasn't actually doing the research. Other students, farther along in their education got that advantage. But, at least I was still on site, and lugging the bulk of the equipment was well worth the price of admission. I loved being in the field. It was why I chose to pursue a degree in Biology in the first place.

The familiar musk of beaver and the chilly spring night etched goose-bumps upon my skin. I glanced over at the two wolves with me. Holy mother, this scenario was beyond imagination. Armand had leapt to the top of the dam, his graceful frame silhouetted against the sky. I literally stood ogling at the image.

Eaen bumped my hand with his warm muzzle.

"Hey," I whispered as I knelt on the wet grass. Our breaths plumed around our heads.

Watch.

The black wolf slipped away to position himself downwind from the tangled alders of the beaver's lodge. Both wolves dropped to their bellies, and I stretched my own frame across the marsh grass.

They did nothing else, except train their attention to the dark mound. The blonde wolf's nose pointed downward with his erect ears framing his face. He was listening to the activity inside the dam. His hunting

46

companion pricked his triangular ears forward, too, and waited for Armand's cue. I squirmed into a more comfortable position, because obviously we were going to be here a while, hence the lesson in patience.

The moon lifted higher into the night sky, and the cloak of early night eased as the glow from the stars illuminated the edges of the marsh around us. It was now easy enough to see the details of the beaver dam.

To my right, water splashed with no more than a quick blurp. The wolves didn't budge, and I held my breath, which sounded too loud in the darkness. The damp mud of the marsh sucked the heat out of my body, and I shivered and clenched my jaw to stop my teeth from chattering.

Armand and Eaen turned their furry snouts toward my position for a brief moment, then refocused on the inky pool. Another slurp gurgled in the darkness. Had the beaver pulled itself out of the creek? The two wolves remained like statues, and if I hadn't been aware of their positions I would have been hard pressed to see them. I racked my brain to remember if beavers were near-sighted.

My heart thudded against the mud. Damn. I hoped like hell the percussion couldn't be felt through the ground, like seismic activity or something.

Focus.

I rotated my eyes toward Armand and Eaen, my brows creasing over my nose. *What?*

Focus.

Okay. Right. I *did* hear that. But how in the hell—? I tilted my weight to my right side to get a better look at Eaen, who was crouched about twenty feet away.

Do not move.

I froze like I was a kid playing Red Light/Green Light. My reaction to what I'd *heard* in my head sent my brain cells zipping across the ice of my skull. I had most definitely stopped moving because I'd heard the command. What the frig? How was that even possible?

I rolled my eyes to Armand, who had turned his head so that his muzzle lay parallel to his left shoulder. His ears were still pricked forward as he focused on the movement in the water. Why didn't he jump in after it? I mean, even *I* could now see the vee of ripples the beaver left in its wake.

Christ, I was getting a cramp in my neck from lying in that awkward position. I never should have moved in the first place. Not only was I uncomfortable, but I nearly alerted the beaver to my presence, and Armand and Eaen would have gone hungry because of it. Shit, I wasn't just effing dumb, I was a liability.

The beaver paddled its slick mass toward the bank, directly in front of the black wolf. Who, I noticed with an inward cringe, hadn't flicked a single hair since he'd positioned himself by the river bank. I remembered then the beaver isn't very agile on dry land. Its defense was the pool it was pulling itself out of. The wolves had known that and had waited.

Yeah, freakin' Patience with a capital P.

With sloshes and slurps, the beaver waddled up the mud bank straight toward the black wolf. How in hell did the guy remain so still? Even Armand didn't turned his head to follow the path of the beaver. And I suddenly understood why he would watch with just his eyes and ears and not rotate his head. From his vantage point, the beaver would have seen that kind of movement, whether it was near sighted or not.

Effing brilliant.

Their cunning struck awe and my pulse quickened. They were going to get this beaver, and my heart thudded with jubilant anticipation. But I didn't move, even if the crick in my neck threatened to crack, and sever my head from my shoulders.

Suddenly, the sough of damp reeds exploded into the darkness around us as the black wolf torpedoed toward his prey. Eaen catapulted himself ten feet in less than the blink of an eye, smothered the beaver with his heavy body, and clamped his great jaws at the back of its skull. The wolf thrashed the heavy beaver from side to side as it shrieked.

My guts tingled and clenched, and before I knew it, I was surging toward the kill as if I could slay the thing. Armand's blonde body streaked headlong into the fray, and he buried his long fangs into the base of the beaver's great tail. I skidded to a halt, panting excitedly, my muscles flexing and constricting in sympathy to the glorious killing. This was life, and I itched like a motherfucker to be a part of it.

The struggle was over in less than a minute, and slowly it dawned on me I was straddled like I was ready to jump, my arms held rigid away from my heaving sides, all set to propel my body forward.

Holy fuck. The rip of flesh and gloating growls clotted the air as the two wolves worked at the carcass. The squeak of rubbery flesh grinding in sharp molars made my mouth water. Some vegetarian I was. But, Jesus, it was brutal, sublime. Exhilarating. And I wanted to be a part of it with every drop of blood in my human body.

Eaen and Armand continued to gorge on the beaver. The musky thing must have weighed around fifty pounds, but they tore into it, rending it between them like it was nothing but a rag. I crept closer for a better view, and watched awestruck as they gnawed and gulped chunks of flesh. The smacking made my mouth water again, and without even thinking, I reached for the eviscerated carcass.

The two wolves lifted their lips from their incisors, and my hand froze in mid-air. Without peeling their shining eyes from me, they sidled sideways to offer me a spot.

Holy living fuck, I was going to do it. I was going to eat raw beaver, stench and all. I stuck the tips of my fingers into blood, then pushed the dripping tips into my mouth.

Oh yeah. Pennies. Hot pennies with a warm, delicious slick that slid like thick cream down my throat. And I wanted more—like I was ravenous. I couldn't fucking believe it. I grabbed, and then stopped myself.

Wait an effing minute. This wasn't my meal. Impossibly, these two wolves, which were shredding sinew with their sharp incisors *and* generously offering me a place as if I were a pack member, needed to eat this. Not me. I pulled away to observe instead.

Eat.

I glanced up from the absorbing image before me, Armand's yellow eyes pinning my attention to him and nothing else.

But I shook my head. "No, Armand. It's yours. You guys eat." Did I just say that? I just spoke to a wolf that hadn't—*couldn't*—speak to me, as if he had. My brain warped, and with habitual reflex, I shoved my hand across my scalp, smearing blood into my hair. Yet, I didn't care. My mind was too confused, too effing hepped up to worry about it.

Tonight was too much on top of an already eventful day. I fell back onto my ass and held my head in my hands while the guttural devouring of flesh filled my ears, and the musk of beaver hide and blood flooded my sinuses. The two wolves continued to eat despite my retreat.

They needed to. It had been almost three days since they'd filled their bellies. I was a little stunned by that. How did they ignore the bite of hunger pangs?

I already knew the answer. Of course, they were used to the cramp of hunger. They were wolves, for God's sake. Their bodies were designed to glut on an available meal because days could pass before they killed anything to eat, just as this instance candidly illuminated.

I took a deep breath, holding it until my lungs felt the strain from the lack of oxygen. This situation was impossible, yet there I was sitting on my can beside the river with a dead beaver and two wolves. *Not* two werewolves, either. By some exceptional anomaly of natural evolution, these wolves could become human-like. Not just because it was a full moon, but because they needed to, or wanted to.

I was harboring highly specialized predators.

Beautiful, generous, fun-loving killers.

Who were in danger of being exterminated because they wouldn't retaliate with the same brutality as their enemy. And I would do anything to help them. Tonight's lesson wasn't just about patience. It slammed home my physical compulsion to protect those who had become as much a part of me as I was of them. Their offering a place at the kill was the evidence of that. These wolves were superior in forming symbiotic relationships, all I needed to do was think about the telepathic messages I'd received to believe that.

I got to feeling all warm and fuzzy again as an acute sense of well-being swelled within me, spreading a shit-eating grin across my face. Oh yeah. Every moment I was with Armand and Eaen I didn't feel like a misfit the way I did when I was around my peers. These guys accepted me for who I wasn't. I was not their enemy, but considered to be as essential to their survival as their friend the crow. I felt that as sure as I was sitting in the dark in the forest beside a half-eaten beaver.

A tremor buzzed pleasantly at the base of my skull as I watched my two brothers fill their empty bellies. And brothers they were. We were connected. I'd jumped into the fray of one of their kills, brimming with sheer self-confidence. Misplaced? Nope. But I would most definitely have to ask the wolf-men about our silent communication.

Was that Luna's influence? Had she altered me somehow, so I would be utterly connected to Eaen and Armand? What a gift, if she had. To feel this self-possession, this unreserved brotherhood with two men who hid nothing of themselves? Damned straight I was thankful.

I sat right there brimming with satisfaction as I watched my new brothers nourish themselves with a hard won meal, and I couldn't help but wonder what other revelations lay in store as I opened myself to the wolf-men, just as they had done for me.

* * * *

The following morning dawned rainy and cold, but I felt none of it since I was snuggled in a heap of super-warm bodies. Taking my cue from their habit of sleeping together, I had offered Eaen and Armand a place in my bed. They'd accepted without reservation, warming more than just my skin. I wasn't so dimwitted to overlook the importance of shared sleeping quarters. Their acceptance was another token of unreserved friendship, of brotherhood. So, I wasn't too anxious to remove myself from that when I thought about the coming day.

Because the morning not only brought the rain, but the bite of reality. I had to face Hersey after my outburst the day before, and God only knew what had transpired after I'd left. Knowing that bastard, he would have petitioned for me to be expelled from campus, and I would have to ready myself for that catastrophe whether I wanted to or not.

I ran my hand across my head, sticking my fingers into a crusty spike of hair. Oh, right. Dried blood from the beaver. I smiled in spite of what awaited me at school. Last night had been beyond belief.

"Good morning, Porcupine." Eaen's voice rasped from the foot of the bed.

How in the hell did he know I was awake?

"I could tell by your breathing," he replied past a deep yawn, and then he stretched until his long legs reached the headboard. Armand rolled over and pressed his back against my side. His breathing was deep and even, so I knew he still slept.

The proof was so obvious I could've smacked myself on the forehead. My breathing had changed, and that's how Eaen knew I was awake. But that wasn't what really nagged and got my pulse trotting.

"I never said anything, so how could you know? Can you, you know, read minds, I mean?" I teetered on the verge of blabbering. *Jesus, Eaen, how about reading my mind now so I don't have to sound like a freakin' idiot.*

"Only if the thought is strong, so never general reflections," he yawned again, his elbows lifting into my field of vision as he put his hands over his face. "Most of what may seem like mind reading is simply the interpretation of physical cues of the one you are with."

Well, that was normal. I had to admit it was also a bit disappointing, like finding out Batman wasn't really a super-hero if you took away his toys. But still, the wolf-people had *some* ability in the mind-reading department and that made me feel a little better. Not to mention they were already fucking awesome in so many other areas.

"Kenrickey?" Armand mumbled from deep within my pillow.

"Yeah?"

"To us you are not human, so maybe that is why." He ground his face farther into the pillow to rub away the sleep from his yellow eyes.

I gushed like a school-girl with a crush, and waited a few seconds before I responded. Christ, I didn't want to *sound* like one. "Wow. Thanks guys. I mean, that's—that's freakin' awesome, you know. I feel the same way about you. Not that you're not human, but like we're brothers. Of course, we're not real brothers, but—"

I was babbling like that school-girl and clamped my mouth shut. Eaen and Armand chuckled, and I grinned in spite of my embarrassment.

"Porcupine?"

"Yeah?"

"Can you bring home more of your books from school?"

"Sure, Armand. No sweat." I'd do anything for the guy. But, as warm and cozy as I was feeling just then, I had to get up and get to that school. It was time to face the music. I swung my legs out over the edge of the bed and planted my bare feet on the cold floor. Christ, why'd it have to be a shitty day out?

I glanced over my shoulder at my bunkmates. Eaen had rolled onto his side when I sat up, and now he and Armand were in an upside-down spoon position. That looked too comfortable, so before I caved and lost all of my resolve, I stretched to my feet and headed for the bathroom without looking back. Their heat evaporated from my skin before I'd even stepped into the shower.

About a half-hour later, I was pulling into the campus parking lot, the windshield wipers of the Subaru squeaking on every upward arc. My headlights splashed across a forest green Range Rover as I pulled into an empty parking space. Naomi and Jeff were huddled in his car, the tailpipe spewing heavy steam into the cold, wet air. They waited for me whenever we had the same classes in the morning, and usually I was used to seeing them first thing.

Not this time. My heart tripped and fluttered at the sight of Naomi's blond head in the steamed up window, and I had to take a deep breath to steady it as they got out of their vehicle as soon as I killed my engine.

"Mornin', bro."

That didn't give me the warm, fuzzy feeling of brotherhood. Never did.

"Hi, Ken." Naomi's lilt sure as hell didn't either. I was not having brotherly thoughts about her.

"Hey, guys." I fell back on my tired, old greeting, forgetting all about the Range Rover. "Hear anything about yesterday, yet?"

They shook their heads as we headed for the Science building.

"Great. I can't effing wait to find out." I pulled my hood up over my head, hunched my shoulders as if I planned to bash through a wall, and strode to class. Jeff and Naomi trotted after me.

I had my hand on the door when Hersey's voice resounded through the cemented hall.

"Mr. Rickey, I'd like a word with you."

Jesus, did they always have to talk like that? All formal and shit? I pulled my hood off and turned toward Hersey's office. "See you guys."

Naomi and Jeff stared silently, looking a little perplexed.

The thing was, see, I was grinning. Nothing could have made me happier than to hear Hersey's authoritative command, because I was looking forward to his little speech. Granted, I was a bit startled initially. I mean, I thought I was dreading the inevitable meeting. Until I felt that little buzz at the base of my skull again, and the images of the previous night flickered like a movie montage in my head.

Oh yeah. I was ready. And this time I wasn't going to mess things up for my brothers.

I looked up in time to see Professor Crandall following Hersey into his office. Her presence piqued my anticipation, and I practically trotted to Hersey's private room.

When I got to his open door, he was already sitting at his desk chewing on the earpiece of his glasses, and Crandall was making herself comfortable on the register under the window, as if she perched there on a regular basis. Maybe she did. The man from the Range Rover sat in the wingback chair in the corner, his ankle crooked up on his knee, like he was trying to seem laid back.

Except there wasn't anything casual about this guy. Not his crew cut, not the running of muscle under his loose button-down, and certainly not the quick, hard flash of his eyes that absorbed every detail without his even trying.

Like Eaen and Armand.

I dragged my eyes off the stranger to look at Hersey, instead. No way was that a wolf-man sitting in this room. No effing way.

Rain splattered against the window, and the noise was another distracting presence in the room. So was Crandall. What was she doing there? Better yet, what was this guy in the corner doing in Hersey's office, and what did that have to with me?

"Come in, Ken," Hersey stretched his arm out to indicate the chair in front of his desk.

I stole a glance at the man sitting in the corner and shook my head. "I'll stand if you don't mind." Sitting beside this guy would've made me feel too vulnerable, and I needed to keep my cajones.

"Suit yourself," Hersey glanced at the others and lifted one eyebrow, as if to say, *See what I mean?*

I had little patience for them, and it felt strangely invigorating to be on the offensive, especially since just a few seconds ago Hersey's visitor almost had me lying flat on the floor. And he hadn't even moved a muscle. "What did you want?"

Crandall's eyes widened in surprise. I was just a student, after all, and should have taken a subordinate tone.

"Well, first I'd like to introduce you to Mr. Randall Wolfe. He's the—"

Wolfe? He's kidding, right? I almost snorted my disbelief. Instead, I looked straight at Randall Wolfe, wondering if he was serious, and if he'd cave under my stare. Blah, blah, Hersey yammered on about the man sitting in front of me.

He stared back, with a subtle twist of his upper lip that could've been a snarl if those sharp eyes of his weren't glittering with amusement.

He let his grin loose, revealing a fine row of pearly whites.

And extended his hand. "Pleased to meet you, Mr. Rickey."

I gaped at it for a second, surprised by the human greeting. This was so effed up. I shook his nice, very warm hand, telling myself there was no freakin' way this man was one of the wolf-people.

Evidence against? His hand was normal, his thumb where it ought to be. I stacked that against the other clues, pretending they didn't matter because of the normal appearance of his hand.

Because there was just no effing way Mr. Randall Wolfe was wolf.

Hersey's voice trailed back into existence. "…Wolfe, here, and his associates, have been generous sponsors of our research. They've been most interested in the results of my field study last fall."

The bastard Hersey smirked, and I backed off from Randall Wolfe to confront the more obvious threat, but kept the new guy in my line of vision. Just in case. Luna made her presence known as an annoying itch at the base of my skull, and I reached up to scratch it.

"You've got no proof of anything." Did I just growl?

Hersey narrowed his eyes. "Yes, well, in spite of that setback, Mr. Wolfe and his colleagues have remained interested. It's because of them, in fact, that Professor Crandall and I have reached a decision concerning your, um…*episode* in class yesterday morning."

So, this new guy wasn't there to expel me, and Hersey hadn't gone before the Board. Suspicion quickened my pulse, and I cast a wary glance at the woman by the window, who up until then had fallen off my radar. "And?"

Crandall slid off her perch. "We've been talking—"

"I'm sure you have," I interrupted. Their keeping the matter of my assault on a professor private didn't sit well on my nerves, especially given the appearance of a new character in this skit.

Hersey pursed his lips and tossed his glasses onto his desk. I suddenly had the random thought that he was an excellent marksman. He had been the one who shot the tranquilizer dart into Grane. The hair at my nape crawled up, and I shivered with a renewed sense of antagonism. But I didn't forget Eaen's and Armand's disappointment at my first outburst, so I shoved my hands into the pockets of my jeans, and clamped my jaw shut.

Mr. Wolfe sat back down in his chair, apparently content to watch the drama unfold without his participation.

"Dr. Hersey, Mr. Wolfe, and I have been talking," Crandall repeated. "And we've all agreed not to recommend expulsion from the university." The whole time she spoke, she looked at Hersey, and kept her arms crossed with her back to the window.

Did she sense the predator in the room?

Hersey trained his attention on his hands, which twisted a pencil he'd picked up when he'd tossed his glasses, and nodded as Crandall spoke.

I addressed Hersey, not the other two. "Is that right?"

Hersey pushed his chair away to stand up behind his desk. "Yes, Mr. Rickey, that is *right.*"

I felt like crossing the room and punching him in the face, but asked the crucial question instead.

"Why?"

"Why?"

"Did I stutter, or mumble?"

Hersey was stalling, and I didn't take my eyes off him. I simply didn't trust the man. Crandall and Wolfe sat in my periphery.

Patience. Right. I had it in spades.

Crandall continued. "We hoped that in return you could explain to us about last autumn. About the wolves." She stepped close enough to me so I could see the worn eraser of the pencil she kept tucked behind her ear.

I stiffened, and took a step backward. *Holy fuck. A goddamned bargain?* I hadn't anticipated this outcome. Which meant Wolfe wasn't who I'd thought. He was just some nosy bastard like Hersey who meant nothing but trouble. But, my step backward practically put me out in the hall, and I'd be effed if I was going to back down from these conspirators.

I crossed the room, brushed past Crandall, ignored Randall Wolfe, and stopped when the front of my thighs hit Hersey's cluttered desk. I leaned toward my professor and pointed my finger at him, a much better tack than what I'd really wanted to do, which was shove my fist down his throat.

So, I jabbed my finger instead, and was pretty surprised by the words that came out of my mouth. "There were no wolves, *Mark*. You have lost your fucking mind, and are blaming me for it. Report me, asshole. I have nothing to give any of you."

I squared my shoulders, turned around and left the room. But not before I caught a quick scan of Crandall, whose mouth actually formed a perfect *O*. And Randall Wolfe? He wore an amused grin, and would it have been my imagination if I thought I also saw approval in his sharp eyes?

I couldn't be sure, but I didn't feel like delving too deep into why he'd be pleased with my reaction to Hersey's so-called bargain, nor did I feel like sticking around to ask him about it. I plowed out of that room without a single hitch in my stride.

My knees started knocking before I reached the exit. If that wasn't bad enough, I could see Naomi standing on the other side of the glass door. Presumably waiting for me. I darted my eyes around the lobby in search of Jeff, but he was nowhere to be seen. At least, that was some relief. I shoved through the doors and stopped for the woman I'd adored since I'd met her four years ago. I couldn't utter a harsh word to her no matter how shitty I felt. I took a deep breath and waited for her to come up beside me.

"Where's the Yeti?" That came out a lot stronger than I'd hoped. Apparently, I could utter a harsh word. I turned to her, and the hurt on Naomi's face dashed away my temper.

"I'm sorry, Nae," I breathed and reached for her, but she stepped back and I let my empty hand drop. My mouth opened to offer some excuse, but then I shut it. She didn't deserve excuses. I wanted her to hear the truth, most of it anyway. And I certainly couldn't tell her in front of the Science building. Plus, thinking about the meeting I'd just

S. C. Dane

had with Hersey got my dander up again. I needed to get my head on straight before I told Nae anything. All I could do was apologize again, and step closer to her, like she was the sun and I gravitated to her like the earth.

She flashed her hazel eyes up to me, and I witnessed the Naomi I remembered. All piss and fire, the feisty sister in a family of brothers. The sight of it washed beautiful, a balm for all the sadness I'd endured while watching her wither away under the spell of The Bear.

I got an erection.

And blushed so hard the blood throbbed in my ears. Sweet living Jee-zus I wanted her, could take her right there on the Quad. Plant my mouth on those pert—I locked down on that train of thought, and dragged my eyes away from her intensely searching, hazel eyed gaze. Nae wasn't some trollop to play my fantasies out on. She was my girl. *My* woman, who had always held my pathetic heart in her goddamned hands. Whether she felt sisterly love for me or not, she had me forever, even if Jeff had his grubby paws on her for the moment.

I lowered my head and backed away before my body made decisions for me. The slap across my cheek stung all the more because I hadn't expected it, and I snatched Naomi's wrist before I realized what I was doing, yanked her to me to plant my mouth on hers, to nail that kiss I'd been too chicken-shit to deliver before.

I stopped with the heat of her lips resting mere millimeters from mine, so close our breaths mingled, hers registering on my cheek in delicate panting puffs. So close, I could snake my tongue out to taste her.

What the hell was I doing? I released her arm like I was stuck to her like taffy and back-pedaled.

"Nae, I'm *so* sorry, I'm—" But I couldn't say anything just then. My thoughts jumbled amidst the memory of her soft skin in my hand, and I knew I'd prattle away and botch everything, ruin the chance I had of introducing her to Eaen and Armand.

My ears throbbed and so did Mr. Plucky. Just fucking great. I spun on my heel and bolted for my car without giving Naomi another chance to either swing at me or berate me, and left her standing alone by the glass doors. I wasn't keeping it together. The combination of my hard-on pressing painfully against my zipper, my possible expulsion, and

Naomi's slap had sent me into a goddamned tailspin. I'd be lucky to drive home without running off the road.

I fumbled the keys and crammed them into the ignition, then just sat there, gulping deep breaths. Man, if I were a smoker, I'd have the whole pack crammed in my mouth. Raindrops splattered on the windshield and then cascaded in rivulets. The drumming on the steel roof of the car pattered rhythmically, and the blood in my veins eased its racing and finally pumped more steadily.

After a while, I wasn't feeling like such a shit, and I wasn't feeling like a rapist, either. I peered out through my fogged up windshield with the hopeless desire to see Naomi still standing outside. Of course she wasn't. She'd gone back in when I'd fled and the rain started.

Boy, I had some major explaining to do, if she'd talk to me. I wasn't so sure she would after the slap she'd delivered. What the hell was that all about anyway? Had she seen my hard-on, the brutal leer on my face, and gotten pissed about it? Maybe I had read her wrong the day I assaulted Hersey, and she really did only think of me as a brother.

Shit. Shit. Shit.

I didn't have a clue.

But, for Eaen's and Armand's sake, I would have to trust that I hadn't ruined our friendship and could still count on her to help us. Especially since I wasn't too sure about my future at the school. I would need someone on the inside to keep me posted on Hersey if I got expelled.

Well, I would obviously have to talk with her later, so I started my car and drove to the campus library to take out as many books as was allowed by law. Hell, if I wasn't going back to the school for a while, I at least wanted to have enough reading material on hand for my brothers.

I filled my backpack and my arms with my loaned choice of literature, and ran for the parking lot. The whole time I wished I could dodge raindrops, and that made me feel as light on my feet as Fred Astaire.

Okay, everything was going to work out. I'd figure out Naomi, where she was coming from, and go from there. Hell, I'd drop to my knees and beg if I had to. Plus, I might have cast a small seed of doubt into Crandall's brain about Hersey's claim. She hadn't seen the wolves, and was standing by her colleague based on his merit as a field researcher alone. Based on evidence that no longer existed. And Randall Wolfe? Yeah, I didn't have a clue about that guy, whoever he was; but, maybe he had some role to play. If I saw him again, I'd find out, especially if he and his associates were the ones funding Hersey's research in Alec's and Luna's territory.

My self-confidence surged back, and I was feeling much better by the time I drove my car down Route One toward home. There would be no running the Subaru off into the trees.

* * * *

Later that same afternoon, we were bunched together in the living room, which was fast becoming our favorite hangout spot where we read, or talked, or were just quiet while we did our own thing. I had finally turned to the two wolf-men for some advice on how to deal with what had happened with Nae.

"You are asking the wrong wolf, brother," Armand held his hands up, palms facing me as he shook his head. "I know nothing about females."

Eaen nodded like he was in church listening to an evangelical minister.

"Nothing at all?" Well, that was exasperating. Apparently, we were a household of virgins. "Can you hazard a guess, at least?"

Some guidance would have gone a long way. I had no clue how to smooth Naomi over, and I didn't want to blow my only chance.

I searched the two sympathetic faces looking up at me.

"I'm on my own, aren't I?"

They both nodded and grinned.

I was all ready to give a sarcastic *Thanks* when Eaen asked about getting another car ride.

"Through town," he added.

I wasn't sure if he was serious. I mean, the last time we had driven through a public place, Eaen had reverted to his wolf form. I cast a questioning glance at Armand, who would have to do a car ride without his fur since it was still daytime. His pursed lips proved that his brother wasn't kidding. Eaen wanted to try another trip in the Subaru.

"Right now?"

The dark haired wolf-man sat up. "Now," he answered.

Armand clutched the arms of the chair until his knuckles turned white.

"You're kidding, right? It's daylight, the place will be swarming with people."

"Then it is the best time to test ourselves," Eaen stated, his expression firmly rational.

"I don't know." My hand raked its involuntary path. "I thought we'd try getting close, you know, not head right into the center of town. If you guys are seen—"

"We will lay low," he promised and grinned, revealing his strong, pearly teeth.

"Aw, man," I groaned, even as I headed to get my keys. They were going to go through with their test, whether Armand liked it or not. I peeked over my shoulder at the stuffed chair. Yeah, he was going to hate it—he hadn't budged from his spot in the living room. If anything, he looked as if he was cramming himself deeper into the chair cushions.

"Come, Arms, it will be all right," Eaen coaxed as he held his arm out to the wolf-man lodged in the furniture. In stark contrast to his brother, Eaen's demeanor was soft and supplicating, in spite of the chiseled muscles and sturdy bones that made up his athletic frame.

Armand shook his blonde head without lowering his yellow stare from Eaen, who dropped his hand to his side when his brother refused to loosen his grip on the armrests. The tall wolf-man wouldn't push, coerce or bribe. He had too much respect for Armand and the situation they were in.

"We'll go first, Eaen," I suggested as I walked over to the two of them and into a wall of heat, like I'd stepped through a portal that placed me smack in the center of the Sahara. Armand was frying. I didn't have to be a mind reader to know how he was feeling. "Besides, it's probably best if only one of you goes. My car's only so big, you know."

Armand managed a tight smile while his Adam's apple bobbed up and down his throat. I knew right then he couldn't have thanked me if he'd wanted to. He was too close to submitting to his wolf form.

Eaen and I both stepped back to give the guy some space. Christ, it hurt to watch him struggle. His muscles were so rigid they looked like they'd pop off his bones, and his chest heaved up and down as he tried his damnedest to steady himself by breathing deep. I couldn't help but think of a pregnant woman in labor. Screw the car ride if it made him feel this shitty.

Eaen nudged my shoulder and jutted his chin toward my backpack.

Oh yeah. Right. A distraction. Armand had yet to paw through the selection of books I'd gotten for him.

"Ha!" My outburst snapped the wolf-men to attention, their heads swiveling in sync to look at me. I grinned sheepishly, and could feel my ears turning red under their intense gazes. I stabbed my thumb toward my bag. "I was thinking Armand hadn't *pawed* through the books, yet. Get it? *Pawed*?"

Armand smiled, and his yellow eyes, which had been hard as glass just seconds before, softened. And then his facial muscles relaxed as he unclamped that bone-crushing jaw of his, so that when he parted his lips he gave the wickedest grin I'd ever seen on a human face. Fangs, I supposed, had a way of doing that.

Eaen busted out with an appreciative laugh, then ruffled his hand across the top of Armand's head, as if he were roughing up ears that weren't there. Armand swatted his hand away and sprung to his feet. But he didn't lose that unnerving smile of his. Oh no. He chomped down on Eaen's hand instead.

The tall wolf-man yelped and tackled his offender, who folded at the waist in a flash of twisting muscle, and wrapped his sinewy arms around his brother's waist as they crashed onto the living room floor like Greco-Roman wrestlers. I stood back and watched with open admiration. I mean, seriously, these guys had technique.

The wrestling ended with Armand fluffing Eaen's black hair. Yet, they both panted happily as they sat in a knot on the living room rug, as if they'd both just played and won at Aerobic Twister. I shook my head, amazed by the spectacle in front of me. Did they ever stay pissed?

"Hey, Eaen? You ready for that car ride, now?"

He gave his brother a questioning look as he licked at the indentations on his hand where Armand had bit him. "Yes, I am ready, but Arms will stay and read while we are gone." He winked so grandly even I didn't miss it.

They untied the knot of their limbs, got to their feet, and shook like they had full bodies of hair. Then Armand headed for his expedition into my backpack, and Eaen strode toward the door.

"Let us go if we are going, Porcupine," he laughed as he swung the front door wide open. Rain fell out of the sky in buckets behind him, which he either didn't notice or didn't care.

I shrugged, shot a parting glance toward Armand, who was already elbow deep in my bag, and bolted for my car. Eaen trotted behind me and slid his tall frame across the back seat.

The Subaru fired up like a saddled warhorse, and we sped toward Machias, population 5,000, through the slashing rain. At least there wouldn't be many people out on a stormy day. I turned my head to get a good look at Eaen, who weaved from one window to the other as he tried to see everything we passed.

"How're you doing?"

Eaen shined a brave smile in response.

"Talk to me, dude. What do you think?"

He swallowed the lump in his throat and gruffed, "It is different with the rain."

I nodded, and then focused on the road ahead. I didn't exactly get the answer I was looking for, but at least the guy could still speak. And he was right. It was different with the rain. For one thing, the ride was a lot noisier, what with the water on the road screaming through the tire treads.

"You want me to open a window?"

"No. I am good."

"We're almost into town, Eaen. You sure you want to do this? We can turn around and go home."

"No. I am good. This must be done."

His determination was admirable, especially given the fact he wasn't just some normal Joe-Shmoe who had a phobia about flying or some shit. Eaen's anxiety precipitated a complete metamorphosis. He became an entirely different species, for Chrissake. And it wasn't like he shifted into a cat, or a dog, even, something safe I could pass off as a pet if he happened to lose his self-control in public. Nope. Eaen changed into a creature that struck a primal, deeply-rooted fear in people. A wolf would not go unnoticed on the streets of Machias.

So, it was a good thing it was raining, and it was a good thing Eaen would stay in the car. I could just put the hammer down if he couldn't hold himself together, and I'd fly out of there so fast there'd be no witnesses.

Lucky for us, it was a typical stormy day in Downeast Maine. Nobody was out walking the sidewalks, and if they were out in this pouring rain, it was to dash from their vehicles to the stores and back again. I heaved a heavy sigh of relief, and loosened my grip on the steering wheel. Turns out it was a good day to experiment, to practice, after all.

I looked into the rearview at Eaen. He seemed to be holding himself together pretty well, and I wasn't feeling like a slice of bread in a toaster.

"What do you think? You want to go where there's more people?"

Eaen nodded his dark head, then as an after-thought remembered our cue. "Yes," he said deliberately, just so I'd know he was fine. "Let us try."

I steered the car toward the Hannaford's parking lot. There'd be plenty of people there since it was the only major grocery store within fifty square miles. I parked at the edge, under the row of seedling elms that every expansive parking lot seemed to have. As if shoppers would be fooled into thinking it was an inviting park, or that the corporate big-wigs were all about the environment. Never mind they had to bulldoze half a forest just to erect their shopping center. The sickly, token saplings were a pathetic substitute.

I draped my right arm across the front seat and turned to look in the back. Eaen had his face practically pressed to the window to get a better view. The ribs at his back were like a washboard under his wet t-shirt, and his lean muscles rippled. The temp in the car ratcheted upward, but he held himself together.

"You're effing amazing, you know that?"

Eaen swiveled his face toward the sound of my voice. His deep, brown eyes shimmered, even in the dull day. "How so, Kenrickey?" he asked with painstaking pronunciation of each syllable.

"You're doing good."

Eaen blushed with my compliment.

"Hey, so does Naomi really smell like snow?" What the hell. He needed distracting, and I needed to talk about the woman who stirred my insides with a swizzle stick.

Eaen cocked his head, and then took a really deep breath. "Yes. Her scent is clean. Sharp like a winter's day."

I inhaled automatically, as if she were sitting in the car beside me, where I could get a good whiff of her. I relished the idea she smelled like that, and I was heartened she wasn't offensive to the wolf-men. Jeff, on the other hand...

"So, what's Armand got about Jeff?"

Eaen furrowed his black brows, so I rephrased the question.

"What is it about Jeff that has Armand so upset?"

Eaen shivered involuntarily, and a low growl slipped from his throat.

Hoo-kay. Wrong subject to talk about if I was trying to keep him human. I strummed my fingers on my leg and fiddled with the knobs on the dash.

Eaen turned his attention back to the parking lot and answered as he stared out the window.

"He is very human. He reminds Armand of the men who shot his sister."

I swung around, surprised Eaen had spoken at all, let alone revealed something so horrific. My mouth dropped open and out fell the words, "What the fuck?"

Eaen kept his eyes on the activity outside of the car as he spoke. "Armand's sister, Grane's first mate, was shot by a human. They killed her because she was wolf."

My stomach sat in my intestines like a huge rock, and suddenly I just wanted to leave, to go back to the forest with Armand and Eaen and order them to go home. I dug my fingers into the base of my skull where a familiar vibration stirred and itched. Shit.

"Porcupine."

I turned my face to the sound, but wasn't really listening. The buzzing in my head mushroomed.

"Porcupine."

65

Eaen's warm hand on my shoulder refocused me, and I blinked like I'd been in the dark and somebody just flicked on the lights.

"We will be all right," he grinned, and I was wholly comforted by the sight of it, even if it exposed teeth too strong and sharp to belong to the average human. "Bring Naomi to your house very soon. I think I am ready to meet her."

The invitation registered, and I craned my neck around to peer out of the Subaru's windows. There were people going in and out of the store, pushing clanging carts, slamming car doors. Through it all, Eaen heroically kept his human form. The guy was freakin' incredible, and my chest tightened like I was going to cry with the joy of it. He had just taken the first crucial step toward keeping himself safe from harm by masquerading as the enemy right under their noses. And anyone who has ever read a spy novel knows, the best place to hide is in plain sight.

"Eaen, you did it." I couldn't have been more proud if he was my little boy who toddled his first steps to Papa.

Suddenly, Eaen jumped out of the car, and my pride-swollen heart shot into my mouth.

"What the—?" I had my door open before I'd even got turned back around. "Where—?"

The wolf-man ripped open the passenger side door, and heaving with the excitement of his Chinese Fire Drill, slid into the front seat next to me. Then he winked as if he'd just pulled the gag of a lifetime. "I just thought I would get a different perspective."

"Eaen, you goddamned, crazy son of a bitch!" I inhaled my heart back toward my lungs, and grinned like an escapee who has just evaded the men in white coats. "You really are something, you know that?" I shook my head in awed wonder, rolled the ignition over, and peeled out of the parking lot.

Our laughter drowned out the hiss of rainwater gushing through the treads of the Subaru's tires.

Chapter Four

That very night, Jeff called to tell me that he had signed up for the June excursion to the Northern woods even though he would have already graduated, and would no longer be, technically, a student at the university.

"Fucking Hersey." I pulled the cell phone from my ear to clasp my hand around the mouthpiece, then pretended to throw the thing against the wall. I took a deep breath and put the phone back up to my ear. Jeff was still talking.

"…they'd give my application serious consideration," he finished.

"I bet they will," *you effing moron.* Of course they would considerate it, and it would have absolutely nothing to do with the fact we hung out together. What a cheese-head.

"Yeah, bro. So, if you could give me some pointers, you know, that'd be great. I mean, you were there. You know what to expect."

"Sure," I answered like an automaton. *I'm also going to tell you everything so that you can report it back to Hersey, you puttz.* Armand and Eaen watched my silent rant from their position on the couch. They were both now sitting up, their curiosity piqued, and neither one was dressed in their human clothes since it trapped the heat they emanated and made them too warm. The two wolf-men clutched books in their strong hands.

"Tell him, Kenrickey, that his going would be a good thing and you will help him."

I palmed my phone again. "What? You can hear what he's saying?"

Armand nodded. "Yes, Porcupine. Now tell him what he needs to do to get his application accepted by our enemies."

"Why the hell would I do that?"

"Tell him," he repeated.

I heaved a resigned sigh, and put the phone back up to my ear. "Sure, Jeff, I'll help." I mouthed *Why?* but Armand just waved his hands at me in the universal gesture that meant *just keep going.* So I did. Jeff was so pleased I'd help him he abruptly ended our conversation because he had to go tell Naomi the good news.

Well, now, wasn't that just a pleasant chat with tea and a hefty slice of envy pie. Really, did the Yeti have no clue how much his news would bother me? The guy mugged me in class so that I wouldn't strangle the professor, for Christ's sake. Granted, I'd been pretty closed mouth about the trip up north, but still. Didn't he notice that all winter long Hersey and I squared off like a pair of alley cats? I was going to have to ask him, find out what kind of rocks the guy really did have in his head.

"It puts him inside, Porcupine. He can tell you everything that your teachers are planning." Armand got up off the couch and headed for the fridge. It sucked open, and he dug into the crisper for a Granny Smith.

I plopped into his favorite chair.

"You guys don't miss a thing, do you?"

Armand crunched. "Not usually."

"It is like hunting with a pack, Kenrickey," Eaen went on to explain, once he'd resettled on the couch with his long legs stuck up over the back of it. "Everyone has a predetermined job to do and every pack member knows what it is, does not even need to think about it. Therefore, the prey is captured because there are no holes for it to slip through."

"But you don't always catch your dinner," I argued, remembering the statistics of successful wolf kills to the number of hunts. But still, it would be to our advantage if The Bear could keep us informed, especially since I was definitely not on the inside of things anymore. That bridge got burnt the second Hersey's data went airborne.

"We are successful enough to keep our pack alive, well-fed, and healthy," Armand rejoined as he sunk his teeth into his apple lustily enough to make the juices fly.

"All right, you two have made your point," I conceded. "I'll help the Sasquatch." I flipped my notes out to study but didn't read a single line. All I could think about was how Hersey had busted my ass all year whenever he got the chance, and how Naomi had noticed, but hadn't ever said much about it. She didn't even ask. Talk about not prying.

Except that I had wanted her to pry, to be nosy and ask me questions. I doubted I would have said anything, because that god-awful buzzing showed up whenever I got my shorts twisted about the wolf-people, but *some* concern would have been nice. She ignored the whole thing instead. What kind of friend did that, anyway?

I stared at the lines in front of me. Naomi's notes, written in her neat penmanship that slanted slightly off because she was left-handed. Mr. Plucky roused himself and pressed on my sweats. Great. Just what I needed. I settled deeper into the chair, and tried thinking about something besides the hazel-eyed imp who had chopped her hair off so it swept the nub of bone at the top of her shoulder.

Okay, that wasn't helping. I scootched further into the overstuffed chair and concentrated on the rain pelting the roof. My balls tingled, then tightened, and my sweat pants turned into a pop-tent. I looked over at the two wolf-men stretched out on the sofa. They didn't seem to notice, or if they did, they didn't acknowledge it, thank the glorious gods of Hard-On Island.

Goddamn it, Naomi. Why now, all of a sudden, are you taking an interest?

My cell buzzed and sent my heart flinging around my ribcage. I snagged the damned thing off the floor.

"What?"

"Hi, Ken. It's Nae." Her voice poured like melted chocolate from the other end. Even the phone couldn't subdue it. "Jeff just called to tell me."

What was she doing calling me? "Um, hi. Yeah." My goddamned penis throbbed like it wanted to talk to the woman on the phone. I should've let it, given I couldn't seem to form complete sentences.

I got up and headed to the bathroom for some privacy. Although, knowing the two wolves on the couch, they could probably still hear me with the wooden door between us. I dropped the lid on the john and sat down.

Sure glad this isn't two-way video. Wouldn't that impress her? Me sitting on the toilet with a raging hard-on and two naked guys on the couch.

I cleared my throat before I dared to utter a single word. "Uh, yeah, he called to ask if I'd help him."

"Are you? Really going to help him, I mean?"

Her tone was ambiguous; I could read nothing from it. Which was just as well, since I was pretty sure she'd be glad I was helping her beef-headed boyfriend.

"Sure." My thoughts drifted to the conversation I'd just had with Eaen and Armand. Of course, I wasn't going to tell her the truth about why I had agreed to help him. Was I?

"Hey, Nae?"

"Yeah?"

"Do you think maybe… Do you think you could come over some time?" What the hell, she called me, right? The silence on the other end of the line made my guts crawl. She was going to say *no*.

"Um, sure. When?"

Right freakin' now, my hazel-eyed deliverer of relief. "Whenever you can come without Jeff."

"Oh, well, I—" She was backing out.

"Please, Nae. I really need to see you. I've…there's someone I really want you to meet. Someone who means a lot to me." Christ, if I keep talking she'll never get a chance to answer.

"Yeah. Okay. Would Thursday night be all right? Jeff's got—"

"Sure, Nae." I couldn't stop myself from cutting her off I was so goddamned relieved. "That would be great. I'll see you then."

"You won't be in class tomorrow?" Was that disappointment in her voice? Please, oh, please let it be.

"No, probably not, given the meeting I had this morning with Crandall and Hersey."

"Well, I'll get your notes then."

"Thanks, Nae," I shut my eyes and cradled the phone like it was her in my hands. "See you Thursday?"

"I'll be there with bells on," she replied, and all I could do was envision her jingling her merry way up my walk on Thursday night. "G'night."

"Night, Nae." I folded my cell phone shut and ran my hand across my scalp. Holy mother of all that's pure, she's coming. Alone. For the first time in nearly three years. Mr. Plucky danced to show his excitement, and I cranked the cold faucet on in the shower. Eaen and Armand were just going to have to wait a few minutes before I delivered the news about Nae's visit.

* * * *

I woke up the next morning to the sunshine streaming in through my window. I loved it when it did that. My bedroom, correct that, *our* bedroom faced east so we got the first rays of dawn, and I could see dust particles floating in the beam. The rain must have ceased sometime in the night, after we'd gone to bed.

I lifted my head off my pillow to get a look at my sleeping partners. The blonde wolf lay curled in tight with his furred back pressed into my side, and Eaen had one leg stretched so it ran the length of the bed, and the other leg folded up so his shin cradled Armand's fuzzy butt. They looked comfy as hell, and I lay there a while longer, thinking about my phone call with Naomi.

Armand had been less than thrilled, and neither Eaen nor I protested when he offered to stay in the bedroom while she was here. We needed her to meet the wolf-men in human form, not have them get so rattled they shifted in front of her. As it was, I was nervous as hell about the meeting between Eaen and Naomi. Suppose he couldn't keep it together? Then what? Would they kill her to protect themselves and their pack?

My mind returned to when I was Grane's captive, and my heart tripped. If Suma hadn't interfered, he would have killed me without a second thought. To protect his family. I covered my face with my hands and took a deep breath. Surely, the two wolf-men here with me wouldn't do that. They would trust my instincts about Naomi, wouldn't they? Should they?

Aw, Christ.

If she wasn't with The Bear I would've said *yes* without hesitating. She was smart, quick to assess situations, and compassionate. And, groan of groans, *loyal*, to the wrong guy. But her behavior the past couple of days had me questioning that, too. What was she up to?

The unease of that unanswered question didn't sit well on my nerves, so I rolled my legs out of bed and placed my feet to the floor hoping that motion would dispel it. Armand stretched his thin, strong legs and wriggled into the warm spot I'd just vacated. He sighed heavily, but didn't wake.

I made my way to the bathroom, and then sauntered into the kitchen. The table was strewn with open books and papers with handwriting on them. None of which were mine. I slid a piece of notebook paper out from under one of the open books. The script curled magnificently, artfully, and I wondered which one of the wolf-men possessed such an innate aptitude for writing. I read the inscription:

> *Wealth was an inferior object, but what glory*
> *would attend the discovery if I could banish*
> *disease from the human frame and render man*
> *invulnerable to any but a violent death!*

I read it three times before finally looking at the book that had covered the paper. Mary Shelley's *Frankenstein*. Jeeze. My English professor really would have frothed at the mouth if he'd had these two wolf-men in class.

"Armand wrote it."

I turned to the solver of the riddle. Eaen leaned against the doorframe, his dark hair disheveled from sleep.

"No kidding? Why this passage?"

Eaen cocked his head.

"Why did he pick that part to write?" I repeated in vocabulary he would understand, as the word *passage* would have had a completely different connotation for someone who grew up in a forest.

He shrugged his wide shoulders. "He liked how the words sounded to his ear."

I nodded. They did have a certain ring to them, and I was gaining another reason to be in awe of Armand. Not only was the choice of words melodic, but the meaning, to a wolf-man or someone privy to their world, was profound. "Pretty effing cool." I shook my head and stuffed the sheet of paper back under the binding of the book. I would definitely have to ask Armand about it.

For now, though, my belly was growling. "You up for breakfast? I'll fix something."

Eaen sauntered to the fridge and pulled the door open. He waved his face around to capture the melded aromas that wafted forth. Ultimately, he snagged an apple from the crisper.

"Yes, we should go hunting later, but I am not sure what you will *fix.*" He winked, turning my offer into a joke. The truth was, I hadn't cooked for these guys yet, since they didn't seem interested in anything except the fruit in the crisper. Eaen bent back over to inspect the interior of the fridge and grabbed another Granny Smith. I should have gone grocery shopping while he and I had been sitting in the parking lot.

Armand wandered into the kitchen seconds later, snatching the apple Eaen tossed to him, the heat from his recent change billowing off from him.

"How did you—?" I didn't bother finishing my question since the answer registered once I'd opened my mouth. Acute wolf senses. Eaen had either smelled Armand, or heard him stir.

"Mornin', Armand. You sleep okay?"

"Yes, Porcupine, even though I am worried about tomorrow's meeting with your woman," he admitted.

I couldn't help but love the sound of Naomi being referred to as *my woman.* "She's not my woman," I refuted with a touch of regret. Eaen and Armand made no other comment about my relationship with Nae. "She's a friend, guys, really," I insisted. Who was I trying to convince, anyway?

Eaen completely changed the subject. "Kenrickey wants to go hunting, Arms," he said.

Armand and I exchanged surprised glances, and then the blonde wolf-man's grin spread across his face and his menacing eyeteeth slid into view.

"Christ, you know how intimidating that is?" I confessed as a rush of blood gushed through my veins.

"Of course he does, that is why he does it. Are we ready then?"

Eaen chomped into his apple.

"For what? Hunting?"

They both nodded. Man, I had to get used to that, because frankly, what on earth did they have to prepare? They were wolves for God's sake, they didn't need to clean their guns.

"Porcupine?"

I turned to Armand, my heart open to the question in his voice.

"Today will you shed your clothes? They stink and give us away."

My ears flushed hot. "Ah, yeah, sure," I stammered, unsure if I was embarrassed to run around naked outside in broad daylight this close to civilization, or if it was because my clothes reeked of human, and every creature in the woods was acutely aware of it. "I can do what you want, but I don't have to go, guys, I mean, I can make myself breakfast here." I babbled, and Armand and Eaen grinned because they caught me doing it, had caused me to do it.

"You guys can shit, you know that?" Yet there were no teeth to my retort.

"Come on, Porcupine. Shed your clothes and let us go." Eaen draped his arm around my shoulders in a good-natured embrace, and Armand slid effortlessly into his fur. I got ready by shoving my heart back down my throat. Someday the fluid metamorphosis of species was going to seem commonplace to me, and I would not have to turn my brain upright after witnessing it.

I opened the front door, felt the rush of cold air on my warm, bare skin and shivered. "At least you guys have fur," I complained half-heartedly. The brisk morning, along with the anticipation of the hunt, revved the blood in my veins as we trotted toward the river. The early morning sun blanketed my skin until we wended deeper into the trees, but by then the running had me plenty warm so the wet peat and pine needles beneath my feet were a refreshing contrast against my soles.

The black wolf dropped his nose to the forest floor and zig-zagged in sweeping arcs, leaping over fallen trees and ledges. My eyes were riveted on the sleek form sliding like a ghost through the tangible. His huffs were the only indication he was working. The rest of his motion was pure grace and effortless stretch of muscle and tendon. Absorbed as I was in watching Eaen, I didn't even realize Armand flanked me until my fingertips sketched delicate lines in the short fur of his broad head.

His command for quiet was a shadow of a bird flying across my thoughts, and I swallowed the breath that carried speech.

The black wolf halted, rotated his great head like an owl, and pierced us with his riveting, brown eyes. My guts rolled. He had found the trail of our kill. When Armand bolted toward his brother, my legs sprung spontaneously, hurling me into the hunt behind them.

We ran for nearly a mile before the two wolves silently split, leaving me in the center to complete the net as we continued east toward the river. I got tangled in a tight cluster of alders and almost panicked as I clawed and shoved my way through them. I was worried that I'd either slowed the wolves down, or left a lucky gap for the deer. The scrape of a branch along the back of my thigh sang a deep path through my skin. I would feel the full force of its sting later, I was sure, but just then my attention was too focused on the mission before me.

Run for the river.

I obeyed like it was a traffic sign.

The ground beneath my feet grew soggy, and brackish water squished over the tops of my bare feet. The crash of heavy bodies broke the stillness of the morning and the cadence of my heavy breathing. Then my heart rammed into my throat and turbo-injected blood to the large muscles of my legs, as a plaintive bleat zapped my nerve endings. I surged toward the sound, bowling through the long grass, then skittered to a slippery stop. Armand and Eaen had a small deer cornered on the mud, its only escape a seven-foot sheer bank. And my position.

Doubt snuck up and weakened my determination. Would a frantic deer run toward me to escape the wolves? Or would the sight of a human panic it so the creature had no choice but to risk the vertical leap and the gripping jaws guarding the river?

My indecision filled me with self-contempt. *Use your brain, Ken, and watch the deer's reaction,* I admonished myself, willing my feet forward as I crouched closer.

Come slow. The command was not my own, and relief cascaded through my body. Armand and Eaen were there to guide me every step of the way. I stepped toward the siege with renewed purpose, a formidable sense of union with my brothers mushrooming inside my skin. I wouldn't let that deer run past me, even if I had to muckle the damned thing myself.

Saliva flooded my molars as I took in the tableau before me. The young stag had made a stand. It stamped its sharp, front hoof into the mud, and sprayed a wet snort from its nostrils as its frond-like ears swiveled back and forth, from Eaen, to me, to Armand. The creature was resplendent in its courage, and I gloried in our taking of it.

In a blur, Eaen thrust his heavy frame at its right flank, then retreated just as Armand parried his brother's attack on the left. Each assault the deer slashed its hind legs in lethal arcs. My breath stopped as the struggle with death commenced for both species, and I truly couldn't determine the victor of this gloriously savage standoff.

Then, as if Fate made her decision, the black wolf rocketed his bulk at the tawny flank, and within the breadth of a millisecond, the blonde wolf snapped his crushing jaws at the soft underbelly. The deer kicked like an AK-47, grazing Armand's skull. Neither wolf retreated or acknowledged, but repositioned for another volley as the deer panted from fear and fatigue.

Grab its antlers.

My muscles flinched as my knees bent for the leap, and the creature blurred as I zeroed in on the curl and nub of horn. My fists coiled tight around my target, and my body exploded as if my muscles were being torn from the bone.

Grab its fucking antlers? Whose bright idea was this? My fragile human body was getting thrashed like it was a silk flag in a typhoon, and just as I thought I couldn't hold on, a black body crammed its bulk between my bare abdomen and the chest of our prey, rendering help like a furred deliverer from the gods.

Eaen sunk his fangs into the muscled flesh of the neck, and locked his powerful jaws in a suffocating vise.

I twisted my torso, braced my feet into the mud and wrenched with everything I had. A roar blasted from my lungs as I dragged the antlers toward my shoulders and dropped my weight to the ground. I was going to take this thing down like a rodeo steer if it killed me.

I succeeded in turning the deer's nose to the air and could go no farther. The fucking thing was so centered I could have been wrestling a pig. Bambi hadn't looked that strong from a distance.

Pull, Porcupine, pull.

The demand disintegrated my doubt and I heaved, twisted and roared again. For the flash of a second, all was suspended—frozen in the pulse of a heartbeat. Then our bodies slammed downward into the mud, and my grip on the antlers was wrenched apart as the spear of one tine impaled my skin and slid across my ribs. Pain flared in a blinding flash, even as I rejoiced from the reassuringly solid weight of Armand stretched across my splayed legs, and his fever-pitched, liquid snarls as he tugged at the deer's exposed belly.

It's down! I felt nothing but the thrill of exultation. Of power. The blood of the deer streamed and smeared down my naked thighs, marking its brutal death, and still I thought it the most magnificent thing I'd ever seen.

The two wolves continued their work amidst my moment of jubilation. The job wasn't done, the deer not yet dead. Death from injury still lurked like a warning stench for the one not aware. My guts landed like they were liquid lead. The hunt was serious business, and no joy was to be acknowledged until the danger had passed. I slid myself out from under the buck, and sat on my ass while the two wolves finished like synchronized surgeons. They were masterful, and I was awed, like I had a front row seat to watch Michelangelo wield his chisel. Then, as the buck's blood eddied and drained down the waters of the river, the deer collapsed and spread lifeless on the mud before me.

"Come, Porcupine."

I stared up into a long, outstretched hand that wafted the heat of fire. Eaen's compassionate brown eyes beckoned.

I was stunned immobile, and my eyes rolled up and down, covering his tall frame, and then darted toward the carcass, where Armand stood on two legs and called for me.

"Come on, Kenrickey. Breakfast."

Eaen snatched my hand, hauled me to my feet, and grinned with a smug happiness. He would eat and live this day. His brothers, too.

Steam curled an invitation from the slit gut of the deer, and Armand drove his arm into the bloodied cavern.

"Ah, wouldn't it be easier," I licked my lips, and had to start again.

"Wouldn't it be easier for you if you were..." I raised my eyes to Eaen's face, and he shook his head.

"No, Porcupine. We share our feast with our human-shaped brother this morning. We share our life."

Tears sprung to my eyes with the enormity of their gesture. This was bigger than the beaver. They had taken the beaver on their own with me as a witness. Today, I had taken part in the hunt. Part of a successful kill, and they were generously honoring that by eating beside me in *my* form. The gesture shook me to the core, the copper tang of blood upon the morning air stirring my whole being, while my growling stomach rumbled in the quiet around the carcass.

Eaen's chuckle diffused throughout my body like a warming glow. "Come," was all he said, and I followed. We descended to fill our empty stomachs, while I took one more step away from the man I used to be.

* * * *

We gorged ourselves on the deer and when we were sated, splashed around in the river to rinse the blood from our bodies. I was covered in it, and rejoiced in every crimson smudge camouflaging my skin. I had stuffed raw meat down my gullet like a man possessed.

Or dispossessed, I thought with a contented smile as we wended our way back to the house. There was nothing human about my abandon at the carcass. That part of myself hadn't returned until I'd bathed in the river, and my first thoughts had been to hide the deer so nobody would find it. It was evidence, and I'd be damned if I'd fail my brothers with that potentially lethal oversight. Eaen and Armand helped me lift what was left of the carcass into a spruce tree, where it would be hidden but accessible should they need to return to it.

My mind meandered over the events of that morning as we strolled along, my guts full. I'd been initiated, and had passed my test. I traced my fingers across the puncture wound lining my ribs. It was beginning to throb now that my adrenalin was ebbing, but how I'd received it overshadowed any physical discomfort I felt. Christ, I'd tackled an effing deer. Sure, I got pummeled; its strength was freakin' deceptive. But none of it mattered.

What really mattered was the unquestioning acceptance of Armand

and Eaen. They'd assumed I would be part of the hunt, had intended for me to play an important role, and that vibrated through my blood as surely as Luna's buzzing did. The consequence of my utter surrender was the connection to other living creatures, where I could hear their thoughts.

Plus, in that primal state, I felt powerful. Capable. Worthy of my new brothers. I turned to glance at the wolf-men behind me, my chest constricting with that familiar desire to keep my family safe. Two wolves trotted behind me, and I could tell at a glance they were as relaxed and comfortable as I was under the strengthening morning sun.

And then we turned the corner of the house and smacked headlong into a human visitor.

Naomi. My heart caressed her presence, despite the shock of seeing her and blurting out her name.

"Naomi!" *Holy effing Jesus.* I spun around to warn the wolves, but they'd practically rammed their muzzles up my ass they were so close. None of us had been expecting company, and there was nowhere now for them to hide. I sure as hell wasn't wide enough to shield them.

Naomi gaped at them, and back at me. She opened her mouth to say something, then clapped it shut as her eyes dragged the length of my naked body, her high cheek bones flushing.

"Nae." *Shit.* I knew I was a sight, but Armand and Eaen. Obviously, she knew they were there, but what the hell would they do? And why in Christ was I loving that blush on my girl's cheeks when I was standing on the edge of a fuck-show?

Armand growled, then so did Eaen. Except I knew, somehow, the black wolf checked his brother, which meant I had to get Naomi the hell out of there until Armand could settle down.

Hell, until we all could settle down. Eaen might have had the presence of mind to interfere on Nae's behalf, but how long would that last? He was supposed to have met her in human form, not as wolf, so I had no clue how things were going to go down.

Nae, dropping to one knee, decided the outcome for us.

"Is this who you wanted me to meet, Ken?"

Huh? Before I could wind my brain back up to speed, and get really embarrassed about standing there buck naked in front of the woman I'd had a crush on for four years, she addressed the two wolves crouching behind me.

"Hiya, boys," she kissed, pursing her lips as she cooed to them like they were babies. Just as every woman seems to do when they're talking to dogs.

Except these weren't dogs. They weren't even animals, but grown men who were getting fussed at like they were infants.

I cringed and rolled my eyes. "Nae, ah, you don't have to—"

But I got no further, because Armand quit growling and flattened not just his ears to his broad head, but himself to the ground. The black wolf fanned his tail in a friendly greeting. Jesus, we weren't just virgins, we were softies, too.

"Come on." I tapped Naomi's shoulder for her to rise as I peered down at Eaen and Armand. "Let's all get inside before anyone else shows up unannounced." *And sees me standing here naked with two wolves.* Bad enough I was standing there nude next to Nae. But what could I do? It was too late to cover myself, and besides, cupping my genitals would probably look a lot worse than pretending that my nudity didn't matter.

I trusted the latter choice, and led the way to the front door. A few minutes later, Nae was standing in my living room admiring two full-grown wolves.

I was a little proud of her, I had to admit, in spite of the impromptu introduction. None of us expected to meet up like we did, but she'd come around pretty quick, had let me steer her inside without a qualm. Even though she'd just caught me running around bare-assed with two predators on my heels. How much did she freakin' trust me, anyway?

And Eaen and Armand? Obviously their trust ran pretty Christless deep, because they followed us into the house and it wasn't to shred Naomi into itty-bitty pieces. They seemed as intrigued by her as she was of them. Eaen was already sniffing the tops of her feet. Granted, he looked ready to bolt if she even wiggled her little toe, but he *was* getting to know her.

Armand, on the other hand, wasn't fairing so well, but at least he hadn't retreated to the bedroom. Thank God he was already wearing his fur. His tense muscles flinched repeatedly, but he still inched toward the woman before him.

But, we had a problem. Now Nae knew about the wolves, but not the men.

"How long have you had them?" she whispered without moving, or peeling her eyes off from Eaen and Armand.

"I picked them up at least a week ago, the days I missed class." I stepped up to encourage her and to ease the wolf-men.

"You picked them up? Where? Are they tame?"

I chuckled softly. "No. I met them where we'd—" Shit. *Shut your mouth Ken.* I had no censor when it came to Nae, and would have to be very careful around her.

Both wolves swiveled their great heads and shot me warning looks. *Sorry.*

They swayed their tails forgivingly. *It is fine. She is nice.*

"Want to meet her properly?"

"One's female?"

I furrowed my brows together. "No. Why?"

"You asked if I wanted to meet *her*?"

I raked my hand through my hair. "Yeah, um, no. They're both men...er, male." *Jesus, moron, think much?*

Eaen backed his furred ass against my bare legs, a playful nudge that made me grin in spite of the seriousness of our situation.

They were enjoying my discomfort. Thought it funny how Nae rattled me.

The moment didn't last as the wolves refocused on the woman standing before them. They stiffened, anticipating any sudden moves on her part.

"Nae," I said gently, "drop to your knees so they can smell you better."

Her eyes darted to my face, but she bent her knees to do as I asked. She was so brave, my stomach flipped at the sight of her. I moved closer to her, and knelt behind Armand. The least I could do was join her, show Naomi she would be okay, that the two wolves wouldn't harm her if she behaved correctly.

"Nae, put your back to the floor. Like this." I rolled onto the rug, baring my chest, thighs, throat to the ceiling, to the predators in the

81

room. My breath caught, I couldn't help it. The scene before me was so unexpectedly beautiful. Naomi lay on the floor, prostrate to her potential death, yet she did so because I asked her. Sweet living fuck, I couldn't let her go back to The Bear.

"Armand, are you all right?"

The blond wolf wriggled the tip of his tail. I'd thought my heart was about as swollen as it could get? I was so proud of him, too.

"Did he just—?"

"Shh, Nae, I'll answer your questions later. Right now, you're doing great. Just stay quiet, like you are, because they're very scared right now."

She nodded slowly, and her esophagus slid along her fair skin as she swallowed. *My Christ, forget the introductions, I could take her right there on the floor.*

Both wolves simultaneously turned their broad heads in my direction, and I blushed to the roots of my spiky hair. They'd *heard* my intentions, and Eaen winked one brown eye.

I stifled a grin, swallowed and clenched my jaw. "Nae, keep your eyes on the ceiling." *So you can't see my hard on.* I got a sudden rush of ownership, and wanted to be so far into her I wouldn't be able to tell where either one of us began.

But that would do nothing for my brothers, or Naomi, and that quelled my longing. A bit. Enough for me to divert some of the blood from my lower extremity back to my brain. Eaen and Armand resumed their investigating of the woman on the floor, snuffled her neck, her stomach, her groin.

I tensed possessively then took a wicked deep breath to calm myself. There was nothing sexual in the wolves' inspections. They needed to determine who she was, what she was like. Hell, even I was curious to see her from a wolf's point of view. Was she dominant? Submissive?

I let my eyes slide over her body as she lay there breathing steadily, her eyes trained on the ceiling. Armand's tail stuck out slightly lower than his back and he wagged it stiffly. He was unsure of the human woman. Eaen, I knew, would give me straightforward signs because he was simply being cautious, and wasn't nearly as afraid as Armand.

He hovered over her stomach, his black, iron-like legs straddling

Nae as he snuffled. Without warning, he swung his broad head toward her face and pressed his sharp teeth across her throat. Her hand lashed out like the swipe of a cat's paw to grip his ruff, her fist disappearing in the loose skin of his thick neck.

Holy shit, she's dominant. There was a fraction of a startled gasp, and then the black wolf was astride the woman on the floor, and I was on my feet to protect her.

From what? I thought madly. From Eaen? Armand whirled, shoving his powerful bulk against my bare legs, barricading me from going forward.

Stay.

I obeyed reflexively, planted my feet, and froze while I witnessed the frightening spectacle before me. Naomi didn't release her grip from the black wolf's neck as she flipped to her stomach to get to her feet. She was going to fight a freaking wolf? What the fuck? Didn't she realize he'd rip her apart?

A groan oozed from my throat. *Not my Nae.*

Armand whined sympathetically, but didn't budge, didn't interfere on my behalf.

He'll kill her, I wailed silently as a black tail ratcheted over a tautly muscled back, and snarls reverberated through my bones, in the air, like shouts in a canyon.

But it wasn't just Eaen's voice I heard. Some of those growls came from Naomi. *My* woman. The female on the floor, who was possessed with something primitive, and the scene unfolding in front of my eyes was primordial. *Base.* Naomi braced off on her hands and knees with her face toward the wolf's erect tail and her hard eyes averted to his muzzle. Eaen's body was fixed, opposite to the human woman but in the exact same posture. They were facing off?

Armand pressed hard enough to push me back, and the movement fractured my focus from the pair challenging each other. The break was just long enough to get my brain working, and my head snapped back up instantly. Eaen challenged Naomi as if she was wolf, not human. He wouldn't kill her, and the realization released the fear from my guts as I fell on my ass to the wooden floor. The waves of anxiety washing away left me as deflated as a leaking water balloon. Armand circled and supported me from behind with his broad chest, while his furry head stuck out past my cheek.

This was effing incredible.

And Naomi? The most gorgeous thing I'd ever seen. If only she was naked, too. But I was too enrapt to discern if I wanted her in the buff because I could still make love to her right then, or if it was because it was more natural without the human clothing. But did it really freakin' matter? It was enough that I wanted her.

As if the tension were too much for the both of them, Eaen and Nae retreated, but did not divert their attention from each other. He stood with his body curved toward her and his tail slightly above half-mast and neither moved for an eternity. Armand and I watched transfixed, neither of us pulling our heads apart as we witnessed the struggle of personality.

Finally, Naomi's shoulders sagged, her eyes dropped, and Eaen pounced as if he'd been wound for it. She fell to her back as she had before, only this time she didn't lash out with her hand to his neck. The human woman unfolded her limbs and stretched them upon the floor, exposing herself to the wolf that loomed substantially above her.

Her name was a sigh from my throat, and Eaen's black ear twitched toward the whisper.

Then he inched back, cautiously, as if she might snap at him if he let his guard down. Her chest heaved, but otherwise she remained still, and didn't move until the black wolf withdrew a few feet. Then she turned her chin and rolled very slowly to her hands and knees.

Eaen struck his deep chest into Naomi's shoulders, shoving her to the floor again. She dropped like a dead weight and rolled to her back without a hair of hesitation. The black wolf hovered for a few moments before repeating his withdrawal.

I held my breath and so did my blonde shadow.

Again, Naomi curled to her hands and knees, and this time Eaen let her while he watched alertly, his brown eyes riveted to the woman beneath him. She crawled toward him and slowly, gently, kissed him on the short hairs of his black chin.

Where in the sweet love of fuck did she learn that?

The black wolf jabbed his muzzle into the air, feigning disinterest, then strutted away from the human woman who remained on the floor.

Introductions were over, as far as he was concerned.

But what of Armand, who remained safely behind me with his head pressed to mine?

Naomi eyed the two of us from her spot on the floor, curiosity mingling with the awe shining from her hazel eyes. We probably looked like some mythical, two-headed beast. If so, then she was my goddess. What woman, I ask, would have challenged a full grown wolf like that?

"Naomi." I hadn't meant for my voice to come out like a squeezed whisper, but *God*, she turned me on.

Eaen circled round to my left shoulder, adding a third head to our mythical beast. Armand whined, and trembled against me. Right. Enough fantasizing. He'd yet to give his own greeting, and wanted to.

"Nae," I said again, this time without the drooling. "Would you mind if Armand, ah, I mean, would you mind if the blonde wolf got to know you, too?"

Her eyes shifted ever so slightly to my right, to Armand, and damned if she didn't suppress a belly tugging giggle, then tried to get all serious by puckering her lips to lose her grin. "Of course."

She seemed pleased as punch, as the saying goes.

Armand didn't exactly rush over and flip her to her back, though. He whined again, too afraid to go to her.

Naomi's demeanor changed as if it had been erased by Armand's second whine, and she grew serious as she dropped her gaze to the floor in front of her.

Then, sweet Christ, she lifted her hand to her blouse, and plucked the buttons free to slip her bare skin from the cloth. The blood drained from my face and shot to my groin. But she raised her gaze to Armand, a cool reminder of why she was undressing.

Armand slid out from behind me and crept toward her, his back roached, and Nae stretched her body to the floor, spreading her limbs like a pagan sacrifice.

"Hello," she cooed, as if she sensed Armand's fear. "My name is Naomi. I'm sure you have a name, too?"

Armand rotated a triangular ear toward the woman lying prostrate on the floor, and whined as if answering. He inched closer, sliding his nose the length of her body, and stopped his muzzle at the base of her bared throat.

I held my breath, and Eaen stilled behind me. Would Armand do as his brother had done? Would he challenge Nae? Would she challenge him if he clamped his jaws around her neck?

Moot questions, because the blonde wolf's tongue flicked out to kiss Naomi under her chin.

She giggled her pleasure, then ever so slowly reached her arm out to cup his jaw in her palm. Armand pressed his head into her hand like he wanted her to scratch his ears. Then he flopped to his back, curled his legs, and coiled his bushy tail up to his exposed abdomen.

He was subordinate to her? What the hell?

Nae's reaction? She rolled to her knees to drape her arms around him in a gentle hug, trying to collect him to her like he was still a nursing pup.

She struggled to do it, though, he was so damned big, and before I could interfere, she giggled again and nuzzled her face into his ruff.

Armand's yellow eyes glazed like he'd just entered the gates of Heaven. Then he squirmed to free himself, flipped around in a tight circle, and stuck his furry ass into the air.

Nae dropped her upper body to the floor to bow from her knees, and snatched at one of Armand's mammoth paws.

Armand exploded, raced around me and Eaen then bounded back to Naomi to kowtow playfully. Nae leapt to her feet and dashed off toward the kitchen, then circled and bowed in front of the blonde wolf.

Holy kindergarten, they were playing. Eaen practically plowed over me to join them, and I scrambled to catch up. My sweet Naomi hadn't just passed her test with Armand and Eaen with flying colors—she'd passed directly into the realm of the wolf-people like she'd been born there.

* * * *

We cavorted for quite some time—chasing, snatching, biting. Armand, once he'd gotten over his initial fear, darted around just as uninhibited as the rest of us; although he and Eaen were careful about shifting in front of Naomi.

I, on the other hand, shed all of my inhibitions, and the mock hunt for Nae escalated seriously. I wanted her bouncing ass all to myself, and her playful screams were jabs of electricity to my groin.

She didn't run very fast once she caught me ogling her like she was an entrée. Good ol' Nae. She even feigned a limp so that I could corner her in the living room. She darted her eyes around like a trapped deer, and wedged herself into the corner by the book shelf, protecting her back. Then she lifted her upper lip in a warning snarl, even as her hazel eyes glistened and her pupils stretched to turn her eyes almost black. Her blonde hair was tousled and sweaty, and I'd never seen a creature more inviting.

My mouth found hers before I could say *no guts, no glory,* and sweet living jackrabbits, she opened herself to me. It was all I could do not to slide Mr. Plucky into home once the ump signaled for me to steal. Her tongue teased, tasted me, then retreated maddeningly, and I withdrew just far enough to clamp my teeth across her windpipe and cup her ass in my hands. She gasped, and my groin ached as it grew more swollen.

The ringing of her cell phone was like the screech of a car crash, and we both flinched at the intrusion of it. Naomi groaned as she slid away toward her pile of clothes on the living room floor. Eaen and Armand stood with their legs splayed, sides heaving, and wore tendrils of frothy spit on their fur. I stood with my need so obvious my balls hurt.

Christ, guys.

Eaen winked, the teasing turd. He saw. He'd noticed we'd all gone a bit nuts, and he loved it. Armand's waving tail gave him away, too, but the three of us paid more attention to Nae's cell phone call.

It was The Bear, and he wanted her and his car. She'd been gone too long already, judging by her end of the conversation. She'd promised to be back before lunch and it was past that. My, how time really does fly when you're having fun.

She told him she'd be right there, then snapped the lid shut on her phone. And I got an unexpected explosion of jealousy in my guts.

"Don't go, Nae. Stay with us," I offered, and fought like hell to keep my anger from boiling over into my voice. A feat beyond me, I wasn't exactly successful. "Tell him to fuck himself." Oh, yeah, I was really trying.

"I can't, Ken. Not yet, anyway, but soon," she promised.

Was she crying? "Aw, Christ, Nae, don't cry." She effing leveled me. I was a mud puddle waiting to catch her tears, and before I knew it, my feet crossed the room and my arms were wrapped around her. I'd have sacrificed daylight for her.

"Come back later, then, huh?" I pulled her away to lose myself in her shimmering eyes, which had turned green because she cried. "I'll come get you. Just call me, and I'll come, okay? Whenever you want." My fingers combed her tousled bangs, tucking their length behind her seashell ear.

She nodded and sniffed, and my heart cracked. Jee-zus, how was I letting her leave?

I wiped her tears with the pad of my thumb, pulled her warm body close, then ripped myself away and edged a fair distance back to stand between Eaen and Armand while we watched her dress. Weren't we the gentlemen? When she finished donning her clothes, the four of us huddled to say good-bye.

"We really have to talk, Nae. Soon," I said, before she slipped out the door and into the Yeti's car. Within moments, she was gone, but even I could still smell the snowy day in our house.

* * * *

I drove to class on Thursday morning, just like I'd told Nae I would. *Ah, Naomi.* My brain wafted the images of her in my head, teasing my groin. She'd been remarkable—in fight *and* play, and Eaen and Armand were quite taken with her in spite of the fact she was human. It had been her kiss beneath the black wolf's chin, Armand said, that had given him the courage to properly introduce himself.

My heart squeezed a prideful smile across my face when they complimented her. I'd chosen a woman the wolf-people liked. But we still had a problem, no matter how much they admired her. We didn't have anyone for them to practice being human with now that Naomi had met Eaen and Armand as wolves.

I'd held out the vain hope she wouldn't put two and two together, but neither wolf-man thought that was likely. As Eaen pointed out, Naomi had been quick to figure out the language of wolves, she'd notice their strange hands and teeth in an instant. Armand had yellow eyes, for Chrissakes.

I pulled the Subaru into the campus parking lot, and the real Naomi replaced my memories. She and Jeff were standing at the back of his car. She was wearing the sweater that brought out the gray in her hazel eyes, and the leggings that hugged her slender calves and accented the length of her thigh. Shit, she was gorgeous. *And mine.*

A knot of jealousy twisted my guts when The Bear put his arm around her as they walked toward the car. A low growl built in my chest, and I was shocked when my upper lip lifted from my teeth in a real snarl. Eating raw meat had its advantages. Jeff had his arm around my woman, and I felt like ripping the limb from his shoulder to beat him with it.

But I couldn't, so I swallowed and took a deep breath instead. Naomi had asked for time to break up with Jeff her way, and I'd give it to her, even if it tore my insides out. Besides, The Bear was still our connection to Hersey, and I had no inkling as to how things now stood since I'd refused to give the bastard any information. I would find out in the next few minutes, when I stepped into his classroom.

"Hi, Ken," Naomi's sweet voice stirred Spring's morning air.

"Hi, Nae." My voice sounded too heavy, too saturated. So much for the practiced greeting I'd used for three years. Her eyes locked onto mine for a brief second, transporting me to my living room, to Nae's searching tongue, her soft throat in my mouth. *Jesus*, I wasn't going to be able to be near her anymore without wanting to take her down.

"Hey, bro," Jeff's deep voice slapped my thoughts back to the ground, and I yanked my bag from the car, and headed for the Science building.

"Hi, Jeff." *Play it cool, Ken.* I readjusted my bag on my shoulder and kept walking. Nae and the Yeti fell in beside me like they always did. The distance to the building stretched before me like an empty highway, but Nae striding alongside was the life-blood pumping through my veins with each step forward.

"I think Hersey has about six other seniors who signed up for his trip north," Jeff puffed and pouted, just as my hand reached for the glass door.

I clenched my jaw, and dropped my eyes to the ground. No way could I have looked at Nae just then.

But she slid into the conversation like an otter on a river bank. "Don't be so worried, Jeff," she teased. "You'll get chosen because Ken will help. Isn't that right, Ken?"

My God, she was insistent. Did she know we needed The Bear on that trip? She wasn't that quick, was she?

I nodded, even though my heart fell flat in my chest as if it had suddenly gained six hundred pounds. I couldn't mate with Naomi as long as we needed Jeff. But, she had to know why. I owed her that. *We* owed her that, especially if she'd already figured out The Bear's importance.

"Nae, we gotta talk." My urgent whisper as she passed by me into the classroom fluffed a tress of her fine, blonde hair.

"Tonight," she managed, before Jeff interrupted.

"But you'll help, right?" His eyes rounded with worry. He was so wound up about going north with Hersey he didn't notice my exchange with Nae. A very good sign.

"Yeah, I said I would, didn't I?" With my promise confirmed, I strode straight to the back of the room, as far away from Hersey as I could get, and prepared myself for whatever I'd have to deal with in the coming hour.

* * * *

Turned out, not much. Hersey acted his usual pugnacious self by ignoring my presence in his classroom, clearly his way of using reverse psychology. Maybe he figured if he pretended I didn't exist, then I'd get all in his face about it.

I fell for it once, when he'd announced his return to the north woods, but I wouldn't again, especially with so much riding on my keeping control.

Except, I wanted another look at Randall Wolfe before I said anything to the guys back at the house. Not bad enough to initiate anything with Hersey, mind you, but still. Wolfe was just a bit too weird, a little too off.

Naomi wasn't though. Uh-uh. Before yesterday, I'd learned to ignore her effect on me, but now it was if I was a freshman again and wanting her with an intensity that bordered on pain. Right in my goddamned dick. Seems I was fighting Mr. Plucky again like I did when I'd reached puberty. The effing thing had a mind of its own, and that mind wanted the woman sitting next to me. Badly. I could smell her for God's sake. The lavender in the shampoo she used, the scent of snow, just like Eaen said, that drifted off that tender spot behind her ear now that her hair was short enough to fan it.

Christ.

I peered over at Jeff to take Mr. Plucky's mind off Nae. He was leaned forward, as if gobbling up every word Hersey crapped out of his mouth. *Good.* I wanted him distracted.

I nudged Nae's foot with mine, slid her my note.

Her lashes lowered provocatively to read it, the corner of her luscious lips lifting into a conspiratorial smirk. Which I could have erased with a teasing swipe of my tongue, then kissed away the blossoming blush from her creamy cheeks.

On the edge of her notes she wrote *5:00-ish.*

She would come by the house while the Bear played his out-of-town baseball game. Perfect. We'd have all kinds of time to figure out Nae's part in this adventure, if she played one at all. I'd leave that decision to Eaen and Armand since they were the ones risking their lives. I wouldn't fault them if they chose not to trust her enough to be human around her. Like they said, she was quick, and would most likely notice how Armand's eyes were exactly like those of the blonde wolf.

I sat through class, half listening to Hersey as I doodled his lecture in my notebook, while the other half of my brain imagined Nae meeting up again with the wolves.

By the time we parted ways after class, my nerves were so hepped up at the thought of seeing Nae alone again, it took a few seconds for my brain to register who the person was leaning against my car.

Randall Wolfe.

I'd bristled long before my brain caught up, and strode across the parking lot with every intention of telling the guy to get away from my car. Pleasantly, of course.

He pushed himself away from the Subaru as soon as I got near.

"Hi, Mr. Rickey." This time he didn't extend his hand for the usual shake, but leaned in as if to sniff the air around me.

91

I pulled back. *What the frig?* But sharp on the heels of my surprise I got defensive, forcing myself between the guy and my car. Had he smelled Eaen and Armand around it?

Great Christ. If he had? Now my brain hit overdrive. If he was scenting me out, then my instincts about Randall Wolfe had hit dead on. He wasn't the average human, but one of the wolf-people, even if his hands were like mine. His sharp eyes and teeth agreed, especially now that we weren't in Hersey's office.

My blood ran so fast through my veins it actually got very hot, and I felt the sweat itch to the surface of my skin as I braced off to confront him.

My visitor took a polite step backward, softening his entire demeanor so that I automatically relaxed at the sight of it. A little. I didn't let my guard down even if my body intuitively responded to his.

"I was hoping I'd get the chance to meet you outside of class. I'd like to ask you a few questions about last fall, if I may?"

He actually asked, so I didn't feel like I was being interrogated. But still, I kept my guard up. I didn't quite know what, or who, I was dealing with, especially since he spoke with contractions. He didn't speak like the wolf-people I knew.

Except for Beth. And speaking of that wolf-woman, where the deuce was Luna and her buzzing? Her absence seemed most troubling of all. Wasn't the presence of a possible, *strange,* wolf-man enough to set off the warning bells? Obviously not, since I remained upright and could see straight.

"There's nothing to tell." I tried sniffing the air, like I might get a whiff of Wolfe, who hinted a smile at my attempt.

"Mr. Rickey—can I call you Ken? Is there someplace private we could talk? In your car, perhaps, where we won't be overheard."

Did the guy think I was a total jackass? Let him into my car? The same one that probably reeked of Eaen and Armand? Not a chance in hell.

"How about yours, instead."

I saw full on the look I caught in Hersey's office. *Appreciation.* "Of course, Ken." He stepped off for his own vehicle, which was parked across from mine, facing out. He punched his key ring to unlock it and waited for me to start getting in before he slid behind the wheel.

He turned the key to crack our windows, and the cool spring air filtered in to replace the stale atmosphere of the closed up Range Rover.

"Why does Hersey think you sabotaged his research?"

"Going for the jugular, eh, Mr. Wolfe?" I joked, but the question kept my blood running hot.

"Rand. Friends call me Rand, Ken. And I'm hoping I'm going to count you as one of them." He leveled those sharp eyes of his on me, but I didn't look down. I studied the color of them, instead, to see why they shined like they did, and noticed the golden flecks warming the gray, and the layers, like the eyes were truly the windows to the soul.

Rand, here, had levels. His nostrils quivered before he turned his attention to the parking lot in front of us.

"I didn't *sabotage* anything," I said, And while I had an interested audience, I figured, why not inflict a little more damage to Hersey by spewing forth a few lies. "The man based his research on rumor, and when we found nothing, he had to blame someone. So, why not the kid who couldn't fight back. My word against his, and who would people believe, me or him?"

Randall Wolfe, or Rand as he said he liked to be called, kept his gaze straight ahead as he clenched the muscles of his jaw like he chewed on his thoughts.

My question was rhetorical anyway. I didn't expect a reply. "So, he makes my life hell, does his level best to keep me on shaky ground as a student of this fine campus, while I keep my mouth shut about his accusations."

This time I got a response. Randall Wolfe swiveled his head to face me. "Except when he announced a return trip to the very place where he'd previously gotten no evidence."

Man, could the guy break skin with that stare? I almost pushed my back against the door. *Almost.* I had Armand and Eaen's safety riding on this, and I'd be damned if I'd back down. Not when Wolfe brought up the very mistake I'd made by assaulting Hersey.

He had me on that one, since I had nothing to fling back at him in the way of denial. I locked my jaw, and glared at him.

He gazed back, his expression void of the antagonism I expected to see there.

"I've got nothing," I said, grabbing the door handle to get the hell out of Wolfe's presence.

"Wait, Ken. *Please.*" If the guy had triangular ears, I just imagined them laying flat on a furry head, and that halted my exit. Who the hell was this man?

"Look, I'm interested because I happen to believe you up to a point. Professor Hersey did not find wolves in northern Maine."

The way he said that would have had *my* triangular ears pointing forward, if I'd had any. Still, though, he piqued my interest.

"I believe the two of you found something up there, Ken, but it wasn't wolves. Not the kind to be tagged and documented anyway." He held me with those gold-flecked gray eyes of his, and for the life of me I couldn't deny the layers dwelling in them.

I practically flinched when he reached for his wallet. "Look. I'm not here to accuse anyone, but I could use a little help. Here's my card. If for any reason," he hardened that all-too-familiar gaze of his, "*any reason whatsoever,* Ken, you call me. Even if it's two o'clock in the morning, I want to hear from you. Understand?"

I nodded. Christ, what else was I going to do just then? My thoughts were tumbling like a loaded clothes dryer, and I felt just as hot in the confines of his vehicle.

"Yeah, sure." I reached to take the business card he offered, but he snatched it back before my fingers closed over it.

Then I watched, stunned to my planted ass, as Rand swiped the little card across his cheeks and along his neck, like he was slathering it with his scent.

"Here," he held the thing back out for me to take, watching me close the whole time for my reaction, like he was reading me for any signs I might think he'd fallen off his rocker.

Couldn't have passed him that look if I'd tried. The man was far from crazy if you'd already been immersed in the ways of the wolf.

Shit.

I snagged the card so he wouldn't see my hand tremble.

"Thanks, Ken. And I mean it, get in touch with me. I'll be hanging around for a while, so any time you want to talk, I'm there. Got it?"

Yeah, I got it like white on rice. I hopped out of his vehicle and strode as nonchalantly as I could for my own, and beat down the urge to peel out of the parking lot straight for home.

Instead, I forced myself to be careful with my memento from my meeting with Rand. I didn't want to contaminate it with other scents if I could help it. The man hadn't wiped himself all over it for nothing. Uh-uh. He'd marked that card, and the reason why made me more nervous than a long tailed cat in a room full of rocking chairs.

What did he know? Better yet, how much did he know? I kept my eyes trained on the rearview mirror as I drove back to the house, just in case a certain green SUV decided to tail me.

Chapter Five

I left my stuff in the car when I got home, and headed straight inside to see Eaen and Armand, to let them get a whiff of Rand's card before his scent faded. Eaen pinched it between his long fingers and waved it under his nose as he inhaled quick, little puffs through his nostrils. He handed the card to Armand.

"Recognize anything, Brother?"

I stood there practically dancing like I was a little kid who had to pee, and shifted my rapt attention from one wolf-man to the other. "Well?"

"No one I know." Armand looked at me as if I'd grown an extra head. Without a brain, I should add. Because he had a good point. How would the young wolf-men know, given they'd lived in the woods their whole lives.

"So, it's not someone from your old pack, then? I mean, you should have seen this guy, Armand. He was wolf, I'd swear it, even if his hands weren't like yours."

"You say he rubbed his face and neck on this?" Eaen took the card from Armand to smell it again, then shrugged. "It is no one we know, Kenrickey, but perhaps he was giving you a clue about himself. Perhaps he suspects you are like him."

Huh?

Eaen laughed. "Armand, I think our new brother has a question or two. Come on, Kenrickey, come sit with us while we tell you what Ane and Elga had to say about the porcupine traipsing around in our territory."

Ane and Elga who? And how did this conversation become about me, when we'd been discussing Randall Wolfe and his card-giving hi-jinx.

"Ane and Elga, Kenrickey, are our eldest pack members. They have much of the wolf-people lore in their blood, and their stories are wise. We hold them in very high esteem. Even Luna does."

"Really?"

Eaen and I plunked onto the couch, while Armand removed an open book from his chair to sit down. "They do not think your finding Grane was any accident. In fact, they say your finding of us, once you were so close, was inevitable, and Luna's strange mental connection to you was the clearing of the channels in your wolf spirit."

"My what?"

"The old women called it your wolf spirit. They suspect your blood has ties to the Schism. They thought it important Armand and I show you the ways of the wolf, Brother, so you might remember your lineage."

"Get out of town."

Eaen and Armand exchanged glances, and both turned puzzled looks toward the front door, then back to me.

"No, no guys." I waved a hand to reassure them, like I was erasing my words as though they floated in the air. "It's an expression. You don't really go anywhere. It means I think you're kidding, that I think you're playing a joke on me." It was my turn to give them the puzzled expression. "You are kidding, right?"

Eaen shook his head, his brown eyes bright. "Not about something so important, Kenrickey. So far, Ane and Elga seem to be right about you, and what we have been taught by them may help us identify this wolf-man who left his card."

"This is crazy." I scraped a path through the top of my head. Crazy talk, yes, but I wished it were true just the same. I'd love to be able to become a wolf like my new brothers. I mean, how great would it be to run and keep up with them, to hunt as an equal beside them without getting beat up so easily? But, my wanting and the old women's stories didn't make it so. As the saying went, I could want in one hand and shit in the other.

"My parents are very human, guys. I'm not like you in any way, no

97

matter how much I might want it to be true."

"Kenrickey, we hear your thoughts and you hear ours." Armand wiggled his blond eyebrows over shining yellow eyes.

True. Very true. Maybe those old wolf-women were onto something.

So, what about Rand, then. What were we going to do about him? If it turned out he was a wolf-man, then we just might have an ally in our mission against Hersey. Or, I thought as my stomach turned to rock, his arrival made things even more complicated and possibly outright dangerous. Would he hurt my brothers if he learned about them?

"Christ, guys, could things get just a little more complicated?" I couldn't hide my exasperation. I'd promised to keep them safe, and so far I wasn't doing a very good job of it. Two new people, Rand and Naomi, knew or suspected I was involved with wolves up to my eyeballs. How was that holding to my promise to Luna? Or, most importantly, to Eaen and Armand themselves.

"Let us hope not," Eaen replied, ignoring my rhetorical lament. He put his arm around my shoulders, hugging me to his bare chest to offer me comfort from my worries, to share them, even, like a strong pack leader would.

"I am getting hungry, we should go hunting." Armand stood up and stretched, his sinewy muscles bunching.

Eaen unfolded his tall frame from the couch and held his hand out to me. "Good idea. Come on, Kenrickey."

My heart sped up, and I couldn't hide my grin. The wolf-men wanted to take me out in the woods with them again, *to hone my wolf skills,* which they seemed to think I had, given that we could hear one another's thoughts. I wondered what else they would've noticed that I didn't, aside from my getting in touch with my inner assertiveness. "Yeah, okay. What are we going after this time?"

"Whatever comes across our noses first," Eaen announced, then promptly collapsed onto four paws.

"Mother of—" I faltered sideways. Someday, goddammit, I was going to get used to that. I resisted the urge to clutch my hand to my heart, and shucked my shirt instead. I'd leave my pants on until we got into the woods. Naomi would be dropping by later, and this time I didn't want to be caught bare assed in front of her if we didn't get back before she arrived.

I headed out the door with two wolves, and felt the tweaks of envy. Yeah, I wouldn't mind being able to shift into wolf like that, to hunt with their killer senses. But it wasn't going to happen. My parents were as white bread as the average American got. Think Ward and June Cleaver and you got my folks.

So, no, I wasn't wolf, even if I could hear their thoughts. Luna had done that to me with her mojo; there hadn't been any opening of my wolf spirit. Had there? I shook my head, and chased after the black and blonde wolves, my adrenaline already pumping through me.

It was time to get focused on the world surrounding me, to tune into the woods, to what was going on right then. I could fantasize about the changes in me later, after the hunt. And after I'd learned a little more about Rand.

* * * *

We returned from the hunt with sated bellies. Eaen's and Armand's fuller than mine, but still, I'd killed and eaten a squirrel Eaen had trapped under his huge paw for me. He got bit for his efforts, but he didn't seem to mind, not if his fanning tail and lolling tongue meant anything as he and Armand watched me fumble with my first bushy tailed rodent.

My hands, arms, and bare stomach got clawed to bits as I tried to subdue it, and the scratches stung like a mother effer. The squirrel dug deep in its frantic attempts to get loose, until I finally managed to cup my hand around its gnashing, little head to wring its neck.

Its body had hung limp and warm in my hands. I still felt it, even as we made our way back to the house, its death weighing on my heart just as heavy as the impression in my palms. A universal truth learned and accepted with the full force of its reality. Killing another living thing was not done lightly, or just for fun.

The life taken had not been given freely, and it would be a sacrilege to disrespect that fight, no matter how small the battle. Christ, these wolves humbled me to my marrow.

It was that mood I nursed as I watched Naomi's car pull up the drive as we rounded the corner of the house. My sweet Nae, who wasn't to be

S. C. Dane

taken for granted, either. I never had in all the time I'd known her. I ached for her, for shit's sake, and I wanted to bury my face into the warmth of her nape as I watched her get out of her car.

Still emotional from the hunt with Eaen and Armand, I strode right over and did just that, seizing the opportunity no matter the risk. I squeezed her hard to my chest, my face nuzzled right where her scent of snow contrasted with the warmth of her neck, and felt her arms coil around my waist.

She readily opened for me, just as she'd done the day we'd romped in the house with my brothers. Sweet God, I loved her. Always had.

"Nae, you came." I pulled away from her just enough so I could look at her. She didn't say anything, because we both knew that a year ago, she wouldn't have come. Jeff the Bear had her on a short leash, and she'd been content enough then not to stretch its limits.

But now? I wondered what had changed, but didn't want to look that gift horse too close in the mouth. She had come to see us, *me*, and I'd take it as the present it was.

I pressed her to me again, her clothes warming in the heat of our embrace, drifting her scent up to my nose. *My God*, she felt glorious against my bare chest, and I beat down the urge to cup her ass in my palms, to pull her hips so she could grind against me.

I pulled back once again, this time releasing her from my desperate grip, so the wolves could greet her, too. As much as I wanted to, I couldn't hog her all to myself. Armand and Eaen needed their chance with the human, even if she was my sweet Naomi.

Who dropped to her hands and knees to kiss the black wolf under his chin, just like she did before, like she was wolf, too. Man, the guys were right—she was quick. Armand sidled close to rub his muzzle across her upper arm, while Eaen curled behind her to stroke his back to hers. They were reclaiming her just like I saw the other wolves do in the forest.

"I think they like me," Nae laughed as she scratched the blonde wolf's ears, her face beaming her pleasure.

"Yeah, I think it's pretty obvious." I pegged Armand with a knowing smirk. "He let you rub his ears."

Naomi glanced up, and all I could do was gawk back at her with cartoon hearts bubbling out of my eyes. She seemed utterly enthralled

100

with how the wolves acted toward her. But then she frowned, narrowing her eyes as she scanned my bare torso.

"Ken." One word, dropped like an admonishing brick from her, and we males fell still.

"What?" Like I didn't know what she'd noticed. As if my upper body wasn't plastered with scrapes and scratches from our hunting, or sported a bruised and scabbing hole from a deer's antler.

She jutted her chin at the puncture wound as Armand slid himself under her hands. "That. How'd you get *that*?" She hadn't noticed it the other day, then.

I lifted my arm to get a better look at my side and grinned sheepishly. Eaen padded over to sniff at the scab, and I saw Nae's thoughts churning behind her eyes. I lost my guilty grin.

"It's nothing. Not infected," I said, trying to slow her diabolically clever brain. But, I should have known, should have seen her setting her trap. Naomi wasn't at the top of our class because she was slow witted. I pushed my fingers to the base of my skull, preparing myself for Luna's electrified punishment I was sure would come.

With true affection, she hugged Armand closer to her, twirling her fingertips through his mane. "Remember when you asked if I minded meeting the blonde wolf? What did you say his name was?"

"Armand. His name's Armand," I answered, still gullible as a liquid eyed fawn. Guess who swished his tail at the mention of his name.

"And the black one?" she asked blithely. Oh, she was good.

"Eaen. Only he doesn't spell it like we—" *Aw, shit.* The buzzing was going to strike hard enough to kill me.

"Really, now." She turned, sat on her buttocks and locked eyes with Armand, who dropped his head as a whine escaped his deep chest.

"So, tell me, Armand," Nae addressed the wolf directly, "How did you and Ken meet?"

Surely, she didn't expect him to answer. And I had my head stuffed up my butt if she wasn't.

Armand shot a worried glance at Eaen, scrabbled his paws beneath him, and pulled himself out of Naomi's embrace.

As soon as her arms were empty, Nae shifted her weight to the balls of her feet and faced the black wolf. Like she expected another confrontation. "And you, Eaen? How is it you know Ken?"

Eaen curled the corner of his lips away from his fangs.

Naomi paused, but didn't retreat. Or put her back to the ground. Nope. Her beautiful fingers pinched the edge of her shirt, and then she pulled the garment over her head. She slid her pants off just as methodically, all without dropping her challenging gaze from the black wolf.

Eaen stiffened, but didn't budge or take his brown eyes off the naked woman crouched in front of him.

"Nae," I whispered, entranced, mortified.

She ignored me to lay herself prostrate before us.

The black wolf shot his bulk onto her, and pushed his sharp teeth into her neck. Naomi flinched as if to bear the brunt of his weight, then lay frozen under the cage of Eaen's legs and fangs.

I stood there stunned as she relaxed under him, and she didn't offer to get up when the wolf eventually backed away from her to stand beside me. I could feel him trembling. We both knew Naomi suspected something wasn't right with the wolves. Whoever said she wasn't smart had an empty suitcase for a head.

I bent down like my legs were noodles to retrieve her clothes and hold them out for her.

She looked up, the hurt on her face unmistakable. Then I saw her expression shift, like she thought she knelt before me like a beggar looking for a handout. She snatched her clothes from my hands, threw them on in a huff, and ran for her car.

"Nae, wait." *Christ Almighty.* "I didn't mean—"

But she didn't stop to hear what I'd intended to say. She hurled her body into the driver's seat, slammed the door, and spewed a shower of gravel at the side of the house as she peeled out, speeding the car to the main road.

"*Naomi!*" But my howl bloomed out toward the empty, evening air as I watched my woman run away from me.

* * * *

"What the fuck have I just done?" I bellowed as the taillights disappeared around the corner. My legs turned mushy and I nearly dropped to my knees. Armand pushed his body against me in sympathy, and whined as he nudged my legs.

His gestures offered little comfort. My heart had just sped out of our lives and I couldn't think straight without it. I couldn't breathe right. "How the—?" I tugged at my hair, glared at the stars, the house, as I pivoted like a dysfunctional monkey in the driveway. "What the fuck just happened?" My heart kicked my sternum like it wore work boots. I really wasn't breathing right.

"Kenrickey."

Yeah, we were fucked. What did she think I'd meant as I'd held her clothes out for her? Right. She thought I'd told her to leave, for shit's sake.

Kenrickey, breathe.

I inhaled and then looked around me, trying to refocus my brain.

"Breathe again, Porcupine."

I obeyed as I stared up into Eaen's concerned face, his brown eyes shining in the waning daylight as he blasted heat from his lean body. I stepped back from the force of it.

"Eaen, what did we do?"

The tall wolf-man shook his head apologetically. "She yielded after her assault. It is what we always do. She understood or she would not have—"

"She knows," Armand's deep voice threaded into our bewildered fear. And the fact, once stated, wouldn't go away.

Because she did know. She'd asked direct questions of the wolves, for God's sake, as if they could answer her. She was too effing quick-witted, and had jumped the logic rail with mind-numbing accuracy.

"She has superb instincts," Eaen complimented with a twinge of awe shaking his voice. "She caught us all off guard."

"Jesus, guys. I love her, you know. I want to have her kids, I want to wake up—" I let my angst spiral and scatter my thoughts like a cyclone in a trailer park. I didn't care if my skin blew off in front of Armand and Eaen. I'd just driven the woman of my dreams away from my home.

Because I swore to protect my brothers at all cost. That truth had no trouble sticking in the eye of the tornado that was the spiraling of my tormented thoughts, and it was anchored there because of the fucking buzzing. It was back, and so goddamned present my hands flew to my ears to muffle the sound.

My knees finally did buckle, but I never felt the gravel bite into my flesh, and a moan curled out of my throat like smoke. My stomach soured and bile washed my molars. I was going to puke.

"Jesus, Luna, can't we have her?" I groaned, and spit the contents of my stomach onto the driveway.

The buzzing ceased so abruptly my head teetered in the vacuum.

Eaen and Armand knelt on their knees beside me, and Eaen slid his broad shoulders under my arm to lift me to my feet.

"Porcupine, what happened? Are you all right?"

Poor Eaen. His evening was turning out to be just as bad as mine. Somehow, we'd gotten tickets on the rollercoaster from Hell and couldn't get off. Except, of course, when you went shrieking past the conductor and left a trail of vomit streaming behind you like a comet tail.

"Why did you talk to our sister?" His confusion furrowed his brow, and he cast an anxious look at Armand.

"The buzzing," I pointed to my head. "She gave me this buzzing, I don't know, not for what you guys or your old women think, but to help you, or something. To warn us when things get too crazy. I don't know—it never went away after I left the woods."

I rambled but didn't care. My stomach was freakin' knotted, my mouth burned, and my heart just vacated the premises. I wasn't exactly doing great enough to get my shit together.

Well, at least I hadn't pissed my pants, but why end the suffering there?

"Luna is still in your head?" Eaen's face shed its distress, and his luminous teeth emerged in a blissful smile.

I nodded, not sure where he was going or why he was so happy about it.

He beamed his brown eyes on Armand. "Luna is with us, Armand."

The blonde wolf-man warmed beside me, and I snuggled myself closer to him. I still had no idea why that should be so heartening. If anything, I could do without her presence, thank you very much.

"You do not know, Kenrickey," Eaen cupped my face in his long hand as he and Armand exchanged knowing looks.

"Know what, Eaen?" I asked, because I was the monkey with my hand caught in the hole and refused to let go of my prize so I could be free. "What do you know that I don't?"

Eaen pointed to his lower leg, where a thin, nasty scar glowed white in the dusky light. "See that, Porcupine?"

I nodded.

"That was a very bad wound from a steel trap," he bragged, prepared to continue even if my eyes hadn't bulged and the buzzing hadn't started to vibrate at the base of my skull again. Before my anger got a foothold, he continued, and the droning ebbed.

"Luna healed it. She saved my life. And Armand's life, too." Eaen was smiling joyfully. He wasn't finished.

"We have been inside of her, Kenrickey. We have seen her power. If she transferred some of that to you, do you know what it means?"

"Is your question rhetorical?"

Eaen laughed outright, and a reluctant grin lifted my lips.

"I will answer your question with another question." He wiped his mouth with his hand and rubbed his palms together.

I nodded, and looked to Armand for some support against Eaen's tidal wave of enthusiasm. Got none. Nada. The levee was gone. Armand's face glowed with the mania of his brother's threading logic.

"Did you hear Luna's buzzing when we first met your woman?" His shining eyes searched my face.

"Nooo…" Was that a drop of water?

"You did not hear or feel the least little tingle?"

I shook my head. The flooding tide submerged my feet.

"Not even during our second encounter with your woman?"

My feet slid out from beneath me in the current.

"You did not hear it until she left, and it did not stop until you beseeched Luna's help?"

My mind cart-wheeled backward, to when Naomi addressed the wolves directly. There had been no paralyzing buzzing in my head. So far, I'd only received its punishing intensity when things were going very wrong for the wolf-men, like when I'd tried to attack Hersey. Once I started thinking about it, the vibrations were comforting until I got angry or really frightened for Armand and Eaen. "She's supposed to know," I crowed.

Eaen's laughter exploded into the early evening air.

"Yes, Porcupine. I think it is okay for her to know about us."

I whooped at the stars and hopped around, then planted my feet to cast an anxious glance at my brothers. "We have to go get her."

Even Armand grinned expectantly. Obviously, the notion of Luna looking out for us did wonders for his self-confidence. It didn't hurt, I thought as my resurrected heart thumped ecstatically, that he was rather taken with Naomi, too. I'd seen how he snuggled her.

"Come on, guys, get in the car. We've got a woman to catch."

* * * *

We got to Nae's apartment a little later than I thought we would, given how enthusiastic we all were about chasing my woman down. Armand still had trouble with the car, and to top it off, he was doing his damnedest to stay human in order to meet Naomi on two legs.

So, we had to go a little slow, give him time to reconcile himself to two major events happening to him at once. I didn't mind, though, since we were going after Nae, and were going to let her in on our secret.

Thanks to Luna.

I parked the Subaru up a ways, away from the streetlight so it sat in darkness, and had Eaen and Armand wait in the car while I went into the building after Naomi.

I leapt up the steps leading to the main door, and pounded on it until one of her roommates let me in. She wasn't a biology major, but the campus was small. We'd bumped into each other occasionally.

"Which one is Naomi's?" I asked as I blazed by her without waiting.

"Hi, Ken. How are you doing? Me? I'm great. Thanks for asking."

In any other circumstance, I'd have loved the sarcasm.

"Naomi!" I strode down the narrow hall, banging on every door.

"Third down on the right. Sheesh."

Rude me didn't even say thanks.

"Nae, open up." I pounded my fist on her door. "Come on, I know you're in there."

"Go away."

God, I loved the sound of her voice, even if she was mad.

I rapped my knuckles on her door, softer this time. "I'm sorry, Nae. Just come out so we can talk, okay?"

"No."

Shit. I took a deep breath to quell the urge to kick her door down. Man, but it felt good to finally be in touch with my cojones. Plus, I had two wolf-men waiting downstairs in my car, and I didn't have time to stand there being all tactful and diplomatic. I kicked her door in anyway, and the thing smashed open on its hinges, nearly ricocheting back into my face if I hadn't barged in as soon as the latch broke.

Naomi jumped off her bed. "Ken!"

The sight of her in her skinny tank top and Victoria's Secret boy shorts stole my breath, and I stood stock still for a second while my thoughts jumped ship.

Never mind I'd seen her undressed before. Then we weren't standing in her bedroom, with her too tantalizing close to her bed. And, her cheeks weren't flushed then, like they were now.

"Get dressed. You're coming with me." Now where, I wanted to know, had those orders come from? My lips, obviously, but at least that brought my brain back to the present scenario. "You've got two friends waiting in the car to meet you. *Again.*"

The thought of Eaen and Armand waiting in my car, unsupervised and unprotected from prying human eyes, kept me from tackling the woman in front of me. But, still. "Hurry up."

Nae didn't hesitate, as if she'd once again connected the dots faster than a computer. She leapt off the bed, yanked the clothes she'd been wearing earlier over her very feminine p.j.'s, and crammed a hooded sweatshirt over her head.

"Ready," she announced as soon as her ruffled head poked out.

My God, when she was breathless and excited she was smashing. Utterly beautiful. I snagged her wrist, drawing her body to mine, pinning her arm behind my back as I pressed a not so very gentle kiss to her lips.

She responded by sucking my tongue into the joyful playground of her warm mouth and by grinding her hips across my bulging groin.

Sweet Christ. I peeled myself away with a regret that churned my guts, and ran my tongue across my lips to taste the remnants of her. "I'll collect more of that later. Right now, I've got something else that will

S. C. Dane

blow your socks off. Come on."

She followed me out of her apartment. Really, I'd given her no choice since I didn't let go of her wrist. Although she didn't even balk when we got closer to the Subaru, when I knew she saw the silhouettes of two men sitting in the back seat.

I stopped by the passenger side door to give us all a minute to take a breath, to get ready for what was about to come next. Eaen and Armand were about to meet their first human being since my introduction in the northern woods, and despite our excitement, we were all three nervous as hell about it. Especially since Armand had yet to prove himself capable of even maintaining his human form around anyone but me. And how Nae would take witnessing a man change into a wolf was anyone's guess. Suspecting such a thing was possible was one thing, but for her to witness it would, I had no doubt, knock even her diabolically clever brain for a loop.

I took another breath, and looked down at her. "Ready?"

Naomi nodded, and stepped back so I could open the car door for her. "Your chariot awaits," I announced like the king's footman, and shut the door as soon as she was ensconced in the front seat.

I ran around the hood of the Subaru, and hopped into the guts of a furnace, as if I'd left the car sitting under the summer sun in a paved parking lot, not in the cloaking shadow of a huge pine tree in the thick of night.

Naomi was already twisted in her seat getting a look at my two passengers, at the two friends she'd already met.

The suspicious incredulity on her face settled my dancing nerves. So did the rigid outlines of the wolf-men in the back seat.

"Ken, what's going on?" Nae lost a bit of her brash self-confidence as she eyed the two men sitting in shadow.

"Shh, Nae. Just move slow, okay, like you did when you first met the wolves."

She reached tentatively to touch the knee closest to her. Armand flinched backward and yelped like she'd burned him, and my heart seized up.

"Armand?" Nae gasped the name, her guess nailing the right wolf-man, and she peered deeper into the back seat, then shot me a look of

108

disbelief. "This is impossible, right?"

I grinned as if I was telling her the best secret in the world, because I was. I shook my head. "No, your leap in logic is spot-on, Nae, but just go easy. Armand isn't used to the car, let alone meeting people."

Naomi pulled her knees under her and wedged herself between the Subaru's bucket seats. "Armand, let me see you." Her hand shook as she reached across to touch him, then hovered as he whined, gripped his hair, and panted heavily. Still sensitively attuned to the blonde wolf, Nae pulled her hand back to give him some space.

"We're going, guys. I'm starting the car, so just hold on."

Eaen's silhouette nodded, but he didn't speak.

"You all right? Speak to me, Eaen."

The wolf-man's voice rumbled thick, like something primordial. "Yes, Kenrickey," he answered. "But hurry."

Naomi's voice squeaked Eaen's name, and suddenly she didn't seem to be doing so great either. I punched down on the accelerator to fling the car out of town like I piloted the space shuttle. The sooner I got us home, the better for all of us.

We arrived in a spray of gravel, and three people fell out of the Subaru before I barely had the thing in park. Nae gazed up and took a step backward as Eaen stretched himself upright and took a tentative step toward her.

"Eaen," she huffed, her chest heaving laboriously. Then her legs crumpled and her body spread across the driveway, as if instinctively adopting a submissive posture while her brain worked to piece itself back together.

The wolf-man shivered, and took several gulps of air even as his strides led him inevitably toward her prostrate form. Eaen bent to all fours and reached for her neck, but then checked himself and smiled fearfully, as if revealing his teeth would send Nae running hysterically.

He had good reason for his trepidation: Nae had whined.

But then she clenched her jaw like she gritted her teeth, and without peeling her eyes from the wolf-man kneeling toward her, she rolled up onto her hands and knees to kiss him under his chin, just as she'd done when Eaen was wolf.

"Sweet mother of mine," I muttered. Nae was some kind of savant, she had to be.

Eaen's nostrils billowed as he sniffed the air around her head, and Naomi froze to let him do it.

"Eaen," I scolded, even though I felt awful doing it. But it got his attention, and he quit sniffing Nae to look up at me. "You're human," I reminded him.

He quirked an uneasy grin, then straightened to his full height, planting his two bare feet under his tall body.

Naomi rose with him, and stuck her hand out for him to shake. Would she notice the difference, the placement of the wolf-man's thumb? "Hi, Eaen," she smiled up at him, her hazel eyes sparkling in the starlight. Nae had rebooted her brain, and it was working as sharp as ever. "This is where you take my hand and say *Hi* back."

"Hi back," he repeated, and this time he let Nae see his full smile, without the fear of her reaction.

Nae stared, but then seemed to remember her place, because she dropped her gaze and tilted her chin to bare her throat to the man standing in front of her.

"It is okay," Eaen reassured her, quickly adapting himself to the situation. "I am human, remember?"

"I'm sorry. I didn't mean to offend you." She kept her lids lowered.

"Kenrickey's woman, it is all right. We are friends, we have played together," Eaen gruffed a teasing laugh to ease her, to remind Nae they'd already met before, that he was the same being, no matter his shape.

She visibly relaxed as she looked up at him, then seemed to remember something important, her breath catching as she glanced around where she and Eaen stood. Her worry pinched her brows, coloring her call with alarm. "Armand?"

God, I'd been so engrossed watching this scene play out I'd forgotten all about the blonde wolf-man, who squatted by the bumper of the car with his head gripped in his hands. He panted as he fought himself, and the thick muscles across his broad back buckled and coiled beneath his sweating skin.

He couldn't stop his reversal to wolf, no matter how hard he was trying. Yet he hadn't retreated, and that said a lot about his feelings for Nae. He trusted her, and I'd be damned if I'd stand there like a gawking moron while he struggled.

I dropped to my knees in front of him, and pulled off his shirt to help. "Easy, Armand. Let it go in just a second. We'll get this shit off you first, okay, then let her rip." I slid his pants off his hips as he kicked his legs free.

Just in time, too. I glanced up at Nae as Armand's body refolded itself into its truest form.

"Ha," she gushed, then plopped to her pretty ass like the bones melted in her legs. I knew how she felt. It would be a long time before I ever forgot my first view of a man shifting into a wolf. Hell, it still knocked me sideways.

As if pulled by an invisible string winding between them, Naomi crawled toward Armand, who hadn't budged a muscle since covering himself with fur. He watched her though, his yellow eyes darting from the woman nearing him, to the ground, then back again.

Like she'd done before, she gently cupped his cheek, and the blonde wolf pressed the weight of his head to her palm, then pushed his face to her chest.

Nae closed her eyes as she wrapped her arms around the man who was now a wolf, and she cradled him just as she'd done the first time she'd met Armand, when she didn't yet know what he truly was.

And like that first time, Armand savored the feel of being within her embrace. Then he squirmed, flipped to his massive paws, and stuck his bushy tail into the air in a classic play bow.

Nae squealed her delight, sending the blonde wolf into the stratosphere. He bounded around us in a couple of speeding circles, then fell against Nae, who hadn't managed to find her legs yet, and stretched himself prostrate in front of her, completely exposing his vulnerable underbelly to her.

"Well, that's that."

As if my pronouncement unleashed us, Armand twisted to his paws again, drove his muzzle toward the night sky, and released a howl so hearty it lifted him off his front legs. Eaen and I joined him in raucous celebration before he could yip twice.

As he had done with me that first time, Eaen collected Nae into our little group, and I didn't hesitate to wrap her in my arms. Seconds later, I felt the taller wolf-man drape himself to encompass us all, his harmonizing howls reverberating the length of my spine.

Eaen was claiming us as his pack, and we unhesitatingly bound ourselves to him. Our beautiful Nae lifted her tear-streaked face to the diamond chip stars, and howled her joy, too.

* * * *

"She did well to last as long as she did," I whispered to my two companions, who hovered beside me as I carried Naomi into the house. Her cheek rested against my chest, and her long eyelashes tickled my nipple.

"She is special, Kenrickey," Eaen complimented, then blushed proudly. He was still full of his own accomplishments, as he should have been. Armand said nothing with his tongue, but his tail rode high and waved soft arcs behind his great back. He obviously thought Nae was special, too, or he would have never transformed in front of her.

We got her into the bedroom, where I lowered her gently onto the bed. Her tiny sigh thrummed the blood in my veins and it was all I could do not to slide in beside her and take her in her sleep. She was a nymph, a fairy—*something*. I mean, she had intuitively known about the wolf-men. Plus, she looked so freakin' delicious laying in my bed I wanted to drag my tongue over every inch of her woman's skin.

I slid my body in alongside hers but denied my urges, and cradled her to me instead. Then I rubbed my nose across her rumpled hair to inhale her crisp scent. *Mine.* She was ours and she was mine. The reality of her belonging filled me to bursting, and I snuggled deeper into the bed with my prize.

Armand and Eaen slipped away, but didn't return to the bedroom. They were giving us the privacy due a mated pair. A *mated* pair. Funny how I adopted the wolf-men's language so easily when it came to Naomi. She was mine, but not as a possession. Most definitely not as that.

On the contrary, Nae owned *my* heart, she owned me. She always had, right from the early days when I'd realized she was moving closer to me in the classroom. This beautiful, extraordinary woman wanted to be with me.

And I thought I was like a brother? Didn't I have any self-confidence? Not when it had come to Naomi, I hadn't. Christ, I was stunned for a whole year just thinking someone like her wanted to be around a social outcast like me.

I tightened my arms around her and buried my face into the crook of her neck. *Sweet living Jesus.* Her scent hardened me, reminding me that she wasn't wholly mine yet. But I didn't want to wake her, didn't want to press with my needs. She'd been through way too much already.

I nuzzled into her to drift off to sleep. It had been quite a day for us all. Yet before I shut my eyes, I lifted a silent prayer to the moonbeams glowing through the windows, asking that we share a billion more days as brimming with love as this one had been.

* * * *

The morning sun brightened to a mellow haze, and I cracked my lids to greet it and the woman who snored quietly beside me. My grin radiated from within as I listened to her steady breaths. Nae snored like an infant, and it touched me to the core, tickled my feet. I stroked the hair from her temple and pressed my lips to her soft skin.

The morning, I was beyond pleased to realize, didn't put things straight, didn't make them better in the light. I slid out from the tangle of Naomi's warm limbs and headed for the living room to check on my brothers. They'd had one hell of a night, too, *and* had lost their comfy bed.

The two wolves were curled up on the couch, butts touching.

"Good morning, guys. You sleep okay?" I whispered as I crouched in front of them. Eaen lifted his furred head, but Armand was slow to wake as usual.

The black wolf stretched his jaws wide, unfurled his pink tongue in a huge yawn, and uncoiled his limbs so the bones could roll, slide and shift. Eaen, the human oven, lay curled in front of me.

I snapped my gaping jaw shut.

"That's pretty effing amazing, but you already know that." I shook my head as I stared at the wolf-man who grinned back at me. Yeah, he knew that, knew how it still thrilled me to see it.

"Did you sleep well, Porcupine," he winked.

"Yeah, but not like you think, you nosy turd." I reached out to tousle his dark hair like he still had his ears, and withdrew my hand before he could chomp on it. Armand flung his paws toward the back of the couch and lay on his back with his legs akimbo. His head was twisted upside down, but he was awake and watching me and Eaen.

"Good morning, Armand." I stood up and made my way to the kitchen for apples, dug into the crisper, and by the time I turned around to offer breakfast, I had two, full-grown wolf-men tangled up on my couch. They snagged the apples I tossed, and the three of us munched while we waited for our woman to emerge from the bedroom.

"Maybe we should go and wake her," Eaen suggested.

"Maybe we should let her wake on her own so we do not frighten her," Armand countered. I raised an eyebrow, and took a closer look at the blonde wolf-man who was endearingly protective of his human.

"Armand, you are a gentleman," I complimented. "Those were my thoughts exactly."

Eaen didn't mask his disappointment. He wanted to practice staying upright some more. Yet, I couldn't blame him. It was a huge deal among his people. I knew because I had been the test model for Suma and Alec. For Eaen, though, it was a gargantuan personal milestone, one that gave him an edge in their war against the human intrusion of their territory.

"You'll get your chance very soon, I promise."

"I know. Here she comes."

Both wolf-men pulled their feet beneath them to crouch on the sofa, their heated bodies shivering in nervous anticipation as they stared toward the bedroom. Naomi, disheveled and dreamy, leaned against the doorjamb and came no closer. I lobbed my attention between the wolf-men and Nae like a spectator at a tennis match, then stood back to let the game play out as it would.

Nae's voice, scratchy with sleep, lilted across the room and struck the wolf-men inert.

"I thought I'd been dreaming."

Armand whined, but couldn't tear his eyes away. Nor could he move. Eaen was only a little better.

"Good morning, Nae." I kept my tone low, but grinned, then dropped and lifted my lids in salutation. My stomach twisted like a dishcloth when she blushed, and I had to squirm like the wolf-men, just to readjust my balls that had sucked up tight.

Eaen finally managed a gruff good morning to Naomi, but Armand was still struck silent. Naomi's instincts concerning the wolf-men were as dead-on accurate as they'd been before. She did not advance directly toward them, as if she could sense how close they were to losing it.

"Good morning, Eaen. Armand." Naomi dropped her chin and eyes in deference. "May I come near?"

Her voice was the nectar of flowers, the plack of raindrops on the leaves.

Eaen's voice carried the timbre of his ancestry. "Yes, Kenrickey's woman, you may sit with us."

Nae's ears pinked like delicate seashells, and the two wolf-men stood, as if their manners overrode their fear of the human. Armand sidled over to his favorite chair, but Eaen remained, standing stiffly erect in front of the couch where he'd been sitting. I stayed put, not trusting Mr. Plucky, who fidgeted when the words *Kenrickey's woman* rippled across the room.

Naomi tip-toed her way toward the tall wolf-man until she was only a foot away from him, then she tilted her chin to the ceiling, leaning forward as Eaen lowered his head toward her so she could kiss him under his smooth chin.

I sucked in my breath as the muscles in Eaen's strong jaw clenched and his nostrils flared.

Naomi stepped back slowly as if she registered his difficulty. She probably did. So far, she'd been eerily in tune with the wolf-men, as if her senses were preternaturally heightened when she was around them. Images of Nae flickered like snapshots through my memories. No, her sensitivities were not drawn out by the presence of Armand and Eaen. My woman had skill. Her actions and reactions concerning the wolf-men were already honed to the finest point, I was sure of it.

Because it explained her relationship with The Bear. She constantly assessed and behaved accordingly when she was with him. She protected herself to the Nth degree.

A knowing smile tugged my lips because Nae didn't always act like that. I'd seen her with her hair down, so to speak. I'd seen her eyes shine without inhibition. The most recent time was just last night.

And she didn't seem wary here, even with two naked wolf-men in her midst. Odd, but heart-wrenchingly so. She belonged here, and she dropped her defenses as the wolves shed their fur, without effort.

As if to prove it, she sat down at Armand's feet, her slender legs curled beneath her, her delicate arm draped across his knee. The blond wolf-man sat in his chair with his long hands on the armrests, the fingers of his right hand wiggling forward to touch her hair. One finger barely brushed a strand, and Nae tilted her head closer to his tremulous touch.

Loving Christ, she was an angel.

With sharp teeth. "So, boys, tell me why *Kenrickey* is covered with bruises." She pushed her head into Armand's hand as she turned to look up at him. A playful grin lit her hazel eyes, and damned if Armand didn't succumb to it. He grinned back, his luminous teeth dazzling forth without restraint.

Eaen was the one to answer. "We take him hunting."

That caught her off guard. She snapped her head erect and ogled Eaen. "No way." Then she turned to me, but the whole time she remained curled up at Armand's feet.

I lifted my arm and pointed to my ribs. "An antler," I explained.

"The Porcupine is a brave hunter."

"Wait, what did you call him?" Naomi's playful smile returned.

"My brother nick-named him Porcupine, and it stuck." Armand caressed the hair at his fingertips absentmindedly, while he grinned at me. Both he and Eaen relished revealing my nickname to my mate.

Nae, bless her acute senses, snorted a quick laugh. "That's perfect."

The wolf-men laughed with her, and I couldn't help myself either as I joined Eaen on the couch to close our circle.

Still smiling, but missing nothing, the woman at Armand's knee asked, "There are more of you?"

"Your woman is sharp, Kenrickey," Eaen chuckled with approval. "Yes, there are more of us. Armand and I are here with your mate because we need his help. Your teacher discovered our pack's territory, and we need to keep him from coming back to harm us."

Naomi rose, crossed the short distance to the couch, and burrowed in between Eaen and me. Then she patted the foot of space beside her, asking Armand to snuggle in with us. He swallowed, then unfolded his muscular frame from the chair. Gently he squished himself in so that he nestled like a pup between Nae and Eaen, and his tall brother draped his arm affectionately across the other wolf-man's shoulders.

Could Nae do anything more perfect?

Armand turned his yellow eyes to me, and promptly lowered his lids. "Is it all right that I sit with your mate, Kenrickey?"

"Absolutely, Brother. It warms my heart that we are so close." Did I just say that? Man, I was picking up more than just hunting skills from the wolf-men. But my response sat well with every one of us, and just then I really wished that Luna and Alec, and Grane and Suma, could see the young wolf-men piled up so comfortably with two humans. We had formed our own little pack, and my shit-eating grin had company. We all looked as though there was no dreamier place on earth than where we were at that moment.

"Tell me more," Naomi invited as she swiveled her head so she could see us all, which pushed her deeper into my side, curving her like a silken glove against my skin.

"You remind me of my sister," Armand confessed.

Naomi's periwinkle ears flooded red she was so pleased.

"Tell us, Armand," Eaen urged. Apparently, neither Grane nor Armand had spoken much about her, outside of the obvious, that she'd been shot by human men.

Armand took a very deep breath and let it out slowly. The air around us warmed as if the morning sun shined directly onto the sofa. "Her name was Misha, and she was brave and quick like you, Naomi." The blonde wolf-man lowered his head, focusing on his knees as he spoke with a voice laden with sorrow and admiration. "She was my only sibling, and when she mated with Grane, I followed her to Meron's pack so that we would not part."

The mention of Meron's name chilled me as I recalled how the gray wolf-man had made short order of three of his wolves. Which made Grane a traitor, didn't it? Running quick on the heels of that thought was the image of Luna and the brown wolf and how they'd greeted Grane and Suma with such love. I quashed my ugly suspicions, knowing full well I'd have done the same to be a member of Alec's pack, too.

"Misha and Grane took care of me like I was their wolf-pup, especially since they were forbidden to have any of their own, and our life together was beautiful when we were not under Meron's watchful eye. Too often our pack leader took chances with us, pitting his subordinates against the humans. They killed my sister while she was out hunting for me."

Here Armand stopped his story telling and raised his face to view the two humans crammed with him on the sofa. His yellow eyes glimmered with unshed tears, which threatened to spill if he lowered his lids again.

"Armand," I whispered with the breath that exited my lungs. I knew his sister had been shot, but to know why was unendurable. Meron had betrayed his own. Misha had died because she'd not only been a brave wolf, but a loyal one as well.

Nae's whisper was the dust particles in a sunbeam, and she captured Armand's mournful gaze with her own.

"I'm sorry. You loved her very much, and knowing I could be thought of as your sister, to be compared to her? You've no idea what that means to me."

"You're crying."

I didn't know I had a stereo. But damned if the three of us weren't right about Naomi's tears. She *was* crying. I pulled her to me, kissed her temple, while Eaen and Armand fidgeted, hovered, reached for her, withdrew.

Why was it a woman's tears could demolish us?

But so could her words.

"To be your sister," she whispered while concentrating on her bare, precious toes, "would've meant I wouldn't have been beaten by my father while I was growing up."

We froze in spite of the fire igniting around our little group.

I spoke in slow motion. "Say that again, Nae."

But she shook her head against my side, wiping her tears into the hole in my ribcage. Despicable Jesus, the only pain I felt was in my heart. And the wolf-men?

Lost it.

Two pissed off, emotionally wired wolves paced the room, and I

118

wouldn't have been Naomi's father for all the tea in China.

She sniffled, wiped her tears, and God bless her, laughed appreciatively.

"Guys," she sputtered, pouring forth a smile that would have mended the broken hearts of Romeo and Juliet. "It's okay, really. I never see my family anymore, they're far away from here, from me."

Both wolves came to her, pushing their whiskered noses into her clasped hands, waving their lowered tails, while I smothered her with delicate kisses. It was as if our comforting was all we had to give her and we lavished it freely, giving her whatever solace was in our possession to give.

Oh, Nae. Armand. You two have just spilled my guts all over the floor. I squished my woman in my arms, reached for the blonde wolf, and shed tears for her pain, and for Armand's.

Because theirs was mine.

Loving fuck.

Right at that moment, right there, the four of us were safe together. And if it was in my power, I would've kept us all in that moment, in our circle, where the only thing present was our compassion for one another.

But of course, I wasn't a superhero, and Naomi, who was because she had skills, redirected her three men back onto the trail, allayed our protective anger, eased our hurts, and refocused us. I took a deep breath, Eaen leaned his weight into his brother, and Armand received it as he gazed adoringly at the female on the couch.

"My handsome boys," she complimented as she leaned forward to cup Armand's great head in her palms and kiss the bridge of his muzzle. "It's getting late, and I really need to go so that I can get ready." She lifted her shimmering eyes, and stab my skin with a thousand pencils, but never had I wanted to learn they turned green when she cried. And knowing what she meant did nothing to quell my fear for her. She omitted mentioning she had to get ready for The Bear on purpose, to keep our fragile emotions from spilling again. She did it for us, for her boys.

"Yeah, okay." I got up slowly to give Eaen and Armand time to back up, to let Naomi uncurl herself from the couch.

"Do you two want to come with us?" Stupid question. Of course they did. They'd follow her into her apartment, to class, anywhere she went. She was cemented, bonded to them like a sister of their pack, and that really did make me feel better. I lifted my coat from the hook by the door, gave it to Nae, and jingled my keys.

"Let's go if we're going."

Because as Naomi artfully didn't say, we had to get her back before Jeff came looking for her. Before the human came here to look for her, and found two wolf-men instead.

Chapter Six

After dropping Naomi off at her apartment, and returning home to drop off Eaen and Armand, and get myself cleaned up, I finally pulled into the campus parking lot just in time to catch Jeff go into the Science building with Naomi tucked possessively in his beefy arm. They hadn't waited for me to show up, and that lifted the hairs on my nape. Did Jeff know about Nae spending the night at my place?

My stomach wasn't liking this at all, either. It fluttered as if it was a glass jar with moths inside. I jumped out of my car and jogged after my woman as a familiar feeling sharpened my nerves. Naomi needed help, or protection, or *something*. I ripped open the door and skittered into the classroom, just in time to see Naomi turn and shake her head, warning me not to come near.

What the fuck?

But her gesture cemented my feet to the floor, and I darted my eyes around the room before pinning them on Jeff. He glared back as he wrapped his gorilla arm across Naomi's shoulders.

Why didn't he just piss on her while he was it?

Obviously, he knew something. Either Nae had fessed up about where she'd spent the night, or one of her roommates had ratted her out. No matter. Jeff was jealously guarding his woman, and I could have done without having my hunch about him proven right. He *was* keeping Nae away from me now that he knew my true feelings for her. I just hadn't expected him to act like a damned Neanderthal about it.

I took a deep breath for Nae's sake. She'd warned me off and I had to trust she knew what she was doing. *Christ all freakin' mighty.* Like it wasn't bad enough I had to contend with Crandall today while I sat like a good little boy and didn't make trouble. But now Jeff was acting like Naomi was a prized possession, a trophy won easily from the geek. I wanted nothing more than to saunter over and punch the smug look from his face. Nobody should wear a look like that when they held a living creature in their arms.

What a disgusting thug.

I stabbed Jeff with a look of warning and plunked down in one of the desks on the other side of the room, away from The Bear and Naomi, but situated so that I could keep them in my field of vision.

If he so much as hurt one hair on Nae's head, he'd learn the true meaning of fucked up sideways.

Crandall entered the room, and I snapped the lid on that line of thinking. It was time to behave so I could actually graduate from this shit-hole. I wouldn't do the wolf-people any good if I didn't have a piece of paper giving me access into the field of Biology and its various projects. I was going to have to find a way to separate my personal life if I was going to be effective.

Except now, my personal life was a part of the mission. Naomi knew about the wolf-people, which meant The Bear had become a dangerously loose string we had to tie up.

I listened close enough to Crandall yak on about multivariate analysis to write down what she said. She would quiz us on this lecture before putting it in the Final, making sure her students understood the material. She was a good teacher, in that respect. Unlike Hersey, who devised methods for culling the masses so only the cream rose to the top, Crandall wanted all of her students to pass.

It was the fundamental difference between the two professors. Crandall understood the sciences were broad enough to employ even an average brain. Hersey felt they diluted the art. Those were his words, too. That was the privilege of camping with two professors, you got the skinny during private moments.

But Hersey's passion for perfection made him dangerous. He wouldn't stop until he proved there was a thriving pack of wolves in Maine, and somehow we had to figure out a way to stop him. It didn't matter if his intentions were noble or not. Proving the existence of wolves to safeguard their habitat didn't protect the wolf-people.

I turned my attention back to Crandall and the diagram she painstakingly etched out onto the blackboard. But then Naomi shifting sideways in her seat distracted my focus to the back of the room.

This wasn't going to be an easy few weeks. I could barely concentrate on anything besides Naomi, The Bear, the wolf-people and our trouble with Hersey. It was a mighty fine thing my grades were good enough to withstand a slide downward. The son in me cringed a bit under the ramifications of that. So much for proudly showing the folks a high GPA. I was going to have to juggle chainsaws just to keep my shit together until graduation.

Sweet, swaying snotgrass, this classroom smells like snow.

Crandall finally wrapped up her lecture, and I bolted out the door before she told us to have a nice weekend, then waited impatiently in the Quad for Naomi and the Yeti to emerge from the building.

When they finally did, The Bear looked directly at me, sneered, and pretended to smear an obscene track across Nae's head with his tongue. Then as they walked by, from behind her he made a circle with the fingers of his left hand and jabbed the index finger of his right through the hole, miming his screwing her brains out.

My legs pistoned my body upright so fast it took a second for my brain to register I was moving forward. All I could think about was striding over and tearing the asshole's windpipe from his neck. I didn't even notice the itching at the base of my scalp detonated until I was looking at the cement real close and personal, and had my hands clapped across my scalp to keep it from shredding off. The buzz was back like a fucking siren inside my head.

Warning heeded, for pity's sake.

Right there in the center of a hundred milling students I was curled in a mewling ball, fighting to keep my bladder tight and my thoughts my own. The first part I managed. The latter idea I threw to the wind, and tried my damnedest to accept Luna's electric intrusion as a gift.

But I didn't have a clue why I suddenly found myself kissing the concrete. Who gave a shit what I did to Jeff? It had nothing to do with Eaen or Armand. I bet they'd be glad to know I protected Naomi from his insults. Hell, I knew they'd do the same if they were in my position.

Aw, Christ. They would, and there was the problem. They liked Naomi a lot, and Armand was particularly protective of his new sister. Would they expose themselves if Naomi's and The Bear's break-up turned shitty? I rolled to my knees and dug my fingers into the base of my skull, where the buzzing had shrunk back to an aggravating itch.

Armand would kill the bastard if Jeff laid a finger on her.

Which was our problem, wasn't it? But I already knew the answer to that. It was telegraphed straight to my electrocuted gray matter.

Jeff wasn't an ally to use in our battle against Hersey. He was going to be as much of a menace to the wolves' safety as the professor. As sure as I was kneeling on the pavement.

* * * *

I skipped the rest of my classes and sorely tested the road handling capabilities of the Subaru during the drive home. Eaen and Armand were waiting expectantly inside the front door when I burst through it.

"What is wrong, Kenrickey?"

Once I was back in the house, I took a deep breath to calm myself. I needed a moment to rearrange my emotions, my thoughts, so I wouldn't sound like a ranting idiot when I filled the wolf-men in on my latest visit from the electric company.

I went to the fridge, snatched an apple from its cool interior, and wound up leaving it untouched on the counter when I assessed the concerned faces of my brothers.

"Luna hit me with an electric skillet today before I could tackle The Bear." I looked from one to the other. Their sage eyes registered confusion. Right, they didn't cook. I changed my vocabulary.

"Luna buzzed in my head to stop me from tackling The Bear."

Their wolf eyes widened appreciatively and then narrowed with suspicion.

Armand voiced their thoughts. "Why would you *tackle* him?"

I shrugged, but not disrespectfully. Their question was necessary. "Why would you think?"

They both bristled, and in that instant I understood fully the weight of Luna's warning.

Thank you, wolf-witch.

They were wolves who accepted Naomi as a pack member, just as they'd accepted me. For better or worse, Nae and I were under their protection as much as they were under ours. Except the repercussions of protecting a member of their pack came at a far higher cost for them than it would for me or Nae. And damned if the image of them strung up by their hind legs didn't come into focus.

"It's not good, guys," I admitted blackly, scratching at the spot where my spine was attached to my skull. "Not freakin' good at all, and I'm wicked sorry for dragging you into this mess."

"We are all dragged into a mess, Porcupine. It is always so when humans are involved. Armand and I knew the dangers when we started."

Which did absolutely nothing to reassure me. If anything, it only amplified just how vulnerable they were, how dangerous this mission really was. They'd probably taken their biggest risk by getting to know Naomi. Who, I didn't need to remind myself and kick that horse when it was down, arrived on the scene because of me.

"Come, Porcupine," Eaen wrapped his strong arm around my shoulders. "Let us go hunting and pretend we stalk bear."

I forced a grin, and then let the idea swirl around and take hold in my heart. A good run and a little killing would go a long way toward making me feel better. Pretending it was The Bear would lift my spirits even more.

* * * *

I waited, crouched under the long boughs of an old spruce, downwind of the wolves' trail. It took me a minute to figure out they weren't hunting deer this time, though. We were after coyotes. Eaen and Armand were looking for a kill that would ease their tension, and satisfy their urge to hunt The Bear instead. They knew I needed the same outlet, so they'd invited me to come along, but only after I'd sworn to take precautions, such as waiting under the tree for them to bring the coyote to me.

They were not hunting an herbivore, after all, but a predator, and as badly as I felt like kicking some ass, I knew a wild animal would kick mine instead. Armand and Eaen were keeping me safe, and I would do exactly as they instructed. I sure as hell didn't want my blood on their paws either. So, I waited with my ears trained on the forest around me, and my eyes straining into the dense brush.

I barely heard the coyote's approach as it slid through the underbrush. It wasn't loping along at a leisurely pace, either, but racing as if something chased it. My heart hammered into my throat as I witnessed the two wolves thread themselves along the coyote's trail. They were in no hurry, and of all the images I could have concocted, I thought of Pepe LePew prancing unhurriedly behind the frightened kitty with the painted stripe down her back. The enamored skunk in no hurry because he knew he would get his prize.

I smiled and shook my head to erase the image. Well, at least I had enough good humor left to conjure up something funny, because when I returned my attention back onto the chase unfolding before me, I got an eyeful of that lethal grace the wolves possessed. The coyote was doomed, of course. Without effort, Armand sped up and swept to the side, passing the coyote and turning it back toward the spruce. Back toward me.

I thought my heart hammered when the coyote ran by? It freakin' whaled like a sledgehammer when the little beast started running toward me, the noose Armand and Eaen fashioned drawing up tight, with me at the knot.

This most definitely fell into the category of *Shit You Saw Coming But Did Anyway*. I was about to tackle an effing coyote and was going to get my ass kicked in the process. Scratch that, I was going to get my ass bitten.

But who had time to think? I was on the balls of my feet, and the coyote was coming toward me as if it had death on its heels. It did, but it also had death waiting for it up ahead.

Wait a sec? Death? *I'm a goddamned human.* But not unarmed, this time. I wore no clothing, but I had a knife. I needed a fang, Eaen had said as he'd placed the blade in my outstretched palm. Oh yeah. This hunt definitely fell under the chapter of Shit You Saw Coming.

So fucking right, I was Death, too, and so wired my skin crawled.

Rapid panting huffed rhythmically with each stride, the sound of the galloping coyote expanding as it raced closer, the little beast unaware the trap was set in the path ahead. Finally, it burst from the underbrush, its yellow eyes bulged so far as to reveal the white ring lining the iris.

Don't shoot 'til you see the whites of their eyes, boys!

I lunged, and wrapped my arms and legs around the coyote when it shot by so close I could see how its hair grew in layers. Of course, when I muckled it, the coyote swung its head around and bit first. Nothing needle-like about those teeth, no sirree. Wooden chopsticks punctured my flesh, and I almost released our quarry when the sheer agony of the coyote's bite ripped like lightning down my arm.

Suddenly, my body was smothered in a tumult of fur, fangs and snarling, and I dropped my knife in the fray as Eaen and Armand pushed in with their broad heads and whipping tails. The coyote's jaws gaped wide, slashing its maw defensively until the black wolf clamped his crushing molars across the back of its face, one of its large, triangular ears sliding to its shoulders as the skin of its muzzle and neck stretched fatally. Eaen's grip was so powerfully clamped onto muscle and bone the coyote's mouth was unable to close effectively.

Armand, frenzied, gripped the coyote's flank with his fangs and thrashed his head side to side. The coyote screamed, its voice pitched with fury, terror. My skin crawled, yet I couldn't cease tearing at its skin, its flesh bunching in my fists, until finally my grasp found the coyote's neck. My spine and muscles stiffened as adrenaline exploded. Rational thought snuffed out like a candle flame. I squeezed that windpipe for all I was fucking worth.

And didn't realize, until the thing sagged like a wet dishrag in my clutches, the wolves had backed off while I was wringing the life out of the coyote.

Holy sweet living Jesus, I just killed a predator with my bare hands.

I swung around to face Eaen and Armand, who stood panting with their bushy tails waving fluidly behind them. I grinned back with so much pride busting through me I shivered, reared, and then roared into the sky.

The wolves' yips shot my short hairs into spikes along my skin and I bayed with the ecstasy of it. They slid and rubbed their massive bodies across my legs, my thighs, until I dropped to my hands and knees and rubbed my torso all over them, too.

Brothers.

Pack.

Abso-freakin'-lutely.

I snatched the coyote up by its hind legs, pulled it to my chest so that its head swung loose between my knees, and stretched my fists in opposite directions, fully intending to rend that thing into pieces for the sheer joy of it.

The wolves descended in a charge of fur, and snagged the coyote's head and shoulders in their vice-like jaws, so that we played a gruesome game of tug-of-war. The yanking of the wolves pitched me forward until I squatted, dug in my heels and locked my shoulders.

The skin ripped like fabric, creasing the air, which was thick with possessive snarls, my own growls filling the space as I claimed my chunk of the carcass. I tugged back willfully until the flesh of the coyote could take no more, and the wolves and I fell apart, each of us holding a limp, ragged body part.

It was base and it was beautiful.

For us, anyway. The coyote would have had a different opinion about having its leg proudly pumped in the air like a trophy hard won.

We did not eat our conquest, but sat on our haunches panting and savoring the moment.

I, Ken Rickey, recently converted vegetarian, just mutilated an animal with my bare hands. What the fuck was happening to me? The two wolves lapped their fur, each slick slide of their tongues scraping away the evidence of the kill.

I scraped up some black earth and rubbed my arms to slough away the blood, and without thinking ran the dirt across the wound on my upper arm. *Jeezus tits*, I winced. I'd forgotten the coyote got in a fantastic blow before succumbing to the gang-style fury of three killers. My blood oozed from the four perfect punctures in my skin and dripped from the tips of my fur-encrusted fingers.

I was turning into a pincushion, so my smug smile was all wrong. I should've been worried. Christ, I now had two, no wait, *five* open wounds, and enough scratches and bruises on my body to make me look like a UFC fighter. And that was from only three hunts? My fragile human body wasn't cut out for the sport. But I had no intention of not doing more, even though I now had a realistic grasp on the old saying about the spirit being willing, but the flesh weak.

What I needed was fur and fang. My eyes rested on my partners in crime, and for the first time gave serious consideration to Randall Wolfe, and the wise, old wolf-women Ane and Elga. Could I actually have a little wolf blood in me somehow? Christ, it explained my recent metamorphosis from meek vegetarian to the assertive, aggressive, raw meat eater I'd become.

But I was barking up the wrong tree. As much as I'd changed on the inside, outside I was still bare skinned and beat all to hell. Yet, I would relish what gifts I'd been given and not pine for what wasn't to be.

I turned my face to the sky to soak up the sun dropping in the western sky. Our foray had taken longer than I thought. It must've been late afternoon, but I was content to stay where I was for a while longer, before I had to go pick up Naomi.

If I could go pick up Nae, I reminded myself.

I studied the shredded coyote carcass and wondered aloud why the wolves didn't bother eating it. I mean, it was food right there in front of them, right? I looked at two wolves and laughed at my mistake. I'd completely overlooked what shape they were in and was talking to them like they could chat back in their present form.

"Sorry guys. It's just getting wicked easy to not notice, you know?"

The black wolf spread his jaws in a gaping yawn, shook his fur, and then tumbled his bones in an effortless shift to human. My heart squeezed like my chest was too small.

"Fine. You got me, Eaen. *That* I may never get used to."

Armand transformed just as effortlessly, so within seconds I did have human company. Well, not really human, but they could talk in full sentences with me as if they were.

"So, why don't you? Eat coyote, I mean." I got right back on topic.

"We have before, Porcupine, when we have been hungry."

"But not today?"

Eaen stole a sidelong glance at Armand, and then they both shook their heads solemnly. "You have inflicted so much damage, there is nothing left to eat."

My mouth fell open and I snapped it shut, but then it dropped open again so I felt like a goldfish in the forest. "Guys, I'm so sorry. I didn't realize. I thought we—I thought this hunt was to, you know, take out our frustrations on The Bear. I didn't think—" I was an ass, too, apparently, because when the two wolf-men turned their faces to the ground to hide their grins, I realized they were teasing me.

"That is for the ruffling of my ears," Eaen delivered pompously, adding a so-there nod of his head.

I tackled him.

And once again, the three of us ended up in a pig-pile that would have had our pack leaders tsking with dismay. But at least I got in one good hold Armand almost couldn't break, before I wound up on the bottom of the heated heap.

Chapter Seven

I didn't notice how much of a mess I was until I got back to the house. I had gobs of dried blood all over me, not to mention a ton of bruises and scratches, and leaves stuck to my bristled hair.

Criminy, I really was a porcupine. Why hadn't I noticed that before? Probably because I was seeing myself as Naomi would, and yeah, my hair did stick up in spikes because I couldn't keep my hands out of it. A gesture that was intrinsically me. I couldn't recall when I didn't scrape my fingers across my scalp.

What I didn't possess was the congenital ability to lick myself clean. I turned the hot water on for a much needed shower, instead, and let the steaming water jet into the bite wounds on my arm, hoping that would flush out any infection that might take root. The coyote didn't have rabies. Hell, the coyote didn't have legs anymore, either, or entrails. So, where was my remorse? Well, it went packing with a little bandana on a stick. Along with my aversion to eating flesh.

I shut the water off in time to hear my phone ring.

Armand came in with my cell in his long hand. "It is Naomi."

My heart fluttered. "Answer it, Arms," I tossed my chin toward the phone in his palm, water splattering from my soaked hair.

His yellow eyes widened as he shook his head. I'd caught him off guard. Meanwhile, the phone kept ringing.

"Here," I laughed, holding my hand out while I still stood dripping in the tub, "I'll take it."

Armand dropped it in my outstretched hand as if he was passing off a peeved skunk, but he stuck around for the end result. I flipped the phone to my wet ear.

"Hey, Nae." The twinkle of her voice on the other end of the line set my stomach into fluttering, even though my heart fell flat. I nodded my head as she kept talking, but didn't take my eyes from Armand. He'd tensed sympathetically, since he could easily hear what Naomi was saying. I sincerely liked how he worried for her. Somehow, his being protective of my girl was downright endearing, as if he *was* her big brother or something. His feelings for Nae weren't polluted with jealousy, and that was refreshing as hell. His attitude toward her grafted him stronger to my own heart.

Christ, these wolf-people.

I said good-bye to Naomi with the promise I would see her the next day. Early. As in, the second Sasquatch left for the weekend to go play his baseball games in Vermont.

"She can't get away tonight, Arms, as you know, but she will be here tomorrow. Then we'll have her all to ourselves for two full days."

My repeating Nae's message cheered him up, and so help me I swear I saw invisible ears prick forward and his missing tail wag.

"Maybe tonight we could try spying on Hersey instead."

"Yes," he snarled, drawing out the *ess* through his sharp teeth.

"Good, then. Let's go scope out his house and see how we can mess with him."

Armand left me to scrape the towel across my goose-bumps and went in search of Eaen to deliver the news about the up-coming hunt.

Jeeze, did the fun never end?

* * * *

I drove the Subaru until we were about a mile from town and ditched it on a side road. The moon was still around half full, so I wasn't completely blind, but it did mean we wouldn't have the protective cover of full darkness. Plus, Eaen and Armand didn't need the extra light to see by, either. But I wasn't going to be the one to say our reconnaissance mission wasn't a good idea.

Thank Helen Keller that Armand, the blonde wolf, was the one leading us through the forest, not Eaen, whose fur was pitch black. I wouldn't see him in the woods if he walked right in front of me.

132

Maybe I really was a porcupine.

"Hey guys, you know, if you come across food instead—"

"We will hunt it, Kenrickey," Eaen assured me. He knew I worried about them, how they didn't eat every day, except for apples. "But it is normal for us to go days between meals, so please do not worry."

Right. He had a point. It was feast or famine, and since the wolf-men had arrived, I'd been doing the same and was, surprisingly, feeling pretty freakin' good despite turning into a carnivore. Well, I ate the apples, too, but basically my caloric intake had taken a drastic side-step. And my body was beginning to show it, if you erased the bruises, lacerations, punctures, scrapes, scratches, et cetera, et cetera. I just hoped we didn't add any more during this foray.

Yes, I am a naïve man.

What was it about running through the woods in the dead of night that made me think I wouldn't come out of it scratched all to cat crap? Well, at least I kept my clothes on. Once I pointed out how illuminated my bare ass would be, Eaen and Armand screamed with laughter, and finally admitted, amidst their hooting I should add, that perhaps I made a valid point. Eaen's words, not mine.

So, here we were on our way to spy on Hersey, and hopefully find out a little something. Thankfully, Armand turned out to be a wicked good leader and kept to the clearest trails. It probably added a shit-load of time and distance, but who was I to complain? We made it to the professor's sprawling house, and I still had enough energy to continue. Meaning, I wasn't sucking ass or copious amounts of air.

Armand stopped behind the hedgerow lining the back property and shifted so we could talk. Hersey's house was lit up as if it was on fire, and there were several cars in the long driveway. One of which belonged to Randall Wolfe, and the other to The Bear himself.

Wonderful.

Sarcasm aside, it was a good thing since it probably meant they were discussing the very thing we needed to know. I informed my partners in crime.

"Can you guys tell if Nae's here? Can you smell her?"

"Not yet, Porcupine, but we will tell you as soon as we know."

Armand sniffed the air again for good measure.

"And," I added, "We probably shouldn't show ourselves to her if she is. Right?"

We all agreed with that.

"All right then. Let's go have ourselves a listen," I choked out, as Armand's human form tumbled and stretched into wolf before me without warning. At least I managed to finish my sentence without my brain draining out of my ears. Thusly encouraged, I followed the furry asses of two wolves, which were stealth personified and made no sound.

Which made me sound like an elephant crashing through an echoing canyon lined with dried leaves. *Must work on the skills*, I reminded myself. We skulked toward the north side of the house where the kitchen was, and followed the voices from there. Slowly, I raised my eyes to the windowsill and peered in while I cursed the size of my forehead. Everyone was gathered in the dining room, sitting around emptied dishes and half-full glasses.

Hersey was entertaining those chosen to assist him up north, the elite of his student body. Not that the Yeti was a top scholar, but he did have me as an acquaintance and that, I was sure, tipped the odds in his favor. Nae, seated beside him, tripped my heart so it pattered like running ducklings. Man, she was so under my skin.

I opened my mouth to whisper the news, but I *heard* a firm *We know* before I could breathe a word. Yikes, did my heart thump so loud they could hear it?

Smell you.

Oh. I lifted my arms to sniff my pits and got sat on by Armand. As I fell, I oofed, and Eaen plopped his gi-normous paw on my lips to shut me up. My lord, we were the Three Stooges, and what I was missing was a double finger poke to the eyes. Moe swiveled a black ear toward the house. The din from inside didn't change, so we'd lucked out. They hadn't heard us, but I had the outrageous desire to laugh hysterically.

Except this was serious. A lot hung on a successful outcome. Loved ones counted on us.

The thought did nothing to stifle the urge. Made it worse, actually. Like laughing at a funeral. I took a super deep breath and held it as I thought about Luna and Grane.

Right. The thought of those two settled me quite well because A, I didn't need Luna's crippling buzz in my head; and B, I didn't need Grane ripping me a new asshole when he found out we botched this reconnaissance mission because of me.

I raised myself for a final look through the dining room window, and then crawled to the back of the house, where I figured the living room would be, or an office. The wolves followed tightly.

I peeked into a window and into Christmas, then spun and squatted with my back against the house. "Jackpot, guys. I see equipment."

The two wolves swished their tails.

"What say we go in and take some?"

They swished their tails harder.

"All right then. Wait for me and watch. Tell me if someone comes." My pulse ratcheted upward and I was already feeling like a criminal before I even got inside the house, which lucky for us was in Downeast Maine, where nobody locked their doors or windows. I slid the sash upward, and scraped my carcass through the opening, only to land in a pile along the wall.

I heard a scratchy thump behind me and turned to see the black wolf with his front paws on the sill peering in.

"What?"

He pointed his muzzle toward the dining room, to the part of the house we'd just left.

"Yeah, go listen. Good idea."

Eaen dropped to all fours and out of my sight, and I crawled on my hands and knees across the darkened room.

Why was I scurrying across the floor like Inspector Clouseau?

I stood up to finish my path across the floor, to the pile of gear in the corner. It was all familiar, even though some of it was new. I recognized the type of collar, and my stomach plummeted. It was the type Hersey and I had attached around Grane's neck. The kind designed to stay put for a long period of time. But why would he store it here and not in his office at the university? Probably because he didn't put it past someone to sabotage his next excursion.

Well, that just pointed the finger right at me, didn't it?

Shit.

I had two options at that moment: either stay, commit the crime and

S. C. Dane

be rightfully accused, or leave the stuff for now and hatch a better plan. I opted for the latter, but wasn't going to leave without something. I circled to the back of Hersey's desk and sat down in his swivel chair, then hooked my fingers under the middle drawer and pulled. The drawer slid easily, but its skid sighed loudly in the dark.

I glanced up to see if anyone noticed, but the conversational tone in the other room continued in a steady stream. Hopefully Eaen was getting an ear full. I turned my attention back to the desk and its contents.

Finally, in the last drawer I looked, of course, I found a clue in the form of a map. Hersey had outlined the area he planned to target. The map was definitely exiting these premises. I set it aside for the moment while I continued rummaging, though all I came across were a few shell casings, and a couple of charts for tranquilizer dosages. I lifted the map, and tiptoed back toward the open window, pushed through the slit, and dropped to the ground.

The blonde wolf snuffled me all over, making sure I was fine, and it warmed my heart to see his tail make bold, circular arcs in greeting. I'd seen the helicopter motion before when Suma and Grane were reunited with Alec and Beth. Armand was glad to see me, was happy I had come back unharmed.

I hugged his thick body to me and rubbed my torso from his shoulder to his flank, just as I'd seen the wolves do when they wanted to spread their scent, reclaim their positions, their relationships.

"Ready to go?"

Armand slowly squeezed his lids over his yellow eyes in affirmation, then we retraced our steps to find Eaen. I could just make out his shadow under the dining room window. He was sprawled along the grass on his stomach, with his nose pointed upward, toward the lower sill of the window. The blonde wolf and I crept closer, to hear for ourselves what was being discussed.

All I could catch was the blurred murmur of human voices, and finally the scraping of chairs as the guests moved away from the table.

"Shit," I hissed. "Their leaving. Did you get anything?"

Eaen raised his dark bulk and got his paws underneath him, then he turned on his tail and trotted toward the back of Hersey's property where we had emerged when we'd arrived. Armand followed him, and I

136

gravitated after them, irresistibly drawn to their retreating backsides.

* * * *

The next morning, Naomi was waiting for us on her doorstep, like she didn't want to waste another minute not joined with us. Seeing her hepped up like that got my heart fluttering, and it was all I could do to pull the car to the curb without slamming on the brakes.

She hopped in the front passenger seat and mushed a kiss right on my surprised lips. Then she promptly turned her attention to the two in the back seat.

"Hi, guys."

Eaen and Armand wriggled to lean toward her, found their way blocked by the front seat, and settled back in without a proper greeting to the woman who had just joined us.

"Good morning, Kenrickey's mate," Eaen offered by way of a salutation, and pushed his long hands between his knees since he couldn't touch Naomi appropriately.

"I love hearing that," she confessed, and beamed sunshine throughout the vehicle.

Armand sat silent, as he still wrestled with sliding along in the car, but he smiled beautifully for Nae. As did we all.

Naomi shoved her overnight bag behind her feet and turned in her seat as I pulled back onto the street. "Guess what?"

She had an attentive audience. We three automatically leaned toward her as if she would share an important secret.

"I went to Hersey's for dinner last night." Naomi glanced around, full of herself that she had the skinny on what Hersey was up to.

"We know," I confessed.

"How did you know? I never said," she gushed, and my heart fluttered again, taking my stomach with it.

Armand finally discovered his voice, as if the woman's fresh enthusiasm was a tonic to car sickness. "We went hunting for him, and saw The Bear's automobile." His voice carried the weight of pride.

"We saw you at the table," Eaen finished.

"You were spying." Naomi's peals of laughter resounded like the giddy chirps of chickadees, and the two wolf-men shivered and burned, ratcheting the temperature in the car so I was forced to lower the windows. Naomi's shoulder length blond hair fluffed in the breeze, and I watched in the rearview mirror as Armand lifted his face to catch her scent as it billowed around.

"Yeah, we were. But we didn't get much, just a map of where Hersey plans to go. Otherwise, we kind of struck out," I admitted while keeping my eyes on the road ahead.

"Well, Jeff is on the team."

"We figured as much when we saw his car there," I replied, trying to keep the anger out of my voice. But hearing it from Nae irritated me, and I shifted my shoulders against the seat to ease their tensing.

We rode in silence the rest of the way, each of us lost in our musings about Jeff being selected to go up north. I couldn't help wondering what Randall Wolfe thought of the whole thing, given he was one of Hersey's guests at the dinner. If he was wolf, as we suspected, then what the hell was he doing there? Keeping his enemy close? Could we be that lucky?

Armand's question to Nae pulled my attention back to the four of us in the car.

"Kenricky's mate, you are not all right?"

Naomi frowned. "No. But yes, as soon as we get this mess with Hersey straightened out."

She'd guessed at the ramifications of Hersey's next trip north with her usual lightning strike accuracy. Hey, she wasn't a 4.0 Biology major for nothing. But I also couldn't help but wonder what she planned to do about Jeff personally.

Armand grew quiet again, too, but I could see him watch her, as if he suspected there was more to her plunge in happiness than just Hersey's plans.

"It's just that—" Nae sighed, dropped her chin, started again. "It's just that Hersey's invasion of your territory is just as sinister as the abuse I suffered growing up, you know? I mean, waiting for danger to descend has a way of undermining everything that makes a person whole, and you and your family don't deserve that."

Well, she rendered us dumb with her philosophy, and I cast a worried glance into the rearview to get a good look at my brothers.

Then Nae turned in her seat to speak directly to Armand, who knew too much about death and pending doom. "You are hard to fool, blonde wolf. I *am* scared. For you, for your family, and if I can help, I want to."

We arrived at the house, and as soon as we were all out, I wrapped myself around her back. Nae closed her eyes and took a deep breath as if she was inhaling my scent. Man, what an aphrodisiac. Armand and Eaen waited patiently while the mated pair reunited.

"We aren't mated yet, you two," I teased half-heartedly, releasing Nae so she could stretch to her tiptoes to kiss Eaen's chin. Then, as she released her cupped hand from Armand's smooth cheek, she dropped her news about Jeff and how she planned to stay with him until the mess with Hersey was resolved.

"You're what?" Like she'd just walloped me in the head with a brick. "You did not just say what I thought you did."

Naomi opened her mouth to explain, but no sound came out, like our disappointed faces rendered her speechless.

"Nae," I managed to breathe, shaking my head. "No."

I swear Eaen's and Armand's missing ears laid flat.

"It's for the best. I can get the information you need."

"No. There are other solutions, Kenrickey's mate. What you do is wrong. It is not truth." Eaen spoke plain enough for us all, and his words hit with the precision of knowing one's heart and being loyal to it. He was wolf, and he couldn't lie, was incapable of it.

Armand knelt in front of her, and lifted his face to hers. "Naomi, your loyal heart is a beautiful thing, but it belongs with us, with Kenrickey. To leave it elsewhere betrays our pack because you are not able to give us all of yourself."

Naomi sucked in a sharp breath as the eloquence of Armand's heartfelt words hit her. Obviously, she had no idea how much she meant to us.

I folded myself across her back again, wrapping her close. "Nae, you belong to us. *To me*. Break your ties and be with us."

I felt her tremble, and she turned within my embrace to snuggle her face against my bruised chest, but I locked my mouth onto hers before she could. She softened, accepted my advance. I sighed, lowering her to the ground, and she yielded so that her body molded to mine, her nipples pressing against her shirt.

Holy Christ. "Nae."

She opened her eyes at the sound of my plea. I knew she felt me quiver against her.

"I can't," I squelched through my clenched jaw. I bowed my head and retreated backward to crouch on my haunches.

Naomi sat up, dazed, and supported herself on the heels of her hands. "What?" She seemed stunned by my removal.

"Nae, I want you," I seethed, my ferocity singing in my blood. "But not while," I swallowed and ran my hand across my scalp. I needed the right words. Shit, I couldn't have her running off again, and I sure as shit didn't want to say anything to hurt her. "*Jesus woman*, I have wanted you for four years."

Well, it wasn't eloquent, but she didn't run.

"I'm yours," she assured me, even as her tears welled, as if the truth snapped its teeth across her throat, constricting it. She was not mine, yet. Not until she severed the relationship with Jeff. "I want every scrap of you, Nae. Every damned scrap."

Naomi's head dropped, as if she was ashamed, and that about wrecked me. "Nae, come here." I didn't wait for her to move, but went to her, cradled her against me and nuzzled the top of her head, breathed in the snow of her scent.

"Woman, I am yours. Sweet Jesus, please don't forget that." I squeezed her to me with a ferocious desperation I hoped didn't crush her. "*I will take you*," I promised, my urgent snarl surprising me, and I released her before I caved to the need swelling within me. I wouldn't wait for her to end it with Jeff. I would claim her right then if I didn't put some distance between us.

Naomi slid from my arms and stood up, shook her spine back into place, and squared her shoulders.

"Well, Porcupine," she teased, her hazel eyes bright. "Stand up here and share a friendly weekend with me instead." She beamed her bravest smile at me.

Shit, I loved her. I accepted her offered hand, then stood with Eaen and Armand.

Naomi eyed the three of us, her lids narrowing as she bit her lower lip, her gaze stopping on me. "Tell me about your wounds while we study, then, because you sure as hell didn't get those shopping in the produce section of the grocery store."

Now that I would be very pleased to share with her.

* * * *

"You really hunt?" Naomi was seated in Armand's favorite chair, her notebook spread open on her lap, and she cocked her head back, her expression of confusion softened by her disbelieving smile. "You're a vegetarian."

"Yup, and nope to the second part." I enjoyed that look of fascinated surprise on her face. It lit her hazel eyes like a sunny day. My woman looked to Eaen and Armand for confirmation.

"Yes, and he is very brave. For a human." Eaen winked a brown eye at me, which is the only thing that kept me from tackling him. Well, Nae was also present, so he should've counted himself lucky.

Armand marked the page in the book he was reading and set it down. It was Sun Tzu's *The Art of War*. Man, the guy read as fiercely as he hunted. And protected. It didn't escape my notice he kept himself as close to Naomi as he could without being obnoxious. I would have to watch him very carefully if he ever got around The Bear. Although I had to admit he was very careful not to overstep his bounds, even though technically Nae and I weren't mated, or in very human terms, not going out, yet.

"Which, I'd like to say, I'm ready to go any time you are. I'm starving."

Nae was incredulous. "You're really going hunting?"

"Yep." I nodded, and was surprised at how proud I was to say it to another human being, to Naomi especially. "What do you say, guys? You ready?"

Eaen let his *Plant Toxonomy* book fall from his lap as he stood up. In his eagerness he'd forgotten it was there. Quickly, he scooped to place it on the stack tilting haphazardly beside the sofa. I could already feel his heat escalating.

Of course, Armand was in if we were. He loved the hunt more than Eaen did, so I was a little taken aback when he hesitated for a second before opting to join us. *Ah, right.* Nae wouldn't be with us, and he was

S. C. Dane

reluctant to leave her alone.

"The Bear is very far away, Armand, I promise you." Naomi uttered her words tenderly, so as not to slight his brotherly affections. Man, she was so in tune with the wolf-men, and more of my pride radiated. My heart had chosen well, even if it had taken me four years to act on it.

"Besides, I really need to study. This stuff doesn't come easy like it does for someone else I know." She sneered at me and stuck out her tongue, even though we all knew she was playing down her smarts.

I was part of Hersey's cream, too. Or had been, before I'd been selected to go prowling around in the north woods looking for wolves. Now, I wasn't even the caked-on ring at the bottom of the glass. Oh, well. At least he was letting me sit in his classroom, provided I kept my mouth shut, and my hands to myself.

"So," I said, just to get the proverbial ball rolling.

Eaen and Armand folded to the floor, and within seconds, Nae and I were in the company of two very impressive, very hot wolves. At least my curiosity for Naomi's reaction to the shift kept my mind off from my own. She was agog. Mouth gaping, eyes shining. Stunned.

"Cool, isn't it?"

She tore her eyes away from Eaen and Armand and breathed her answer. "Yes," was all that she said.

I leaned in with my hands on the arms of the chair and kissed her gently on the lips, and Nae's eyes reflected my image, even as I pulled away and stood up. "Don't laugh, but I go naked," I warned as I started undressing for the excursion into the woods.

"No way."

I winked. "Way." Then cast an accusing glance at the blonde wolf. "Armand says my clothes stink and I scare the bunnies."

Naomi snorted a laugh, stretched out her long leg and shoved me playfully with her foot. "Get out of here so I can study."

The two wolves turned toward me and Naomi, and stood rigidly, their ears pricked forward and their tails waving in unison.

I jabbed a thumb in their direction. "Don't get *them* started. We'll never get anything to eat." I backed away from the teasing woman on the couch and headed toward the front door. "Come on you two, I am not going to wrestle Nae."

We trotted off toward the river, following the same path we'd used the day Naomi discovered our little secret. When I turned, she was standing in the kitchen window watching us, so I waved, and without waiting to see if she waved back, I returned my eyes to the trail to follow Armand. Eaen trotted close enough behind me I could feel his warm breath on my calves.

God, I hope she doesn't think I'm nuts. From her perspective at the window, I was a naked guy traipsing to the river with his two dogs. How much odder could it get, really? Thankfully, Nae was obviously the type to keep an open mind, and I'd have to hold onto that redemptive thread until I could get back and talk to her about it. Feel her out.

Right then, though, there wasn't much time to think because Armand's pace picked up as if he'd caught something's scent. Within a few minutes, Eaen and Armand fell off to each side of me while I continued on in the center. It was becoming our pattern, and my heart thumped with more than just exertion. This was how wolves hunted in the wild. Every wolf on the hunt collaborated to the ultimate end, working their strengths and weaknesses. Just as Armand and Eaen were doing with me, and it was freakin' exhilarating.

We pushed our line to the river.

Deer.

Oh, this was going to be good. I shoved my way through thickening alders as brackish water oozed up over my feet. We were in one of the swampy sections where the deer would be feeding on the new shoots of swale grass poking like little green spears out of the lion's mane of dead, flattened reeds.

There was deer sign everywhere. Lots of pebbly poop and pointy hoof prints. The black wolf appeared to my left, his lean body rolling stealthily along the contours of the earth, his panting tongue lolling and snagging scents like a lollipop gathers lint. He loped with tireless grace, and floated like fingers of fog.

A crackling explosion to my right had me turning my head in time for me to see a small doe fling herself in ten foot leaps. The blond wolf rushed in a fluid line on her sharp heels, pressing and dropping back, relentlessly driving the deer toward us in crucially accurate intervals.

The doe darted nearer, zig-zagging dramatic arcs in her panicked flight, and still her death bore down, dictating her direction across the swale grass.

My Christ, I'll never catch her.

She was fast, but she was not designed for the incessant stamina of a patient wolf, and Armand continued his pursuit, ducking, then striding in bursts of speed as he herded the frightened creature.

I bolted right, and the black wolf slipped along to close the void, tightening the circumference of the deer's arena, fatally barring her advantage, pushing her to the mud where the points of her hooves sunk too deep, worked against her.

We shrunk the distance between us as we closed in toward the doe. Her tongue pulsed in her panting mouth as she locked into position, reassessed her situation. The blonde wolf ceased, guarded her flank as he waited for my insurgence. I inhaled, forgot the cold muck beneath my feet, and charged.

The little doe crouched, tilted and flung herself backward. Her thrust was a costly expense of power. She scrambled her skinny legs even as their fluid grace sagged and they were rendered to jabbing sticks, stilts whose strength was wooden, not elastic, and her lunges deteriorated to fatigued, awkward steps.

The pack descended.

The blonde wolf plunged his head between the shafts of the doe's hind legs, brazenly risking the slice of her sharply edged hooves to sink his fangs into her tender belly. The thick muscles of his jaw clenched, and she bleated frantically as he thrashed his head and ripped her entrails through her torn skin.

Eaen clamped onto her heaving flank, his ears flattened to his skull as his shoulders braced against the strength of her pelvis, and yet he yanked until the suck of bone pocked the heated atmosphere, and the doe's leg stretched away from her prone body. I stifled her screams with a crushing grip to her windpipe, my pounding heart rejoicing as her life bled out onto the mud.

We would break our famine.

But not until I dragged the little deer to the edge of the alders, where we wouldn't be easily seen by humans, but could still keep a wary eye out for black bears or desperate coyotes. Eaen gobbled at the tender liver before the body landed on the flattened grass, while Armand worked his molars like scissors, cutting away strips of hide to bare the tenderloin.

I drooled and wiped my mouth with the back of my hand, and smeared deer snot across my lips. The lack of any revolt on my part blipped on my conscience then disappeared as ethereally as it had appeared, and I entwined my fingers into the doe's warm hair. My stomach twisted as skin peeled like tape from muscle, and before my radar blipped again, my body dropped and my mouth closed over the exposed flesh.

The wolves snarled their pleasure, and I looked up into two pairs of gratified eyes, one set a shimmering, soft yellow, the other an invitingly deep brown. My heart learned in the depths of those eyes what they saw and we gorged until we fell away from the shrinking carcass, our guts crammed with the gift of an easy kill.

I flaked out to let the sun dry what blood I couldn't wipe off with the wet reeds.

"We are becoming a formidable trio, brother," Armand observed, his voice scratchy from his recent shift.

I nodded as I stared up at the darkening sky, my body stretched comfortably along a bed of soft moss. The sun was dropping toward the western tree line, and the low clouds blushed salmon.

"I am stuffed."

Armand and I turned to Eaen, who was sprawled out on the damp swale grass, his body producing more heat than what the cold mud could suck from him. He yawned and closed his eyes, and my own lids drooped heavily, as did Armand's. We dozed in the fading heat of the sun.

It was dusk when we woke, yawned, and stretched our rested muscles. Two crows were balanced on the deer carcass, and were picking away niblets of meat even as we neared. Unafraid, they remained with their prize, but squawked their disapproval at our intrusion.

I halted and crouched as the two wolf-men descended on the doe once more. The crows didn't fly off, but hopped back out of reach, their black wings fluttering in protest. Eaen perched his large frame on one distended front leg of the deer as a counter-weight, while Armand wrapped his sinewy fingers around the other slender shank. Both wolf-men pulled until the shoulder separated from the chest cavity in a loud rip.

Blood oozed from the exposed flesh, and *God help me,* I licked my lips. This was not eating meat in the passion of the kill, it was sheer want of meat, and my guts constricted anxiously.

What in the hell was I turning into?

I halted my progress forward to study the scene before me. Armand and Eaen were hovered over the dead deer, their bare backs rounded as they crouched on muscular legs, the spring of their ribcages subtly revealing their core strength as the tendons in their arms bulged with every bloody tug for food.

The crows hopped back onto the carcass, unconcerned that the wolf-men feasted in their company, and I ran a sticky hand across my scalp.

The image should have been macabre. They should have looked like ghouls.

Instead, they were beautiful.

They were laughing, and Eaen stretched his strong arm and clasped Armand's broad shoulders in a quick hug before pulling away to smile, to let his face shine openly. The blonde wolf-man turned and held his arm out to me.

"Come, Brother, fill your stomach again. The crows have not eaten all of it."

I stepped forward, my chest expanding with pride, like we were on a playground and I'd just been picked first out of all the other kids.

"I'm surprised, because I think we must've slept for over an hour," I said as I squatted in front of them to pinch a good hunk of venison between my thumb and forefinger. I closed my mouth around my bloodied fingers, and my lids dropped appreciatively, as if closing my eyes enhanced the flavor, heightened my other senses.

"This is good," I mumbled as I chewed.

The two wolf-men bobbed their heads.

"When they are small the meat is very tender, much richer," Armand explained, even as he wrested another strip. One of the crows snagged it from his fingers, and he exploded at it with a ferocious snarl, sending the brazen thief into the sky along with his feathered cohort. I leaned back and laughed, then fell quiet as my thoughts eddied and swirled.

"Porcupine, you are all right?" Eaen asked, his brown eyes dark with concern.

"Yeah. It's just that this is so weird. I mean, not weird in a bad way either, and that should be scary, but it's not. You know?"

Eaen and Armand both chuckled and nodded their heads.

"Yes, we know, Kenrickey. You are supposedly human, but Armand and I forget that from time to time. We expect to see your fur and are surprised when you do not produce it." He smiled gently, understanding filling his deep eyes. "You have accepted us, too, as if we were not different, and that is part of what Ane and Elga suspected. You are more like us than you knew, and now you are learning that."

"Will I change? Grow fur and teeth, I mean?"

"I do not know, but I suppose anything is possible. We *are* sorry you do not have our advantage, Porcupine."

"Advantage?" I scanned my scarred, naked body. "Oh. Yeah. The fur and fangs would be helpful," I admitted. "I'm getting stove all to hell."

We shared our laughter and then stilled together.

"But our advantage only goes so far," Armand pointed out. "We do not look human even when we hide our fur and fangs, and that is now a serious detriment for us. For our family."

I released my breath, long and slow. He was absolutely right. Sure it would be fun to be able to shift between species, to physically adapt my body and experience the world from a different perspective. But if it meant I could be killed because of it? Well, that was a hell of a price to pay, wasn't it.

"Which is why you had to trust me in the first place." My words were true, too. "You just lucked out that I was a blubbering idiot who really wanted to live."

"You are very funny, Porcupine," Armand chuckled appreciatively. "But, Grane saw past that, and so did Luna. You would not be alive today if they had not seen your courage, your honest heart. They have faith in you. We have faith in you, Brother."

"And if we don't stop Hersey?"

"Alec will have no choice but to kill him, and we will all suffer the consequences."

Ah, shit. I'd seen the brown wolf's fear, and his hatred. Obviously, he'd already suffered at the hands of humans, and he wouldn't hesitate to slaughter Hersey to protect what was his, to shield his loved ones from whatever humans had done to him. So, if we didn't find a way to thwart Hersey's next attempt at proving a wolf pack existed in the north woods? I shook the unfolding scenario from my head and gazed openly at the wolf-men.

"I love you like my brothers, and I will not let that happen, no matter what I have to do. That is my oath to you, my family."

"And you called yourself a blubbering idiot," Eaen teased and tousled my hair as if I sported ears. I chomped onto his hand with my dull teeth just because it really was the appropriate response.

"Boys," Armand yelped with mock derision, and we turned to tackle him. Before we could though, he spoke seriously, the lowering sun shadowing his features. "Our sister, Kenrickey's mate, waits anxiously for our safe return."

We did not follow through with our puppy play. The sky was growing dark, and we had left Nae alone. Armand was right. We'd taken enough time, had filled our bellies, and now our duty was to return home. To go back for our fourth pack member who had been left behind.

* * * *

The weekend flew by, even though my hard-on made more appearances than William Shatner made cameos. Christ, it seemed like every time Nae sighed, or blinked, my balls constricted and I had to fight the urge to mount her wherever she was at the time. It didn't help that we'd opted to go without clothing for Eaen and Armand's sake. That just made her more accessible; as though if she bent over to pick up anything she may have dropped I could slide into her, as if I just happened by.

It also didn't help I kept catching her watching me, like she was inventorying my body, counting the bruises and scrapes. Which, surprisingly, I hadn't added many more to the collection on our last outing. I'd returned home covered in deer blood instead.

And Nae hadn't batted an eyelash, like it was normal to have three naked men, sticking and stinking with blood, come home to her. What goddess did I get off to deserve her? What Karmic kitty did I have in my favor?

The whole weekend she lounged with us as if it was the most natural thing in the world to do. She and Armand butted heads about certain points in the book he was reading, while Eaen and I eavesdropped, but didn't interfere. Both debaters made valid points, and both loved the hell out of it.

Naomi's shining smile during those times had me clutching my hand to my chest because my heart actually hurt. Armand was helping her heal, and I wondered if the two of them even realized it. The ease and confidence with which she sparred with that yellow-eyed wolf-man? After a lifetime of having the snot kicked out of her for no good reason made it a beautiful sight to behold.

Once, when she'd won her point, he flashed his fangs just to intimidate her, to let her know her victory was short lived. And because my heart could hurt just a little bit more, she squealed her delight at seeing them and asked for a repeat performance. *Heaven help me,* I could have made love to her right there, in front of Armand and his teeth.

The only dark point during Nae's stay with us was when we brought Hersey's map out again, to double check that we had our coordinates right, that he was returning to Alec's territory. It was then Eaen told us the area wasn't the only one we had to watch. His father, Krysh, had territory to the south of Alec's.

"How many of you are there?" Naomi asked, her pale face surrounding her hazel eyes as the kaleidoscope of her irises shifted to green.

"There are eleven of us, counting Suma's pup to be born, and six or more in my father's territory, not counting the pups Fay and Rion may have had after we left."

Ooh boy. I pulled Nae into my arms and snuffled the top of her head, where the scent of snow was the strongest. She relaxed against me, and I hoped like hell it quelled the tears that were coming. She got eerily quiet.

"Nae?" I whispered onto her crown.

No response. Even Armand and Eaen watched her, the worry on their faces pointing their features.

"We'll stop him, Nae. I promise," I reassured her as I looked out into the wolf-men's faces.

When she spoke, Naomi's voice was edged with glass, as if she might shatter into a gazillion fragments. "That's why I chose to stay with Jeff. That's why. Maybe I could help to stop Hersey. You're all just innocents." Her words became a plea. "And the children? They don't deserve—" she hiccupped her sob, but continued. "It's not right, when you just want to live peacefully."

She shivered in my arms, and Armand curled himself at her feet as I pulled her tighter to me, wanting to fold her under my skin, to shield her from pain. Eaen went rigid, straightened his shoulders, tilted his chin to snap and align the vertebrae in his neck, and clenched and unfurled his fists like heartbeats.

"Naomi," he commanded, his deep voice plunging the pressure in the room. She stilled in my arms as she lifted her head in response to him. He stood before us like a wrathful god.

"We will not allow you to pay so high a price. Armand's words were truth, and you dishonor him by your second thoughts." His words rumbled along our nerves, and Naomi's body quivered briefly, before her long muscles stiffened along my own. "You are our wolf, Kenrickey's mate, we fight our enemy as pack. Do not dishonor our strength by feigning loyalty to another."

Nae's sharp gasp strangled on the tears in her throat. And because it was the appropriate thing to do, I claimed her. Penetrated her thighs right there on the floor with Eaen and Armand to bear witness to the union of our bodies.

I pushed my hand between her shoulder blades, and she yielded, dropping to her hands and knees, and spread her legs to receive me. She was already naked, the arched ridge of her spine curling, beckoning.

Sweet loving Christ. I dropped behind her, ran my length along her beautifully rounded bottom, sought the creamy tightness of her opening, and felt her hot juices seep around my shaft, milking me as I slid into her.

She cried my name as she spread wider, and so help me I rammed her hard, then harder, faster, my fingers clutching desperately to the plush of her hips. She arched to take me deeper, crying my name again as she bucked, matching the raw intensity of my thrusts.

Her name scraped from my throat as I felt the spastic quiver wring my seed into her. Naomi surrendered herself, her submissive yelps commanding supreme devotion from us all.

* * * *

"Nae." It was all I could breathe as I pulled through her slick heat, only to have her clench her silken muscles to hold me inside of her. I stayed, *Jesus-fuck* did I stay, with my eyes squeezed shut and my face aimed for the ceiling, my heart smashing against my ribcage, crushing the blood from it.

My Naomi, at last. I could smell her. Her sex, *holy God*, arousing me again even as she clutched me possessively inside of her. She rose to just her knees so she could cradle my head in her hands, and rocked her hips, suckling the thin velvet sheathe of my skin.

My lungs caught, and sucked in a gasping breath.

This was worth the four-year wait. The bliss of the moment shivered up my spine, beading itchy sweat between my shoulder blades.

I snarled, and buried my face into the curve of her neck to inhale her scent, imprinting her to my soul.

She quickened the pitch of her hips as she clenched her core rhythmically, squirting lava upon me.

I squelched her name and cupped her breasts, crushed her against my chest.

Mine, she sighed into my ear, her breath a blanket of a million shivers across my skin.

Oh yes. I was hers. Every careening molecule of myself was hers, and thusly, it made her mine.

Finally, she let me release her. I pulled myself out of her, feeling as I did so the loss of a separation so stinging I engulfed her in my arms just to ease the blow. We lay right there on the kitchen floor where I had taken her, Naomi cradled in my arms where she belonged no matter the surroundings.

I wasn't sorry for claiming her when I did. It felt too right, and if her reaction was any indication of her feelings on the matter, then she thought so, too. Nae had taken me just as readily as I had her. With Eaen and Armand as our witnesses, we mated like fellow wolves.

I didn't even wonder why I did it like that. I'd been sucked in too deeply to their world not to act on what I felt, to be true to my emotions. Those pangs shrieked at every cell in my body to claim what was mine, what was ours, right then, right there. Naomi understood that demand, too. She reacted as instinctively as when she'd yielded to Eaen's jaws clamped around her neck.

She comprehended shit on an elemental level. Apparently, we both did.

So we were mated.

But, we were human no matter how natural it felt to act otherwise. There were certain rules to live by, human codes to adhere to. I had stolen another man's mate, and as much as I wanted to flaunt it, to show the world Nae and I were finally paired, I couldn't. We had to deal with Jeff before we showed him anything.

Naomi snuggled into the crook of my arm, as I kissed the top of her head, then breathed in the snowy day that was her. Now, though, it tingled my nose as the musky tang of her juices blended with the crisp whiff of snow, and my body needed her again, as if my blood thinned without her.

Saying nothing, I gathered her in my arms and bee-lined it for the bedroom, willing my shaking legs to carry us both the distance as her skin flushed and radiated her scent. *Christ God,* I wasn't going to make it as far as the bedroom. My knees buckled, tumbling us to the floor in a sweaty heap, and I claimed my woman yet again as she rode me to the stars.

* * * *

Ultimately, we made it to the bedroom, where we could cuddle where it was more comfortable. Naomi nestled against my chest, and tickled circular patterns around my various wounds.

"You really did kill a coyote, didn't you?" Nae's breath licked across my nipples as she spoke, her voice thick and smoky.

"Mm-huh." It was all I seemed capable of replying. I was too sated, so content. We'd confirmed our union four times, and my Nae had gushed right along with me, and then some, with each reunion.

After the initial storm, I took my time, and it hadn't mattered that we were still in the hallway. I lapped the flesh I'd bruised in our lovemaking, brushed light kisses across her skin. And then, *oh the most delicious of memories!* I tasted her. Suckled her juices with my laving tongue because I couldn't deny any of my senses of the pleasure that was Naomi.

My mate.

I didn't tell her I loved her. I showed her, let her see how strong she was inside of me, like my love for her was an animal within me—ferocious, protective.

In response, Naomi melded her body around mine, crying my name along with her tears as I'd chanted her name.

Now here in the bed with her snuggled tight against me, I felt more of her tears drop onto my chest.

"He was a very bad coyote." I squeezed her closer, kissed the top of her head and left my cheek atop my kisses, as if to hold them there.

She giggled, swiped her eyes, and sniffled.

"Move in with us, Nae." Already I pictured her things with ours, her shampoo leaning against mine, her sweater draped across Armand's chair. All of it.

"Yes," she answered dreamily, as if she, too, pictured her belongings in this house.

"In the morning, first thing. Right after we tell The Bear he doesn't own you."

"*We,* huh?" She rested her chin on my sternum as she looked up at me. "You will be close?"

"Of course. You aren't breaking it off with him alone. I don't trust him, none of us do. You aren't alone in this."

"I like that, hearing you say it with such force," she teased.

We nestled deeper under the covers. First thing in the morning, Nae would drop her bomb on Jeff while I paced anxiously on the sidelines. Just in case.

* * * *

Naomi and I drove to campus together the next morning, leaving behind two concerned wolf-men. Eaen especially didn't feel right about our going alone. As our pack leader, he felt physically compelled to

S. C. Dane

drive The Bear away from us, to keep us safe.

I knew exactly how he felt, even if I was his subordinate. But given the circumstances, we couldn't very well act on our natural instincts. Eaen could not expose himself, or Armand, and it was that line of reasoning which finally checked him. He would never risk his family if it wasn't utterly necessary.

And it wasn't. Nae and I could handle The Bear. It wouldn't be pretty, I was sure, but I didn't for one second doubt I could kick his ass if it came down to it. The wolf-men had shared their skills, had honed my body and brain with every spontaneous wrestling match, with every hunt we'd undertaken. I actually itched for Jeff to try something.

As the Subaru wended along the back roads through pockets of low-lying fog, I glanced at my woman relaxing in the passenger seat, not looking out at the passing scenery but resting with her head back and her lids half shut. Our fingers were twined between us.

I resisted the impulse to declare I loved her by squeezing her hand, instead. Shit, I could tell her I loved her with every breath I drew, and would come off as a wee bit psycho. Which probably really wouldn't phase her in the least. After our weekend together, I was fast learning Nae's extraordinary ability to accept things, for better or for worse. A slow burn crawled up my cheeks when I thought about how I had laid claim to her.

An impartial witness would say I shoved her to the floor and fucked her brains out in front of two other men. Lucky for me there were no objective points of view, not even from Nae's perspective. She'd been just as swept up as I had been. Even with Armand and Eaen standing only feet away.

Naomi closed her fingers, tightening her grasp on my hand. She was extra gorgeous in the slanted sunlight of the car. The skin of her neck and jaw was irritated, scraped to a rash from my unshaven whiskers. Anyone would see we'd been having sex. Including The Bear.

The ringing of her cell phone intruded, as uninvited as my thoughts about Jeff, who happened to be on the other end of the call.

"Hi," Nae's voice fell flat, as if she was conveying through her tone she was finished with him, that she was sending him an oral clue the relationship was crashing to an end.

154

"Mmm, yeah," she continued in response to whatever it was he was saying. I did not have the benefit of wolf hearing.

"We'll talk. When class is over." There was a slight pause, and then she muttered, "Yeah. Okay, g'bye."

Thank God she didn't say she loved him. It was bad enough she was talking to him. I mean, I knew Sasquatch and his temper, but hearing Nae talking to him roused the little itch at the base of my skull. How great was that, huh? It wasn't enough it visited its electric little self whenever Armand and Eaen were involved, now Luna added another to the list of those I was compelled to protect. Unless that wasn't what the itch was conveying at all.

My hand automatically scratched at the back of my head. *Shit.* Like I didn't have e-freakin'-nough to worry about already that morning.

"You all right, Ken?" Naomi leaned forward in her seat to peer at me. "I'll be fine, you know. You don't have to—"

"No, Nae, I'll be there," I assured her, and wanted to stop the car right in the middle of the road to kiss away the worried slant of her brow. "It's just that—" How did I explain it? Whenever Eaen and Armand are in trouble I get a jolt of electricity in my brain and spine that makes me practically piss myself? Ooh, boy. I exhaled a heavy breath, and rested my eyes on hers just long enough to keep the car on the road.

"I get..." *Jeeze,* where was the Ramblin' Man when I needed him? Why couldn't I just blurt out the explanation to her? But I guess I knew the answer to that already, which is why my mouth didn't cooperate. Nae would be devastated if she thought she was the one to bring harm to the wolf-men, even if it was inadvertently.

There was going to be something shitty going down with Jeff and Naomi, and somehow it was going to involve Eaen and Armand. But how? If I could figure that out, I could prevent it from happening. What good was a precognitive zap if it didn't show me anything more than my two brothers strung up by their hind legs?

My stomach rolled.

Nae, being her usual perceptive self, noticed.

"It's okay, really, Nae." Her hand grew cool beneath my own, and I needed to do some heavy scrambling to squash the fear that pulled all her blood to her core, as if she was hypothermic. So, Christ, I had to tell her.

I aimed the Subaru into a parking slot and killed the engine. Naomi didn't budge, but sat as still as a marble statue waiting for me to say something. Well, at least she wasn't the type to go off half-cocked.

"When I was up north," I began, pulling Nae's hand to my stomach, as much to comfort me as it was to solace her. "I met Eaen's brother and his mate, too." A grin tugged my lips despite thinking about the events of that day.

"Eaen's sister is a freakin' wolf-witch, or something, Nae. I don't know," I glanced at my woman then, just to register her reaction. She had her hazel eyes on me, silently urging me on. I couldn't resist her.

"Anyway, Luna put this buzzing in my head to help us, I guess. It's like an alarm or something that warns me when Armand and Eaen are in danger. I got it before, the other day, when The Bear, I mean Jeff, when *Jeff* was disrespecting you in the Quad and I was getting ready to ream him one for it."

"Wait. He was what?"

I filled her in on what Jeff had done behind her back that day. Which pissed her off. She blanched and balled her fist in mine, but I continued because the rambles pulled up a chair.

"So, anyway, it hit and I didn't do anything to him. Because there's something about The—*Jeff,* I'm supposed to be on the alert for, you know. And hearing you on the phone with him this morning touched off the alarm again. The buzz is tickling at the back door, Nae, and I'm not sure why."

There. Now all I had to do was wait for the sickened look to appear on her pretty face. Because it would, and I knew exactly what her response would be. She was going to feel guilty about *maybe* hurting Armand and Eaen. I'd known that and still I confessed everything. I am such a nice guy.

"Nae, I'm sorry. I didn't want to tell you. I know how it sounds, and *goddammit,* I know what you're thinking. It's not your fault."

That fetched her up.

Please, Ramblin' Man, spew forth. "Eaen and Armand already know about it, so Eaen knew exactly what was at stake when he convinced you to be with us, Nae. I swear. I'm sure it's why Armand is so protective of you, too."

156

"Ken," she said. Lord Christ her voice was tiny. Nothing like the confident growls she spoke over the weekend. "What if it's *me* who hurts them? What if—"

"Aw, Nae, don't. No one's getting hurt. We've got Luna looking out for us. I mean, I think this buzzing is telling you and me to watch out today, that's all. 'Cause seriously, it doesn't hit me when we're together, and it sure as hell didn't hit when you found me naked with two wolves in tow." I filled her in on our theory concerning that, too, which did wonders for pumping the blood back into her fingers. I raised her warming hand to my lips and kissed it.

And beat back the urge to suck one of those tapered lovelies into my mouth.

"Come on," I pulled on the door handle instead. "Let's go to class before I make love to you here in the parking lot."

She giggled the choir of angels and my groin spasmed. I shot out of the car and waited for her to emerge on the other side, and didn't approach her until we were away from the vehicle. She leveled her lids enticingly, stroking me with her eyes.

"Christ, Nae, I'm trying to graduate here," I said, even as I pulled her to me.

"I know," she confessed, and then clasped my hand in hers, twirled on her heels, and dragged me toward the Science building for our class with Hersey. I followed like a puppy on a leash, happy to tag along so long as she kept me with her.

Plus, Jeff wouldn't make the first class, so for once I wasn't going to get the usual double-shot of asshole first thing on a Monday morning. I only had to deal with Hersey, and if I could just sit in the back and take notes without letting the bile rise in my throat, then everything would be okay.

Of course, first thing Hersey had to say was that he wanted to see me right after class. To say *No* would strain the already seriously tenuous reasons Hersey allowed me to stay, but to see him directly after class meant Nae would be alone if The Bear showed himself. The bastard was in town. He was just blowing off the first class because the team got home late.

Would it be too much to ask for shit not to hit the fan?

157

Freakin' Christ.

I nodded my head as an answer to Hersey, and took my chair in the back. What did he want now, I wondered.

"See him after class," Nae instructed via a whisper in my ear.

I threw her a withering stare, to which she promptly stuck out her tongue.

Man, but I loved her piss and vinegar. It got my heart rapping and pasted a stupid grin to my face. Hersey started his yammering, so like an attentive student, I turned toward him and away from the sexy distraction leaning into me.

It isn't snowing, it isn't snowing.

I focused on my pen as if it swirled out blue secrets of the universe on a blank page, and shoved Naomi to the periphery of my hankering brain.

Somehow, time crawled by and Hersey wrapped up his lecture, and I hadn't stuck Mr. Plucky into the woman beside me. *My mate*—who was telling me to go see Hersey again.

"Fine," I ceded. "But I'm going to make it quick, and please, Nae—" But what could I say? Be careful? Go hide in the ladies' room? "Just play it safe, okay?" I leaned down to brush my lips to hers, to taste her, breathe her in.

"Okay," she promised, even as her hazel eyes fired with mischief.

I shouldered my bag, and trotted off to Hersey's office as Naomi headed for the car.

I rapped my knuckles on his open door and noticed Crandall wasn't present for this meeting. Neither was Randall Wolfe.

"Ken, have a seat," Hersey stuck his arm out toward the same chair he'd offered before.

"No, thanks. I'll stand."

"Suit yourself." He paused, took a breath before saying, "I'm sure you already know why I've asked you to come."

"Chances are," I clipped, not wanting to encourage him.

"Right, then, I'll get to it." He plunked down in his chair, tossing the pen he'd been holding onto the surface of his desk. "Ken, I know we had wolves up there."

The guy didn't beat around the proverbial bush. "And?"

"And you know where they are. Where the dens are too, I bet."

"No. Actually I don't. Like I said, there were no wolves."

"I saw you run off with them like you were Tarzan of the Jungle," Hersey blurted, losing his temper.

I said nothing, and shoved my hands into my pockets.

"Look, Ken," he inhaled another deep breath to calm himself, and stared out toward his window for a few moments. "We're going to find those wolves and their cubs whether you help or not. I just thought since you had some weird connection up there you'd want your name attached to the discovery. Think of the recognition. You could attend any Grad school you set your sights on."

He didn't know how weird the connection still was, and his offer was insultingly low. It didn't even get my dander up. Until he laid down the ace he had stuffed up his sleeve.

"I'm setting traps this time, kid. And no more collars. It's chip time, and tattooing for the cubs if you don't help me," he warned, trying to force my hand.

"You're threatening me."

"Tit for tat, Mr. Rickey."

The son of a bitch. "I'll do it," I agreed without flinching.

And plotted his death, which was the only recourse I had to stopping the fucker.

"No tricks, kid," he warned as he thrust a pointed finger at me.

"There never were," I retorted, and left his office before I strangled him right where he sat.

Chapter Eight

By the time I reached the glass doors leading to the freedom of the outdoors, Luna's persistent buzz had blossomed until it filled my skull, leaving little space for much else.

Except Nae.

Who was struggling to slip out of The Bear's grasp as he tried shoving her into his car.

I bellowed. I know I did, even with the full explosion of TNT going off in my head. My leg muscles turned to traitorous jell-o so my knees ground into the cement, but I pushed forward anyway, adrenaline thrusting my body toward Naomi, who needed help.

I couldn't hear a fucking thing, just the screaming buzz as my vision tunneled. But I kept running, knew I did so only because Nae and The Bear grew bigger as I neared, and I could hear my chuffing breaths like they left my lungs and went straight to my burning skull.

Along with the rest of me that had been set on fire.

But I didn't have time to worry how hard the buzzing was nailing me. I had to get to Nae. *Yesterday*. Which turned out to be just in time. Nae fought like a hell-cat, and tripped backwards as she wrenched herself free, right into me.

My arms automatically encased her as I staggered to an abrupt halt. I might have heard her say my name. I don't know; I could barely hear a damned thing through the electrical storm raging in my head. I was too hot, and my muscles slithered like electric eels. Holding Nae was the only thing keeping me on my feet.

Then somehow, coming from somewhere, Randall Wolfe jumped in

160

the fray, and was using his body to usher The Bear to the driver's side of his Jetta, to get him away from us. He kept shooting worried glances at Nae and me while he got Jeff out of the picture.

The sizzling in my skull slowly ebbed from red alert to a steady drone, allowing my heart rate to return to half-way normal. Rand came back as soon as The Bear squealed his tires out of the parking lot, choking the air with the stench of burning rubber.

"Are you okay?" he asked me, not the woman who had turned herself around so she was holding me.

"Yeah. Fuck." My hand automatically raked its familiar path across the top of my head. Small wonder my scalp didn't come off in my fingers. But I was shaking, and still too fucking hot. And of all things, it was Nae hugging me that kept me from pooling apart. But seeing Rand clanged bells, and I remembered my meeting just moments before with Hersey.

"Listen," *Christ.* I had to trust him. To what end I couldn't even fathom right then, not with the image of poor Nae wrestling with a man twice her size. "Hersey plans on tagging and tattooing the pups. I saw his equipment." Our gazes locked, and this time Rand didn't look away. I saw his damned pupils swallow his irises.

"Come on. Let's get you in the car." Rand finally acknowledged Naomi. "Are you all right? Can you drive him home?"

"Yes."

Her arms tightened around me as she pulled me toward the Subaru, and she and Rand navigated me into the passenger seat.

"Rand." I wanted to thank him. I wanted to take back what I'd said about Hersey. Hell, I wanted the goddamned buzzing to finally go away so I could think straight, so that my body could actually operate like I had something left of my brain.

He just nodded, not saying a word, and left me and Nae there in the parking lot. He flipped his cell phone to his ear, got in his Range Rover, and peeled out almost as fast as The Bear had.

Naomi didn't say anything, either, but she double checked that my limbs weren't sticking out so she wouldn't slam my fingers in the car door, walked around the front of the Subaru, and got in behind the wheel to drive us home.

* * * *

Relief washed over me as soon as Nae parked the car in the driveway. Eaen and Armand waited inside, and I desperately had to talk with them, to tell them what I'd done. But most important, what Hersey had threatened just before the buzzing in my head electrocuted my entire body like a snaking power line, frying everything its recoiling head came in contact with.

How'd the saying go? Oh, yeah. When it rained it poured. Or the shit's hitting the fan, or anything else along those lines. My thinking wasn't exactly spot-on just then, what with the echo reverberating through my hollowed-out body.

Nae's scent filled my nostrils and my aching head, as she bent through the passenger side door to help me out. When had she gotten out of the car? Who cared. The refreshing whiff of snow was doing wonders for my equilibrium, but I held onto her just the same as we walked toward the house.

I might have been shell-shocked, but I knew she'd just broken it off with The Bear. I'd shown up in time to give her something else to worry about.

"Freakin-A, I'm sorry, Nae," I leaned against her steady frame and snugged her against me. She felt so damned good, and I was a loser for not helping her more, for making things worse for her. *But the fucking buzzing.* Again, I don't know why I didn't piss myself when it struck that hard. Because it had obliterated my frontal lobe, sending it packing like a bouncer at a bar.

Eaen and Armand were right at the door as soon as we came through it.

"What is wrong, Kenrickey? Naomi?" They pressed physically and with questions. Eaen cradled my face in both of his long, warm hands, and peered hard into my eyes.

Nae already had her arm around Armand. "I don't know, Eaen. He showed up when I was arguing with Jeff, and I didn't see what happened, but he was shocked or something when I bumped into him."

No exaggeration there. She'd bumped into me because I was standing behind her like an autistic absorbed by one minute detail.

"Porcupine? Was it Luna?" His brown eyes layered as he searched

162

my face.

I croaked out a *yes* knowing full well what he meant by the name he called the awful buzzing. "It was—" *Christ fuck and any other jumped up Jesusly swear word I could rant.*

Because how did I tell the three people I loved that Jeff had been wearing The Boots. The very same pair standing beside the hanging corpses of Armand and Eaen, which Luna had been so kind as to brand into my brain as a warning of things to come.

* * * *

"I don't get it," I shook my head after telling those three people I loved exactly what I didn't want to. They looked about as stricken as I thought they would, but at least it didn't last. Eaen's eyes darkened as he disappeared into his thoughts, and Nae squashed herself in between me and the back of the couch. Armand sat cross-legged next to Eaen, who occupied the other end of the sofa. The sight of the four of us crammed on the couch together squeezed my heart. We were a pack, in more ways than one. At that moment, we were sardines in the oil of our troubles.

"Ha!" I snorted a quick laugh, painting confused expressions on the others. I shook my head and wiped the grin that tugged. "Nothing, just had a funny thought about us." They smiled sympathetically, even though I probably seemed like a raving lunatic.

"I admit it does not make sense." Eaen picked up the original thread of our conversation. We were all snuggled on the couch together because it offered comfort like nothing else could. "Why would Luna not warn us about Nae, but have us connected to The Bear through her?" He used my nickname for her, yet it sounded natural coming from him. Plus, he reached out to take her hand, knowing his words were a blow to her. She felt responsible as hell.

I squeezed her calf. "Don't. We are pack, Nae, and in this together." I received a kiss to the top of my head, and although I couldn't see her face, Eaen could and he winked at her.

"Let's leave. Go somewhere, anywhere." Nae suggested. "We'll pack up everyone, including Eaen's family, and get the hell out of here." It was a desperate solution thrown out in the open because the reality of what was to be done was so horrific.

I'd sworn to kill Hersey while I'd stood in his office, and I'd meant it with every fiber of my being. If I was going anywhere, it was to prison. But not before I eliminated him from the wolf-people's troubles. Sasquatch just complicated my mission, turning the murder of one man into a killing spree. But I would do it. And that's what had us mashed on the couch in a show of solidarity. The others weren't going to let me go it alone.

Eaen and Armand weren't ready to throw in the proverbial towel and sacrifice one pack member for the safety of the group. Which, I reminded them, went against the law of the pack. Tell me that comment didn't raise some hackles.

"We are not at that point yet, Porcupine. We did not claim you just to—How does that saying go, Armand? Throw you to the wolves?"

Armand dropped his fangs and flashed a wicked grin.

I smiled at their joke, couldn't help it. We had some serious shit pressing, and still we could squeeze laughter into the room, find something to lighten our heavy hearts.

Yet seeing Armand's lethal grin reminded me of Rand, and how I'd spilled what I knew of Hersey's plans. "And what of this other wolf-man, guys? What about him?" His arrival now seemed too coincidental.

Eaen grew serious right along with me. "If he is who you think, and I am inclined to agree with you, then perhaps he may help us deal with your professor."

I didn't dare hope, but it comforted me to know both Eaen and Armand, after having seen Rand at Hersey's dinner party that night, had been able to see what I'd meant about the guy. Without smelling him, though, or meeting him directly, their guesses were only as good as mine.

But I had a raging headache. Too much was piling up way too fast, and my brain cells were having a hard enough time functioning without having their fragile membranes sunburned by Luna's gift. I pressed my fingers to the base of my skull and begged my leave with sincere apologies. I felt like a shmuck for leaving them after the news I'd brought, but I wasn't thinking clearly anyway, and some rest would probably go a long way toward reviving that capacity.

Nae, bless her gentle fingers, came with me. She straightened the covers before we climbed in—a woman's touch. Not that I was the type to determine chores according to gender, but I never would have made the bed just to crawl directly into it. Yet, I had to admit it was a comforting and inviting gesture. She was snuggled in my embrace before she could get the pillows arranged.

Her bare skin against mine was a silken caress, and I buried my face into her nape, snuffled her scent. Then fell into a dead sleep despite the fact the sun was at its highest. It was only noon.

* * * *

Nae merely heaved a contented sigh and fluttered her closed lids when I slid out from under her. The room had darkened considerably since we'd first gone to bed, and I felt rested. The cored out sensation of my body had disappeared, but the itch at the base of my skull remained. Which probably meant it would fester until this whole damned business was over. I stretched, scratched my scalp and sauntered out to the living room.

Eaen and Armand were folded up together on the couch sleeping. I wondered if they shifted in their sleep sometimes without realizing it, if their dreams initiated the change at all. My stomach growled, and I contemplated waking them to go hunting. Yeah, I was in deep when my first thoughts were to go scrounging up dinner in the forest, not my refrigerator.

In the darkness, I heard Eaen's breathing shallow, and what little light there was reflected in his opening eyes. "Greetings, Porcupine." He stretched his long legs as best he could without disturbing Armand. "I trust you slept well?"

"Yeah, the headache's gone, but not the itch."

"I am sorry. I did not know Luna had imparted some of herself to you. That you would *need* to protect us." His deep voice weighed heavier than the darkness, and that saddened me, moved me to want to cheer him up.

"Eaen, it's not Luna. I've loved you guys since the moment Grane risked his own life for mine. In this world, nobility like that is rare, Brother. I didn't know I even needed it until I found you guys in those woods. It sounds wicked corny, but it's true. Luna has nothing to do with

165

my feelings. I'm protective because this world needs you, and Nae and I sure as Christ do."

"But it is not right that you sacrifice—"

I clipped him off. "Of course it's right. After everything we humans have done to you and your kind, taking a hit for you guys is the least I can do. You've suffered enough, Eaen. It's time the wolf-people stopped shouldering all the shit and got a break for once."

Eaen reached his arm out toward me and I clasped my own around it. His bare skin wafted fire, and I knew my words stirred him. Christ, the only thing I regretted was not having enough time. I wanted to be with this wolf-man and his brother always. The four of us together somehow, sharing our lives.

"Us too, Porcupine," Armand's voice scratched through the darkness.

I grinned, even as I wondered that he'd heard my thoughts, the internal connection not registering on my Weird Scale at all. I was simply pleased they could pick up on my feelings so easily, and respond so purely, without fear of recrimination or ridicule.

Human beings could go a long way with that lesson ingrained in their hearts. Instead, they bagged and tagged because they didn't heed other ways of learning from those with whom they shared this planet. And the chances of Hersey knowing the wolf-people existed and leaving them alone? His scientific brain wouldn't allow it. I closed my eyes as if that could erase the image of Alec protecting his family, because it was true what was said in the movies: *if we tell you, we'll have to kill you.*

Which made me and Nae lucky sons of bitches, and the wolf-people too vulnerable.

"You guys should go home, go back to the woods, you know, until this is over."

"Porcupine, you are as near-sighted as your namesake." Armand yawned, stretching his powerful arms over his head then letting them dangle behind him. "There is a solution, and it presented itself when you agreed to help your teacher." His sharp teeth gleamed in the dark when he smiled.

"Oh yeah? How's my helping him going to help you?"

"Eaen and I are going to have the fun of tearing his throat out while you lure him to us."

Even without the details, it sounded good. "Go on."

The two wolf-men sat up on the couch and patted the empty space between them. I nestled in to hear the rest of their plan.

"It has been revealed to us, Kenrickey, that Armand and I do not exist. Not in your world, at least. Correct?"

"You got that from reading?"

They both nodded, showing their wickedly strong teeth in gleeful grins.

"Yes," Eaen continued, acting as spokesman for the both of them. "So, if we do not exist, then we are unfettered. We can do things that you cannot."

"Such as kill humans," Armand summed up.

They could, of course, as long as they kept their human shapes. There were no records of their fingerprints, no one except Naomi had seen them. There were a lot of loose strings to consider before we could go forward with their plan, but on the surface it looked a lot more promising than having me sit in a jail cell. I would be a suspect, of course, but without proof? With a solid alibi?

"I like it," I admitted. I'd be in the hot seat for a good long while, but if I kept my trap shut and let the police do all of the work, then it was highly probable we'd all get out of this mess relatively unscathed. And the wolf-people would be safe, at least for a while, and so would Naomi.

"Good. Now let us go hunt." Eaen rose off the sofa and stretched to his full height, which was effing impressive. Yeah, he and Armand could slay a human with their bare hands. Even one as big as The Bear.

But Armand and I both hesitated, unwilling to leave Nae alone. Who the hell knew what Jeff would do. He'd already called her and left her some nasty messages on her phone since she refused to answer it, and it was very possible he'd show up on our front porch looking for her. The thought was enough to make up my mind about which of us stayed.

"Armand, you go on with Eaen. If The Bear shows up, you need to be out of sight, no matter how badly you want to protect your sister. If this plan of yours is going to work, Jeff can't know you're here." That last part closed his mouth over his protest. He wasn't stupid, and fully grasped the consequences.

"We could take her with us."

"Armand, you're a sly wolf, but with another human tagging along, I'm afraid you'd never get anything to eat." I laughed about it, but it was true, and the two wolf-men needed to feed themselves.

"*Another* human, Porcupine?" Eaen rejoined as he sided with Armand. Then he winked. "We will not know if we do not try. We should all go this night."

"All go where?"

The three of us turned as one to the sound of Naomi's voice, and the image of the Three Stooges flashed in my mind again. *Christ*, the wolf-men lifted my heart. Armand went right over to her, his invisible tail wagging expectantly. I could picture that, too.

"We would like you to come hunting with us, Naomi." Armand dropped his chin to his broad chest and averted his eyes, presenting the epitome of the beseeching, subordinate wolf. It was a potent testament to her effect on him. He was easily the physically stronger of the two, yet her presence enthralled him. He interacted with her far differently than he did with his brothers. She subjugated him, but it was painfully clear he'd level anyone who tried to harm her. It was the reason why Armand shouldn't be left at the house alone with Nae.

If The Bear did show up, I'd have to explain to the cops why there was a mangled corpse on my kitchen floor and a wolf plastered to the side of the only human witness.

Naomi was beyond touched by Armand's offer. She beamed an incredulous smile and followed it with a whopping, "Really? I'd love to!" Which rocketed the blonde wolf-man toward her exposed chin, where he kissed her a number of times and spun on his heels to face his brothers.

"She will come," he said, his yellow eyes sparkling, even though the room darkened with every passing minute.

We couldn't help but laugh at him. His eager anticipation heartened us all. And after a day like the one we'd just had, it was the warmth of the sun beaming in defiance of an impending storm. The rays only shined brighter when Naomi proceeded to strip out of her clothes.

My heart was going to pop right out of my mouth, I was so full. I loved them all so much, and effing right, I would do anything to protect them. With or without Luna's influence.

* * * *

Naomi stood before us, unabashed in Nature's glory, courageous before her boys, then practically hopped toward the front door she was so eager to go.

As soon as we were outside, with our bodies draped in the silver sheen of the moon, I pulled her to me.

"Holy crap, Ken. Is this real?"

"After all you've seen, you're asking me if *this* is real?" I tugged her hand, pulling her toward the waiting wolves. "Come on, let's go."

She trotted gamely along despite the little digs and bites I knew firsthand she felt against her bare skin. But she seemed, as usual, to understand the importance of the hunt and never wavered. Her determination deepened, if anything, her expression shifting as she stole a quick glance back at me.

Her eyes flashed the length of my body, and I knew what she saw. She comprehended the gauntlet I'd run for my body to have become what it had. Every snag and tear of my skin had flecked away the shit of being human until I was stark. Base.

And still I saw her acceptance, her love.

God, but I loved her, too. Yet didn't have time to dwell on the fact. The blonde wolf broke away to the right, while Eaen, his black coat barely visible in the dark woods, sped off to the left. I ran up behind Nae, clasping her elbows to draw her close.

"If you can't keep up, don't worry. *We will find you.*" I stole a quick sniff of her warm neck, then bounded off ahead of her, filling my place in the arc of our hunting noose.

I could hear the two wolves on either side of me, looming closer at break neck speed. Armand was on the tail of something small and quick, and I redoubled my speed to close the gap, just as the black wolf was doing.

We merged in time to squeeze a rabbit into our net. Armand snagged it without wasting our chance, and Eaen and I lunged in, grasping for our share. I worried nothing about the snapping of fangs, or the guttural snarls. The wolves were always aware of their own bodies, so a grazing of fang to my bare skin was incidental, an unintended scratch. And my own growls matched theirs.

We shredded our prey, each of us getting our earned share, and I reveled in the feral pungency of the rabbit's fur on my lips, against my nose, and for the first time missed the absence of fangs, as if I'd expected them to be present in my mouth.

I gobbled the hot, bloody meat anyway, gulping down my parcel of the little corpse. And felt the arrival of Nae sneak along my back as she neared us.

I turned as I rose, and went to her, taking her mouth while the intoxicating scent of the kill still lingered from the blood smeared on my cheeks.

Naomi never flinched. When I drew back from our kiss, she licked her lips. "You taste good," she whispered, her confession strung with a slight twinge of embarrassment.

I grew rock hard from her breathless words. "Guys," I nailed Nae with a hungry gaze. "Finish hunting and come back for us in a bit?"

Eaen and Armand spun on their paws, and like ghosts slipped into the silver shaded forest. Before they were even out of sight, I knelt in front of my woman to bury my face in the balmy crease of her breasts.

"Jesus, Nae, you strike me dead." I inhaled deep of her body's warmth, felt her tremble as my breath drafted along her bare skin, rendering me gloriously savage, feral.

I gazed up at her, delved the darkened hazel of her eyes. "I do not disgust you then, my mate?"

She shook her head. "No." Her tongue slipped the length of her bottom lip. "Call me *your mate,* again," she dared.

I caressed my cheek down her flat stomach then breathed her challenge into her salty core, ushering it into her with a broad swipe of my tongue.

Nae stifled a yip, her fingers clutching my hair. I cradled her buttocks as I lowered her to the forest floor. I hovered inches above her, bearing my own weight so I wouldn't crush her while I spread her legs with my thigh, then slid myself up into her.

170

Naomi's hips bucked, driving me deeper and then deeper still, as if her timidity scattered to the four winds, shattering what was left of my reserve along with it.

Chapter Nine

Eaen and Armand returned with their tongues lolling flat and wide from their jaws. They'd been having fun without the pokey human tagging along. I got up onto my hands and knees to kiss and rub my greeting before they flaked out on the cool carpet of the ground with their sides heaving and their ears pinned.

My woman got up onto her precious bare feet and tiptoed over to them for her own greeting. Her laughter twinkled in the darkness when Armand slobbered her neck.

"Next time, I think I'll wait until you've cooled down, silly brother," she teased as she wiped her neck with an exaggerated sweep of her arm.

"Did you eat, or just run the entire time?" I adopted Nae's teasing tone, easily done now that the strains of the day were completely eased, even though the base of my skull still itched.

Eaen lapped his lips and dipped his chin.

"Well, I'll assume you did both, Brother. Were there any leftovers?" I expected no answer for my question. They had run as wolves and were capable of covering tens of miles within the time they were gone. My dinner could have been twenty miles away for all I knew.

We lay there until the wolves recovered from their romp. It was a beautiful night, with such an explosive pageantry of stars there was barely enough dark sky to display them all. The forest was alight with their silvered glare, so even without the wolves to guide us, Nae and I still could have picked our way home.

But I was glad we hadn't gone back without Armand and Eaen. As soon as we neared the house the wolves' hackles spiked, and they

172

dropped their noses to the ground to sweep the area. Their tails rode high, and they rumbled warnings as they coursed around the perimeter of the yard with lethal vigor.

Someone had been here, and I could guess who without having to smell him.

So could Nae, because she blurted out his name.

"*Jeff.*"

My hackles lifted for Christ's sake, I was so pissed. And ready. The bastard hadn't just gone to the front door to see if we were home, he'd skulked around the outside of the house and peeked in the windows. I gathered that from watching Armand and Eaen follow his scent trail.

My fists clenched reflexively as my stomach knotted.

Protect.

Effing right, Luna.

I tore my eyes from the wolves and stared at the ground, focusing on the absence of the crippling buzz. Just that persistent itch still nagged, so I figured it meant he'd already left the area.

Back to the woods.

I snagged Nae's wrist and didn't ask questions.

Once we were enveloped within the protection of the trees, Eaen and Armand circled, yawned, shivered, and unfolded their long, bare limbs. I waited a few moments before asking them anything, giving them time to recover their voices. Naomi was apparently too upset from Jeff's reconnaissance mission to even flinch at their lightning quick transformation into human form.

Eaen cut the small talk with a scratchy growl. "The Bear went to the ridge to view the house from that angle. He was not alone. Three were here."

"Fuck me," I spat as my hand journeyed across my scalp. If he'd done that, he was coming back. And he wasn't going to knock on the front door this time, which put all three of my loved ones in danger at once.

"Did they go into the house?" Nae's question stilled my blood. Of course, I hadn't bothered to lock it. Jesus, I wasn't even sure where the key was. But it meant that Jeff, and Hersey most likely, had plenty of time to snoop. What would they find? No extra clothes or dishes or used razors, but a shit-load of wolf hair—if they were inclined to peer that close. And Professor Mark Hersey was.

I stared anxiously at Eaen, and then turned toward Armand, who gurgled from the depths of his guts and grated through his clenched jaw, "*We think so*."

I automatically turned my attention to the house where it squatted in the darkness, its windows reflecting the starry night. We'd turned on no lights to welcome us back home.

"There was a third, Kenrickey," Eaen reminded me, his upper lip lifting off his luminous teeth. Whoever it was had Eaen on more of an alert than The Bear and Hersey.

"Who?" Did I really want to know?

"You have met him before. Randall Wolfe."

"Christ Almighty, you're sure?" I glanced nervously from Eaen to Armand, then back again to Eaen. "He was with Jeff and Hersey?"

"Not likely. He would not come beyond the edge of your front territory."

"Because it's our territory, isn't it? Another wolf won't cross it."

Eaen and Armand both nodded.

"Holy Christ, he *is* wolf."

"Wait. Randall Wolfe, the guy funding Hersey's trips north, is like you guys? Huh, well, that explains it." Naomi's surprise over the arrival of Rand near our property overshadowed her fears of Jeff. She got excited, and nude like she was I could see her skin tighten along her curves. "I met him at the dinner, and I was literally biting my tongue and gripping my chair to keep from antagonizing him. I wanted to floor him, you know?" She looked up at Eaen for understanding, then pinched her feathery brows together. "But he doesn't look like you guys. His hands are totally normal, no offense."

"He is different from us, yes, Naomi. But he is definitely wolf. We are certain of that now."

"But you don't think it's likely he's with The Bear." Yeah, it was a shocker to have Rand's identity confirmed, but I didn't want to forget about our other visitors, the ones who immediately threatened us. "Can we find out for sure? I mean, if he's an enemy, we've got to know, and the sooner the better. If he's not, and I'd like to think he wasn't, then we've got to figure out what the hell he was doing here scoping out our territory."

"Perhaps he wants a truce," Armand proposed, shrugging his broad shoulders as he acknowledged my rambling logic.

His idea had us all thinking, and we fell silent under the moonlight. Maybe Armand was right. It wasn't like Rand was going to walk right up and present himself in all his secret glory. Eaen and Armand would kick his ass, and ask the questions after. They had every right to, especially Eaen. Since his arrival, the black wolf had managed to become our leader, the alpha male to our unusual pack. It was his duty to keep us safe, barring the obvious exceptions from living in a human environment.

"Okay. Say you're right, Arms. If he wants a truce, how do we go about inviting another wolf onto the property?"

"Very carefully," Eaen jested, his strong teeth practically glowing in the silver hued night, his dark eyes glinting.

"He comes only if he's in his wolf form, Eaen, which means he comes armed with just the weapons Nature intended." I wouldn't cede on that point. Bringing a strange wolf close was dangerous business, either one of us could get seriously hurt, and I didn't have to be the boy-genius to figure that one out.

Rand was a full-grown man. Yes, Eaen was strong, but he'd never been tried before. Besides surviving a steel trap, this adventure into the human world was his first real test. I didn't want to see him hurt.

"Kenrickey." His tone admonished me, and I dropped my head automatically as my fingers curled around Nae's supporting grip. "This is the way of the wolf. We get hurt from our challenges, but we must take our risks. Life is not static, change comes to us all."

He was right, of course. And his philosophical view stood counter to his voracious appetite for the sciences. Our Eaen was a complex, beautiful being, and I disrespected him with my doubts.

"I'm sorry, Eaen. But don't forget, I've still got this blasted buzzing from Luna in my head. If it goes off again like it did this morning—"

"You will be crawling on your knees?"

I tackled him, and as he absorbed my weight, he rolled backwards with ease, somersaulting us and pinning me to the ground in the short seconds it took to stop our spin. Eaen barked out a laugh and leapt off from me. I snagged his outstretched hand so he could pull me to my feet.

"You can still eat shit, you know that right?" But there were no teeth to my words, and Eaen clapped me good-naturedly on the back.

"Of course, Porcupine. And I will repeat my fondness for you, as well. I will be proud to have you at my back when this Randall Wolfe comes. I am honored you will stand with me."

Well, blow smoke up my ass, because what was I going to say to that? I think my head actually swelled, and I know the grin spreading across my face beamed my pleasure at hearing his compliment.

"Right, so I'll call Rand as soon as we figure out what to do with Jeff."

Nae opened her mouth to speak, and Eaen snapped at her, enforcing his position yet again, and laying waste to his indulgent mood. "Do not say you are sorry," he growled, then leapt toward her so quickly the sound of his voice was still in our ears. He lifted her off her feet as if to carry her, but laid her on the ground instead, his strong hand gently encircling her neck. He was re-establishing his dominance over her, shoving aside her doubts as to her place within our pack.

To her credit, Nae didn't challenge him, but spread her arms and legs across the dirt beneath her. The dark haired wolf-man pulled away slowly, yet kept a stern eye on her. He said nothing else on the matter, and neither did she. Naomi was mated into our pack, was as much a member as either of us, and the sooner she shed her guilt about The Bear, the better for us as a whole. Insecurity was not welcome here.

Finally, he let Naomi up and she immediately crawled under his chin to kiss him and ingratiate herself. Freakin'-A, that woman had to have wolf in her blood. He brushed a passing kiss to her cheek and then turned to Armand. Nae came to me, and I pulled her near, inviting her to snuggle close to my bare skin.

The day had taken its toll, and the wolf-men had been running all over God knew where. I knew their bodies demanded necessary rest, and I know I wanted to crawl into a comfortable spot and sleep. We could deal with Jeff later, if or when he showed up again. The better rested we were, the better chance we had at protecting Nae.

"Brothers, it's been a very long day and I'm ready to call it quits.

What say we dig in here and get some much needed sleep?"

Eaen shook his head. "No, Porcupine. We have been driven away too often, and it is time to protect our territory. We sleep in our home tonight." His impassioned decree wasn't to be questioned, and we all rose and plodded cautiously toward the house.

I didn't bother with the lights, and as Nae and I headed for the bedroom I turned to the two wolf-men, whose lean, muscular bodies were illuminated by the stars shining into the living room. "Sleep in your bed tonight, with Nae and me. Please?"

Naomi didn't wait for either one to answer, but walked over to Armand and circled her fingers around his wrist to lead him into the bedroom. He followed willingly, and Eaen, too, succumbed to the prospect of a comfy bed and a crowded night's sleep.

* * * *

We were all awake by the time the false dawn yielded to the sun, but we remained snuggled up together in a very toasty bundle. Who needed blankets when you slept with two portable furnaces?

"Good morning boys," Nae's trill preceded the haunting echo of the mourning doves.

Like practiced choir boys we chanted *good morning* back to her, and our sleepy faces broke into smiles. It was a wonderful way to greet the day, in spite of what loomed. We lay together awhile longer, savoring the proximity. It wouldn't be much longer before Naomi and I would have to uncoil ourselves to face our enemies. We still had degrees to earn, exams to take.

"What will you do while we're gone, guys?" Despite Eaen's vow to literally confront our problems, my chest constricted with the prospect of their departure, even though it was the safest thing for them to do.

"We will do what armies do," Armand said, surprising the crap out of me.

"What?" I lifted my head off the pillow.

"In the book I am reading, commanders communicate, send dispatches to inform one another. We will do the same."

He meant *The Art of War.* I slurred, "How?"

"You will speak to us on your telephone to tell us where The Bear is, if he has left your area. If he has, then Eaen and I will be ready in case he comes here."

General George Patton would have been so proud of this boy.

Pretending he hadn't stunned me like he'd flattened my head with a rubber mallet, I went logical and offered to explain how my phone worked so they could answer it.

Before we left for campus, we took another precaution by turning the house into a cave as best we could. We hung blankets across the windows so no one could see Armand and Eaen inside.

"Nae and I will be back by noon, then we'll take things from there. I was thinking maybe a drive somewhere, where you two could see more people." Eaen had been right about standing our ground, so we may as well continue with our original plan to get the wolf-men comfortable around people. Besides, there was a second motive. If Rand didn't step up to the proverbial plate to help us, then they were going to have to kill Hersey. The wolf-men would have to do it as humans, and unless they learned to keep their nerves tightly wrapped, that wasn't going to happen.

"Good thinking, Porcupine. We will see you soon."

I clasped them both in a good-bye hug, and Nae did the same. I loved them, for shit's sake, and leaving them was twisting my heart. I headed for the door before I got teary and ditched my classes.

* * * *

The drive to campus was relatively quiet, as Nae and I were lost in our own thoughts. We knew we'd see Jeff that morning for Crandall's class, and I wasn't sure what was going to happen. Obviously, we needed to be ready for any stunt he pulled, but I also had to keep my head on my shoulders should Luna's gift decide to present itself.

"If it does, Nae, leave me on the ground, okay."

"Don't be ridiculous, Ken. I'm not leaving you anywhere."

"I'm just saying, if you have to—"

"No. We're mated, remember. We're in this together. God, I really love hearing that. You know, that *we're mated.*" Nae squirmed in her seat and smiled devilishly, as though she was eating the best chocolate cake on the planet.

178

I laughed. "Yeah, I know." I kissed her hand as we cruised along the back roads. "Me, too."

We drove on without saying more, as if we didn't want to pollute the atmosphere in the car with any more talk of Jeff or Hersey, and when we pulled into the parking lot we scanned for The Bear's car without uttering a word. He was parked in his usual spot, but didn't get out. Nae gave my hand a final squeeze before she exited the Subaru.

When I came around the nose, I refrained from putting my arm around my woman. No point in swirling a stick in a beehive. If Jeff was watching us, we'd give him no reason to go ballistic. Somehow, I still had to make it to class. The semester was winding down fast, and I was teetering on the edge of failure given the number of classes I'd been ditching. To repeat another semester just to get my degree? Yeah, well, I dreaded it more than the buzz that exploded in my skull.

We waited in the lobby until Jeff made his appearance, and then went into the classroom with him not far behind. At least I wouldn't have to call the house yet. I stole a peek at him sitting in his usual spot.

Christ, the guy looked like he'd just stepped out of a barber's shop, all clipped neat and fresh. Which churned my stomach, because his appearance didn't jibe with the desperate calls he'd made to Naomi's cell. Plus, as if I might've harbored doubts, the itch spread its tingling fingers to my spine.

Focus, Ken.

I was missing something I was supposed to be noticing. But what? Was it the fact The Bear was spic and span? I pretended to drop my pen so I could get a look at his feet.

Yep, he had on those boots, but I'd already gotten the jolt for those, so I didn't think that was it. *What else, man? Think.* I had to figure it out before the buzz did it for me. I had to get through this class.

Then, as I returned to the upright position it hit me, and I dropped my pen again for another peek.

G.I. Joe was a fashion designer, because The Bear wore camouflage pants for the first time since I'd known him. He was going Rambo, and that meant we were up against someone who hadn't fully packed his picnic basket. The buzz halted its progression between my shoulder blades and eased in intensity.

I'd solved the riddle. While I scratched at the back of my neck, I sent a silent thanks to the red wolf for her gift, especially since I'd finally figured out how to wield the damned thing.

Nae bumped my shin and mouthed the word *quiz*.

Of course, we were having a quiz, because I liked my shit piled high.

I wasn't exactly prepared for it, and I knew Nae wasn't either, but at least the subject matter was what we'd just gone through the week before. It wouldn't be pretty, but we could pass it. I shoved my notebook into my bag and pushed it under my seat with my heel. Okay, ready. I sent an encouraging wink to Nae, and went to work as soon as the quiz landed on my desk.

Fill-ins. Crandall liked her fill in the blank quizzes. It gave her a good idea as to who knew the answers and who was stabbing with guesses. Smart, especially since she used it as a tool, not a weapon. I filled in the blanks, waited for Nae to finish, then we turned in our papers together and left the room.

I squashed my woman to me as soon as we were in the lobby.

"I got another visit from Luna."

Nae kept her arms around me while she asked about it.

I walked toward the exit like Frankenstein with her hanging off me. It was good for a laugh, which helped to blow off some of the pressure. "I'll tell you on the way to the car."

Nae slid free, put her feet on the floor, and tugged on my hand. "Come on, I'm anxious to hear. You weren't looking so hot for a while there, so I figured something was up."

I filled her in as we made our way outside, right down to how the buzzing had ceased.

"That's good then, isn't it? I mean, as long as you find out what causes it."

"Yep. Except we've got a stickier situation."

"Ken! Mr. Rickey!"

Nae and I froze in our tracks, and I took a stabilizing breath before I turned around to face the body belonging to that voice. *Hersey.* He had his hand up as if I was a cab to be hailed.

"We have a meeting tonight, at my place, to discuss the upcoming trip. I'd like it if you'd be there."

My answer flopped from my mouth without a care. "No."

Hersey stopped as if my one word answer was a command, and I could see his body prepare for his attack. He drew his shoulders together and braced his legs.

What was that I'd said about a stick and a beehive? I re-phrased my answer, even though my guts wrenched at the thought of leaving Nae alone with Sylvester Stallone lurking. "No, I can't. Not tonight. Tonight's not good. I've got some time now, before my next class, though."

Hersey squinted as if he was thinking about my offer. "Sure, Ken. Come to my office," he said, and turned on his heel, fully expecting me to follow right along like a good dog. The bastard. He knew I would, that I had to, especially since he'd already ceded to my request.

"Call the house," I whispered as an aside to Nae, who'd decided on her own to come with us. As we passed the classroom we'd just exited, I caught a glimpse of Jeff hunched over his quiz. Good, he was still occupied.

But we still needed to warn Eaen and Armand. Not only would we lose contact with The Bear because of this meeting with Hersey, but we also didn't share the next class with him. It was the only one on the entire schedule, and for most of the semester, it had been a slice of heaven because I'd gotten Nae all to myself. And the rest of the class, of course, but who cared about that. At least Jeff wasn't there palavering over his property.

But now it was a disadvantage, and the wolf-men needed the heads up.

"Tell them about the buzzing," I added. "They'll want to know."

She veered off to the ladies' room for privacy, and I continued on with Hersey. But the separation was the peeling of my skin, and I wouldn't be able to fully concentrate on Hersey until Nae came back unharmed.

He didn't speak until we were in his office and he'd made himself comfortable at his desk. "I'm glad you're on board," he said, all smug and pleased with himself. I didn't bother answering him, but he continued as if it didn't matter.

"First, I was going to tell everyone at the meeting tonight that the June third date is still a go. The plane is set to drop us off where it did last year." His smug expression disappeared behind his clouded glare. Yep, he was twisting my balls over my James Bond maneuver. We'd be flying over the lake that had become the watery tomb for his lost research.

I continued to keep my mouth shut, while he continued to open his.

"I'm still going to use the traps since it's easier on the subjects than chemical immobilization. I know how to restrain a wolf safely so no one gets harmed, and I want to go over that with the group."

I almost laughed in his face, and would have if my guts weren't sinking. I could picture Hersey now, trying to handle one of his subjects, one of the wolf-people, who weren't ordinary wolves. They'd kill him for sure, and that was what sent my humor into a nosedive. There would be witnesses who would watch as Hersey got mauled to death by a wolf. And then?

And then the real fun would begin. I feigned interest in Hersey's paperweight so he wouldn't see me grimace, and contemplated how hard I'd have to bean him with it to knock him unconscious. He yakked on as if I was all ears and agog with his ideas. "Also, I've decided to go ahead and freeze-brand the cubs, and insert the abdominal implants, after all. Ear tags just don't last, and I only want to use the collars on the adults."

I was so glad we had decided to kill him before he got up north, unless Rand could do something less drastic to stop him. Although, Rand hadn't done anything yet to thwart the bastard. Granted, it had only been a day, but still, maybe we should just kill him and get this mess over with.

"Is that it?" Anger edged my voice like a sharp blade. I knew it did, but I couldn't stop it from seeping throughout my body and manifesting itself on my tongue.

Hersey eyeballed me closely.

Thank the blessed chariots of Heaven Nae arrived at that moment to rescue the situation, and slam the book shut on Hersey's visual inquisition. And our conversation.

"Ah, Miss Foss, how are you today?" His expression shifted like a record in a jukebox as he rose out of his chair, like he hadn't just been talking about mutilating the beings I cared about.

Naomi never let on if she knew anything. "I'm fine, Professor Hersey. Are you finished with Ken? We've got another class in a few minutes." Sweet Nae with her extrasensory perception.

"Of course. And Ken? If you plan to miss meetings with the rest of the group, I advise you to drop in to see me a few times a week."

He was a mother fucker. A goddamned screw turner.

"Sure, *Professor.* I'll be sure to do just that."

I left his office without a word of good-bye.

* * * *

"What in God's name did he say to you? You were gripping that paperweight so tight your knuckles are still white." She exaggerated, of course. My knuckles were flowing with blood just fine, as was the rest of me. As a matter of fact, I was so enraged by what Hersey had said it felt like my blood was boiling under my skin, and sweat prickled between my shoulder blades to prove it.

Even the God-awful buzzing kicked itself up a notch.

"I got in touch with Armand and Eaen. They'll be on the lookout until we get back." She glanced around when I headed for the stairwell. "Where are we going?"

"The back way." I kept hold of her hand like she was a valuable jewel, rubbing my thumb across her knuckles as if to polish them. "We've lost track of The...Jeff, and I don't trust him when I can't see him. Hell, I don't trust him when I can see him."

Nae giggled, which worked miracles on easing my murderous intentions, and helped to quiet Luna's buzz back to its persistent itch. I think Nae noticed too, because she kept giving me coy, little smiles to distract me.

"You can call him The Bear if you want, I really don't mind. It suits him actually." She grinned playfully, squeezing her fingers to mine.

I leaned in to steal a healthy sniff of her neck, that ultra-soft curve of skin from her shoulder to just behind her ear, where her scent of snow radiated. Man, I loved how she smelled.

She giggled and squirmed like it tickled, and I grew hard for her right there in the goddamned hallway. Of course, she noticed, and grabbed my shirt as she pushed her back up against the wall, pulling me along with her.

I clamped my mouth onto hers, and she yielded with a hungry pass of her tongue along mine, her fingers coiling through my hair. Automatically, I grinded my hips against hers to stroke the sweet aching of my balls, and her leg curled behind me to pull me closer so I could grind harder.

Hallway sex definitely qualified as shit I saw coming, but did anyway. But I couldn't let it get that far. Mainly, this wasn't the house with only Eaen and Armand as witnesses. This was the goddamned corridor on campus. Second, I really couldn't miss this class. One more absence and I'd most likely fail it.

I backed off, actually managing to peel myself off Nae. Who was panting, I might add, and not only looking revved with her bruised lips, but smelled divine. Like I should gobble her up. Screw where we were.

"What?" Nae dripped deprivation. "Come back."

Oh, yes. One's mate should never have to wear such a forlorn expression.

"No, Nae," I growled instead, pinning her with my stare alone. "Not now." *Holy Christ, I can smell how ready she is.*

I stepped back and stuck my hand up like a traffic cop, as much to stay myself as her. "No."

"You don't want me?" She teased, playing the wounded coquette.

I caved, and crushed her to me, sliding my chin over her head the way I did when we slept. Naomi folded into me, like melted chocolate to a spoon.

"Nae, not here. Please, Christ, not here. I've got to pass this class." I pulled away to gaze down at her.

"Sorry about that," she lowered her eyes.

"Yeah, well. You gotta know I'm always about one breath away from making love to you. At all times. *Always*, every freakin' minute."

Nae's pleasure spread across her blushing cheeks.

"You're my mate, Nae. *Mine*. And I love the tar out of you. But you've got to keep a tight rein on me, all right? Help me graduate here."

Nae took a couple of deep breaths, then peered up at me. "Are you ready for class, then?"

It was my turn to blush red. "Not yet."

Her eyes drifted downward, then she let loose a taunting smirk. "Oh."

"Yeah. *Oh.*" I needed a minute to get a hold of myself, and snagged Nae's wrist to drag her into the empty computer lab. I could call Rand while we were in there, give my brain something else to think about besides the curvaceous woman with me.

Naomi settled into one of the rolling chairs after handing me her cell phone. I dug Rand's card from my pocket and punched in his number.

He picked up halfway through the first ring.

"Yeah?"

"It's Ken. From the college. You remember?"

"Of course." He sounded anxious, like he'd straightened to attention.

"You said to call if I needed anything."

"Yeah, kid. Are you all right?" Like I was going to tell him anything before Eaen had a crack at him.

"Yeah, but that's not why I'm calling. We need you to come back to the house again."

There was an ocean of silence on the other end, then Rand let out a long breath. "Yeah, okay. When?"

"Tonight, around eight. It should be dark enough by then so no one will see us."

"*Christ.*" He knew what I meant, that I wanted him showing up in his wolf form. I heard him re-adjust his grip on the phone. "You're sure you're all right, though? Not feeling odd or anything?"

Aside from the constant buzzing in my skull? "No, I'm good. You'll come?"

"Yeah, I'll be there."

"Good. And Rand? Thanks for your help yesterday."

"No problem, kid. I'll see you tonight."

He cut off the call before I'd clapped Nae's cell phone shut, and I could well imagine the thoughts running through his head. I'd asked him to meet two other wolves, which could be dangerous. But, I got the impression a guy like Rand could take care of himself. It was Eaen I worried about.

Well, at least the phone call did what I'd wanted it to do. It distracted my tightened balls from Nae so I could sit through class without wanting to drive them flush against her wet heat.

Shit. I couldn't go there again. I raked my hand across my head, which made Nae laugh as she snagged my hand.

"Come on, Porcupine, let's get you graduated."

I went with her because there was nowhere else on earth I'd rather be at that very moment than with my mate.

* * * *

The car ride to Calais had been a real kicker, with Eaen and Armand managing to hold their human forms as we drove around the city, even though we had to keep the windows down so they didn't roast us out of the vehicle. But I was proud of them, and in spite of Eaen asserting himself as our pack leader, I still felt like an indulgent uncle.

We stopped along Route 9 so they could check out the Moosehorn National Wildlife Refuge, which gave them a chance to doff their human attire and shake their fur after trying so hard to keep it contained during their urban tour.

Before they took off, I warned them to be extra cautious. A number of people liked to visit the refuge, and even though it was the off-season, there could still be humans hiking about.

"And," I wagged my finger like an admonishing adult, "if you kill something, do your best to hide the evidence."

Eaen threw his hefty bulk upwards, pushing his enormous paws against my shoulders and knocking me to the ground, where he proceeded to press his open jaw all over my body.

"Cut it out," I begged, laughing, practically screaming like a girl. "It tickles! I give, I give!"

The black wolf stepped off, his bushy tail fanning behind him and his ears tugged back.

I got up, brushing the dirt off my jeans as I threatened retaliation. "Laugh, turd, but I'll pay you back."

He didn't wait to see how, but bounded off toward the woods with Armand loping closely behind him. Nae and I settled onto the hood of the car to wait anxiously for their safe return.

An orange sun sat on the edge of the tree line by the time Eaen and Armand, who toted a deer haunch in his jaws, returned.

"Well, dress Jesus in a bunny suit. Look." I pointed in the direction of the two wolves for Nae. We slid off the hood of the Subaru and trotted over to our providers, where we knelt to greet them. Armand dropped the deer's leg in front of Naomi, then lapped under her chin. Nae giggled her delight, and understood the importance of his gift right off.

"Thank you, Armand. Eaen. Ken and I will be well nourished tonight." She scooped it up as if it was a gift basket with pretty bows instead of a bloody shank from a carcass. We piled into the car behind her, and motored for home. Eaen and Armand crashed out in the back seat, their butts touching.

"Their great, huh, Nae?" I said as I peered into the rear view mirror to steal a peek at the sleeping wolves.

She smiled, and heaved a contented sigh. "Yeah. That was really thoughtful, you know, providing meat for the breeding pair."

My heart swelled in my chest despite the implications. Technically, Nae and I were the breeding pair in this pack, even though Eaen should have been, according to wolf protocol. Which had my thoughts leaping between two topics. A, Nae and I were breeding because neither one of us had even remotely attempted to have safe sex. And B, the wolf-people veered off slightly from the normal behaviors of wolves. Allowing subordinate couples to mate was one way in which their human component asserted itself.

I wracked my brain to think of other things that made them human. If it could help the wolf-people adapt to our civilization it would be a weapon in their arsenal, even if they only used it defensively. I mean, Rand existed, so there was something credible about the idea.

The ringing of my cell phone jangled me from my musings. I recognized the number on the caller I.D. and flipped the phone to my ear.

"Hi, Mom."

"Hi, Baby. You've been too busy to call home?"

"Sorry, Mom. Yeah, you know—the end of the year and stuff." I couldn't lie to her, so played it vague.

"Well, you're father and I are coming for the graduation, but why haven't you sent the rest of the family their invitations?"

I'd completely forgotten about that. Any big deal like a graduation or wedding meant relatives expected to get invited even if they weren't planning to attend.

"Sorry, I forgot. It's no big deal, right? You can just tell everyone I've been so busy?"

"Kenny." I could hear her disappointment for her little man. "Yes. They'll be upset, but they'll understand." She spoiled me. "But what time is this graduation? You're father and I are coming the day before, but it's still good to know."

I palmed the phone, taking my eyes off the road to glance at Nae, who was watching me as I talked to my mom. "What time is graduation, Nae?"

"One o'clock, I think," she nodded, her blonde hair swishing ever so slightly.

"One o'clock, I think," I parroted into the phone.

"You *think*, Kenny?" She sighed into her end of the receiver. "You're father and I will be staying with you, so is there anything we need to bring extra? Bedding, towels?"

Shit. I was going to have to tell her I had roommates who didn't share the rent. But, not just then. "Ah, no, I think we're good. Listen, Mom, I've got to go, okay?"

"All right, dear. I love you, and you're father says to tell his Kenny-man he loves him, too."

"I love you, Mom. Tell Dad I love him, too." I snapped the cell phone shut, and slid it onto the dash.

Naomi wore a teasing smile, and I blushed red so hard I could feel the burn flush my cheeks.

"What? They're good parents. What can I say?"

"I think it's cute," she replied, still wearing that grin.

"Yeah, well." I hoped like hell she hadn't heard my father's nickname for me.

"At least they're nice," she said in a quiet voice, her smile vanishing like the sun behind a bank of clouds. She stared at the glove box.

I treaded very lightly. "Are they coming? Your family to graduation, I mean?"

She flashed a frightened, yet defiant look. "No."

I didn't pry. If she wanted to talk about them she would. Hell, she'd bottled her terrible secret for four years, she probably wasn't going to start spewing the toxic shit until she felt safer with me, and I'd give her all the time she needed for that. Apparently, she needed about fifteen seconds.

"They don't even know where I live. They have nothing to do with my being in college in the first place, so I'm sure as hell not going to invite them to one of the most important days of my life." She spit out some of the poison, and I reached for her hand, squeezed her chilly fingers. Then glanced into the rear view mirror again and looked straight into the blonde wolf's wrathful scowl. He'd absorbed every word, every pained inflection.

"Well," I turned my attention back to the road before we careened into the woods. "My parents, as you know, love the heck out of you, Nae. They're going to be thrilled when they find out we're mated. Except I won't announce it like that. My mother would have a conniption and tell me she raised me to treat women better than that." I flashed her a conspiratorial grin and Nae's smile came back, if a little tremulously.

"Really? I didn't know they wanted us…"

"Hell, Nae. They've known since I met you that I've loved you. Of course they'll be ecstatic to find out we're living together." I kissed the fingers wrapped in mine. Her relief was tangible; I felt it in the heat of her hand.

I peered up again into the rear view mirror, and offered the blonde wolf a sympathetic smile. He lowered his lids over his yellow eyes in silent thanks, and Eaen, whose great, furred head rested against the back of the seat, was very much awake and listening, too. So be it. We trusted them, and Nae, I was sure, never would have said anything about her family if she hadn't. I chalked that up to her feeling secure with her new pack, and that warm, fuzzy feeling visited me again. The four of us were a family. As motley as we were, we forged a unit built on love and trust, and I sent my own silent thanks to the wolf-people up north, who really had bestowed upon me a gift beyond measure.

Chapter Ten

We pulled into the drive a little before eight o'clock. It wasn't fully dark, but the gloaming was rapidly deepening and the stars were twinkling on like they had individual light switches. We'd be blanketed in the cover of darkness soon enough, and Nae joined us in our vigil on the porch once she'd put the deer leg in the fridge.

I took Nae's hand so she'd plunk down beside me, then turned my attention to Eaen. "Will you be able to tell if he's near?"

"Yes, Kenrickey. If he approaches honestly, upwind, then we will know."

I didn't bother asking what would happen if Rand approached dishonestly. I knew we'd all three kick his ass and hand it to him on a platter. But I couldn't help but be nervous for Eaen, who would be the one, as our pack leader, to initially face the other wolf-man.

"You're all right with this, Eaen? I mean, we can call this off, it's not too late."

Eaen's upper lip curled ever so slightly. "No, Porcupine. We have more questions for this other wolf-man than we have answers. We need to know why he is as he is, especially if it will benefit our loved ones back home. If he can help us, then we should listen to what he has to say."

Right. Rand was physically different from the wolf-people up north, and we needed to find out how such a thing was possible. I mean, because of it he was able to mingle with humans without generating curiosity, or revulsion. He blended with the enemy, and that wasn't a camouflage we could ignore.

190

Kenrickey

Eaen pushed his face up into the sky and sniffed. "He is here."

Armand slipped into his fur faster than you can say *fur*. We all stood up, moving like the pack we were to the western corner of the yard where the house would block anyone's view, especially if those *anyone's* decided to spy from the ridge.

A gray wolf paced where the alders bordered the lawn, marking the beginning of the thicker woods. Once we noticed him, he stepped cautiously forward, as if the ground itself burned his paws.

Good. He was being subordinate, he wasn't here to cause trouble. Eaen, who had been standing upright on two legs, folded downward into his wolf form, and trotted toward the other wolf with his tail stiffly erect and his ears pricked forward.

Seeing him so imposingly confident squeezed my chest till I felt I'd burst with pride. I felt honored to be counted as one of his pack members. Although, I didn't have time to savor the splendor of it because Armand pushed against my legs, forcing me forward. I wasn't to be a bystander in welcoming this strange wolf. He would have to be subjected to all of us, including Naomi.

And yet, Armand's insistence I get closer had its other meaning. If things didn't go well, he and I would be right there to drive home our message. No one messed with our united pack.

But our caution wasn't necessary. As soon as Eaen got within ten feet of the gray wolf, Rand shifted back into his human form, and spread his naked self on the new, spring grass.

Definitely no tricks. He'd come with honest intentions.

Still though, Eaen wasn't going to be cavalier about the introduction of another wolf within our ranks. He straddled Rand with tightly reined ferocity, letting him know in no uncertain terms that the black wolf would be happy to rip his throat wide open if he meant harm. Rand would be subjugated while he moved within our familial circle.

To his credit, he remained flat on his back while the rest of us tested him. And I'm no chauvinist, but when it was Nae's turn I hovered close, just in case. So did Armand, whose lip curled up and down, revealing the full length of his fangs should Rand change his mind about being dominated by our female. Nae never let on whether she was put out by our over protectiveness, or not. She smacked her hand to Rand's bare chest, shoving him harder to the ground, if that were possible.

God, she was beautiful, and not to be messed with. I thought of Suma just then, Grane's gorgeous white wolf. She and Nae would have been good friends, I imagine.

Eaen waited to shift until we were finished, but didn't offer his hand to help the newcomer to his feet. As was proper, Rand could get himself off the ground. Carefully. I knew that part, because I'd been there myself. No moving quick, and keep your eyes averted.

Rand knew his wolf etiquette, and didn't even stand fully upright, but stayed crouched as he talked. His excitement was tangible.

"I am honored to be welcomed, black wolf."

"You may call me Eaen. The blonde wolf is Armand, and you already know Kenrickey and our Naomi."

Eaen stood magnificently in his decorum. He shined in his authority, a proud wolf with ample reasons to be so. Rand lowered his short-cropped, gray head, his shoulders softening in respectful esteem, and kept them that way even as Eaen guided us toward the deeper woods, away from spying eyes should The Bear and Hersey decide to pay us another visit.

Walking, too, gave me the chance to assess Rand, to check him out physically. He was lithe and muscular like the wolf-people I knew, but he didn't boast many scars. Apparently, his life amongst the human population was a little cushier, not quite as violent. Which said a lot about Eaen and Armand. They may have been young, but their scars and the sagacity in their eyes told a different story. They were seasoned wolf-men. Untamed.

Eaen led us to a small glade where the light of the fresh moon penetrated keenly, illuminating the darkness around us, yet casting the rest of the forest into deeper shadow. His choice had dual purpose—his human pack members would be able to see better, and the little clearing gave us space to fight if we needed it.

Rand glanced around too, taking his own assessment. He nodded slightly, as if approving of the young wolf-man's choice.

Eaen ignored the subtle compliment. "You have questions, gray wolf. Ask them."

Rand crouched into a comfortable position, obviously intent on talking rather than fighting. He'd lowered his body beneath all of ours to show he meant no harm, but the occasional sharp tic of his jaw belied his total ease. "I do. But first, I must say again how deeply honored I am to meet you. I've never before seen pure, direct descendants of Gor. We've thought you wiped out all these years."

"As you can see, Rand, we are alive and well."

Descendants of Gor? Who was Gor?

"He is our forebear, Kenrickey. The first wolf to walk upright as human."

So, the wolf-people have an oral history.

Rand glanced from our pack leader to me, noticing the silent communication between Eaen and myself, yet he said nothing about it. Instead, he wanted to talk about his reasons for coming, to tell more of what he knew, and Eaen ceded the floor, so to speak, by crouching on his heels. The new wolf-man took his cue.

"Gor was the original, Ken, and retained his wolf-traits even while walking on two feet. Just like Eaen and Armand, who carry untainted blood in their veins. You can see the obvious differences between us."

None of us resisted the urge to glance at the young wolf-men with their dis-positioned thumbs. Rand had our attention.

"You have heard of the Schism?"

"Not in detail," Eaen confessed.

"Then you are not firstborn." Rand thought out loud, but waved his hand as if casting his comment aside. "That's not important, other than to tell me that your pack has maintained the old traditions." Rand chewed his bottom lip, contemplating a bit before continuing.

"I know, black wolf, it isn't your place to learn all of the history, but would you like to?" The older wolf-man bowed his head, deferring to the wisdom of the old traditions. It was up to Eaen to decide whether to remain loyal to his upbringing, or to take a step away.

"It will not be the first time I have had to break with custom. For the sake of our loved ones, Rand, I will hear the story."

He didn't elaborate on why he'd had to betray his old beliefs, but it still seemed as if a piece of his innocence slid from his shoulders, that he bore the weight of disregarding the past for the sake of the future.

"All right. But forgive me my poor handling of our legends. I am no storyteller." Rand finally looked up at us then, offering us a shy smile. Gone was the hard glint of the predator's gaze, replaced instead by the dreamy countenance of a man who believed and treasured his peoples' history.

"You know already the tales of Gor and his mate, so I won't go back that far, but only want to remind you of the reason why he'd been compelled to change in the first place."

"War with humans," Eaen supplied, the slightest bass of a growl deepening his answer.

Rand nodded. "Right. War with humans. One that has never ended because of their numbers. They continue to slaughter us and our brethren, even though we ceased our bloodied retaliation ages ago and chose the relative peace of the deeper forests. Which is why the Schism occurred. One brother believed that the only way to bring about the end of the murders was to take Gor's initiative a step further. He felt hiding in plain sight of the enemy was the only way to end the killing of our loved ones. He sought assimilation."

I could see where his story was going, and could understand the rupture. Hell, *I* felt strongly about Alec's pack staying hidden, so I could well imagine the turmoil the rift in beliefs would have caused. Yet, obviously it had still happened.

"So, the one brother left with those who would follow him, and the other stayed in the forests."

Eaen struck his deep, brown stare on Rand. "Aron succeeded."

If the revelation gave him hope, Eaen wasn't showing it. Nor was he letting on that any of what Rand was saying was a big surprise. Surely, he'd wondered before if this Aron had been able to co-exist with the human population.

"Yes." Rand now directly addressed Eaen, as if the rest of us faded into the background. "Too well, in fact. Neither brother won the war in the end. The humans are still victorious, and both sides of the Schism are faced with extinction. Our side is becoming human, and yours? By now, many of you must be reverting to wolf."

Eaen sat quiet, his eyes reflecting nothing of his thoughts.

I took his cue and kept my mouth shut, even as the memory of the three wolf-men Grane had killed popped up unbidden in my mind. There were probably packs roaming the wilderness Rand had no clue about. Which explained his interest in Hersey, who was committed to documenting the last of the wild wolves.

If other biologists stumbled on the wolf-people like Hersey had done? "Holy shit." I lost my resolve to keep my trap shut and stood up, my fists clenched as I braced off to accuse Rand. "Your pack funds Hersey. You need him to find wolf-people like Eaen and Armand." Who, by the way, bristled their support behind me.

Rand had the good sense to drop to his hands and knees so he could lower his shoulders even more. He'd remain submissive so long as he was outnumbered.

"No," he flatly denied it. "Honestly, we thought Gor's true descendants dead, or irrevocably reverted to wolf. It's you we seek, Ken. We search for those like you."

Was there a spotlight beaming down from the treetops? Because suddenly I felt like a rare bug pinned under a microscope.

"Me? There's nothing special about me." I stepped back, away from Rand and his claim, disconcerted enough to forget I'd just challenged him.

"Quite the opposite." Rand tilted his head toward Eaen. "If I may continue, I can explain."

My brother nodded, and Naomi slipped her hand into mine. God, her touch was the anchor for my drifting balloon basket. I squeezed her fingers and let her pull me back to the ground to sit.

"Ken, you're the reason why I've come to Maine to follow-up on Professor Hersey's report. Yes, we fund his research, but it's to keep an eye over the shoulder of the enemy, if you will."

"Keep your enemies close," Armand provided, his yellow eyes shining. His reading of the *Art of War* was turning out to be an invaluable tool for the wolf-people, as he had most likely known.

Rand dipped his chin, an appreciative smirk gracing his lips. "Exactly, blonde wolf. Especially since our faction experienced another rift." Here, Rand grew still, and before he dropped his head to peer at the ground, I caught the shame watering his gray eyes.

"It turned out we assimilated all too well. Babes born who could not shift were sacrificed. For the good of the wolf-people, of course." His sneer told us how much that rankled. "Needless to say, there were some of us who were outraged, and fearful. The pregnant females lit out, risking exposure and death rather than face the certainty that our pack leaders would murder their human-born infants.

"But what the pack leaders hadn't foreseen was that a few of the human-born pups, once they'd reached their early twenties, started changing. They carried the wolf genes, they just took a while to catch up."

"And they looked human. Like you." Eaen narrowed his brown eyes.

"Yes. But the damage had been done. There are wolf-babes who were cached within the human population to keep them safe. As long as they remain human, all is fine. But if they shift in front of human witnesses?"

"Then we are exposed." Armand stated the obvious, and I felt his worry physically grip my skin, like it had suddenly shrunk and didn't fit my body.

"Which is why," Rand went on, "we keep tabs on the biologists. Anything they hear, we hear. It's worked for us so far."

"And our Kenrickey?" Eaen moved imperceptibly toward me, as if to protect his pack mate, or offer comfort. And I'd take it, every scrap he wanted to dole out, right along with Nae's share. I mean, I have to admit, Rand's story was creeping me out. What the hell did he mean when he said I'd been cached? Like I was buried treasure that time and the elements had eventually exposed?

My hand automatically scraped across my scalp, spiking my hair like the porcupine I was. Eaen shot me a brown eyed wink and a warm grin. Both hit me like a heartfelt hug, and my body gravitated toward my pack leader like he was my hero. God, I was a sap.

"He's definitely wolf." Rand's seriousness sat as heavy as frigid air, sucking the warmth right out of me before I had time to enjoy it.

I choked out a laugh, combed my hand across the top of my head again. "Come on. Really, guys." I attempted to smile, but I knew it came off more like a nervous grimace. Seriously, I had thought it would be cool to have fur and four legs, but Rand's story was making it seem possible.

"We were told by our elder wolf-women that it could be so. We have been watching our Porcupine, initiating him in our ways, just in case."

"And?" Rand scratched his jaw with his normal looking hand.

"He shows signs." Eaen didn't elaborate, thank Jesus. The last thing I wanted to hear was a litany of my bumblings through the woods as we'd hunted. Christ, I'd made more mistakes than a typewriter with missing keys. Naturally wolf? Uh-uh.

"Your elders know of the Schism, then?"

Eaen grew rigid, then very still as a low rumble lifted his lip off his teeth. "Your questions lose their respect, gray wolf."

"Shit." Rand sank back to the ground. "I am sorry. Really, I'm not the one who should handle this. I'm a tracker. I'm meant to find and retrieve our new wolves before they can be seen by human eyes, not navigate a truce with Gor's true bloodline." The last part of his confession dripped reverent, his bare shoulders softening with his regret.

Eaen veered us back on track, away from Rand's certainty I was like him, and never once revealed his interest in any kind of truce. The guy was a born leader. "What of your purpose with Hersey, who plans to invade our territory?"

"I've got a call into headquarters. I should hear back from them soon."

"Crap, Rand." I interrupted. "Don't you guys have a hotline or something? This is urgent shit. Hersey's already nosing around my place, and we won't let him get north, not when he's talking tattoos and radio chips." I started pacing, too juiced up by the adrenaline shooting into my bloodstream. I was sweating, too, and stuck my fingers to the base of my skull, where the itch had revved up its intensity.

"With all due respect, Ken, this isn't the first time we've handled something like this."

Was that a little disrespect? I shot him a withering stare, and wouldn't you know it, he stiffened, like he wanted me to dish out an ass-kicking.

We never got that far. The black wolf descended, his sharp teeth pressed so hard to Rand's throat that one more ounce of pressure would have brought forth a gushing of blood. Eaen snarled his warning, the menace of it unmistakable.

Rand and I both backed off. Well, Rand had little choice, unless he wanted his windpipe to be hamburger.

Armand, who had shifted just as quick as Eaen to his wolf form, stepped up beside Nae. She curled her fingers into his ruff and closed her fist. For ballast, apparently, because she fired off on our guest.

"You get it, Randall Wolfe? Back off from Ken. We've got more important things to deal with than your pissing contest with a—" Nae cast a perplexed look in my direction before turning back to Rand. "A possible new recruit. Get your head on straight, and help us out here."

I almost pumped my fist into the air, I was so cheered by the sight of her. Her hazel eyes glittered hard as diamonds in the moonlight, and damn if I didn't smell her, as if her blood heated to waft her scent.

Rand answered by turning into a cooked noodle under Eaen's fangs.

"All right, then." I sat down on my heels, hoping everyone else would take my cue and settle down with me. We had to keep our cool about this, and my outburst hadn't helped. We needed Rand on our side, regardless of the Schism thing.

The black wolf gave the man some space to get back on his knees.

"I'm sorry. Sometimes it's hard to overcome the instincts, you know?" Rand offered a sheepish grin that morphed into regret. So, it seemed for all the headway the wolf-men of Aron's pack had made, they still had their moments where the wolf rode the human side of them too hard. Just like Gor's descendants, the wolf was the stronger animal within the blood.

"Apology accepted, but not given twice," Eaen growled. Jesus, but these wolf-people shifted too damned fast. I'd totally missed the moment when Eaen reduced the number of his legs.

Rand dipped his chin, chagrined and accepting of the alpha wolf's warning. "Fair enough, black wolf. I get the trouble you're in, and I swear, we'll take care of it. Hersey won't get north, especially given the recent turn in his research practices. He won't be tattooing or freeze branding anyone," he spit the last of his promise from between his pressed lips. Rand didn't like the idea of permanently marking the wolf-people any more than we did, at least.

"Thank you, Rand. Our packs owe you a debt of kindness. Perhaps

198

in the form of future meetings with the four of us here?"

Well, no shit. With one sentence, the four of us had been forged for a future together. One with purpose, a mission to ensure the safety of those up north for all time, and I liked that idea an awful lot. I studied the ground so I didn't show off my shit-eating grin, because one look at the rest of my new pack, and I'd lose it, I'd start quivering like a puppy with a peanut-butter Kong.

Without even looking at him, I could hear Rand's excitement, too. "Yes. Absolutely, Eaen. But, I'll be honest. Like I told you earlier, we've experienced another rupture in the ranks. We're still dealing with that while we search for those like Ken *and* keep track of the various wolf studies that are constantly cropping up. Frankly, we could use the manpower. It won't be easy." Rand extended his hand to shake on the deal.

Armand, Nae, and I moved to stand with Eaen, showing our support by literally standing behind him. Our pack leader reached out to grasp the hand of his history, and you'd have to be blind to miss the symbolism of their joined fists.

* * * *

The rest of our meeting with Rand wrapped up pretty quick after that. Eaen offered him the chance to stay with us while he remained in the area dealing with Hersey, but the gray wolf declined. With regret. The honest sincerity behind his refusal enlightened me yet again as to what, essentially, these wolf-people were. They were wolves, and more comfortable when they were literally packed. The more the merrier kind of thing.

Which I totally got, especially now that I shared a bed with three other people. There was something about the press of bodies, the vulnerability of falling asleep so close to others you trusted to watch out for you. I thought my delight of it had something to do with being an only child, but after the meeting with Rand, I wasn't so sure any more. Was I really turning into a wolf? I mean, now that I realized I didn't have to look like the wolf-people up north, the possibility seemed, well, probable.

And what about Nae, who blended in with Armand and Eaen so

seamlessly? Could she have been one of those poor infants cached within the human population, as well?

I looked up as she walked over from the kitchen, and held my arms out for her. We nestled into the couch with Eaen on the other end, and Armand ensconced in his favorite chair. We were denned in for the night, and the blankets hanging up on all the windows made it seem more so.

Surprisingly, I didn't feel the least bit closed in. I felt safe. Jeff and Hersey wouldn't be able to see inside, and I trusted Armand's and Eaen's senses to pick up on them if they ventured too close. I felt cozy, too. We'd eaten again, and were snuggled together in the living room.

We didn't read or study, but discussed Jeff. Now that we had someone currently dealing with Hersey, we could concentrate on the more immediate threat. We had to end The Bear's siege.

Although Luna's warning had us triple guessing our next steps, we had to carry our rebellion through. Waiting for the image she'd supplanted into my mind to become a reality wasn't an option any more. I kept my fingers crossed the buzzing in my head would at least help to steer us in the right direction.

"We could break into The Bear's apartment and steal those freakin' boots," I offered. Nae's scent tendrilled round me like those aroma therapy candles, and I nuzzled her nape while I talked. "Think about it. If Luna's image is a premonition, then stealing them would pretty much secure Eaen's and Armand's future, right? If there aren't any boots, then there can't be any dead wolves."

My idea was met with silence while the other three contemplated my logic.

"Or," I rubbed my cheek against her soft hair, "if we can't get his boots, we could go to the police for a protection order."

Nae shook her head. "Not an option. It would take too long, and they don't really work anyway." Her sad anger squished the blood right out of my heart, and had me hugging her closer. Armand left his chair to join us on the couch, to squeeze closer to Nae, too. Man, but she wound us tight.

She'd been hurt, a lot. Because how did Naomi know about cops and their worthless protection unless she knew about that sort of thing firsthand? If Eaen, Armand, and I ever got within smelling distance of her father, we'd wound him worse than anything he'd ever done to Nae.

"All right. No police or going to court." I no sooner ceded to that when Eaen spoke up with his plan. I looked over at a very serious and lethal wolf-man, who had one long, muscled arm stretched across the back of the couch, his brown eyes glinting with mischief.

"We wait in ambush," he purled, with just the right touch of peril for me to look at him twice. I'd actually forgotten how dangerous he was. "The next time The Bear comes into our territory, we drive him off so he will not do it again, or we kill him. It is what we do with other predators. There is no peaceful co-existence with them."

"Okay, here's the problem." Nae took a deep breath. She sighed, really, as she pulled out of my embrace to stand up. I didn't like her leaving my arms, and I sure as hell didn't like that look of remorse on her face, like she was already regretting what she was about to say. I sat up, and so did Eaen and Armand.

"Here's something none of you have considered."

We three sat forward on the couch, our full attention trained on the woman pacing a circle in front of us.

Naomi turned to face us and took another deep breath. "Here are the reasons why none of your ideas will work." She held up her index finger. "First, I don't think that god-awful itching of your skull, Ken, is some gift bestowed upon you by Luna. Second," she stuck up another finger, her anxiety ratcheting up along with it, before we could interrupt her. "You're turning into wolf whether you believe it or not, Ken. Have you seen yourself lately? Really taken a close look? You just ate a cold, raw deer leg, for God's sake."

Yeah, I had, even though Nae had fried some up for herself.

"Third, and the biggest reason of all."

She had our devoted attention as we inched toward the edge of the couch cushions.

"The reason you can see Eaen and Armand hanging dead beside Jeff's boots and his gun is because you are his victim, too. You can see your brothers' deaths because you're dying right along beside them. You are the third wolf he will shoot, Ken."

Well, there. Blow candied monkeys up my ass. I hadn't thought of that.

"So, if Luna did give you that buzz in your head to warn you, explain to me why it didn't go off when I showed up." Rhetorical, because she kept talking, and getting stiffer and steamier. "I'll tell you why. It's because she knew the role I would play. And if you three think that for another second I'm going to just sit back and let Jeff harm you, then you are all sorely mistaken. If I go back to him and pretend—"

"No!" We snarled as one fierce, negative force as we launched ourselves off the sofa. It wasn't even an option to put on the table for a vote. Nae was not going back to The Bear.

"Shit-can the idea, once and for all, Nae." I stepped up to her, and Eaen stiffened to his full height of six-foot-six hundred. Armand, Naomi's self-appointed protector, paced around us like a wolf on the end of his chain.

"No fucking way!" Whoops, I was losing it here, feeding off the energy of my brothers. "Do you freakin' see, Nae? Look at us, for Christ's sake, do you see what letting you go back would do? We'll hunt him down and kill him tonight with gladness in our hearts." I spread my arms wide to encompass the other two men in the room, who I should say, were holding it together about as well as I was.

Nae turned to solid ice and braced herself. She locked her stare on each of her boys, and managed to freeze us where we stood as her words slid through her clenched jaw. "No one *demands* I do anything," she hissed. "And if keeping you," she jabbed a finger at Armand, "and you," her talon found Eaen, "alive, then I will do whatever is necessary. No matter how many times you pin me to the floor."

Yowza. Wildcat in the room. The three of us stood there like frozen action figures, staring at the woman who confronted us, who had just sucked the clichéd wind from our sails with her scary logic.

What could I say to that, I ask? Which I did with my bewildered stare at the other two, who blinked back at me in dumfounded surprise.

"She is yours, Kenrickey." Eaen held his palms up in surrender, effectively turning all control over to the porcupine.

Thanks, man. I threw him a withering stare.

"Nae." My hand dug a path across the top of my head.

And then Naomi busted out laughing. We grinned nervously, unsure of the carnival ride she had us on. We chuckled uneasily, looking to each other for reassurances.

"Nae?" I swallowed the frog in my throat who liked to croak my mate's name.

She turned her hazel eyes to me, and they were shining and full of energy. But very far from green. Her kaleidoscopic eyes had turned gray.

"My boys," she held her arms out. "You are mine. You're me. Everything I do is with the three of you in my heart. The sacrifice I make *is* for our pack."

Now how could we argue with that?

Nae spoke on to her gawping, riveted audience. "My going back to The Bear keeps all of you safe. While I'm with him, I can get rid of those goddamned boots, and I can keep track of his whereabouts so he doesn't come sniffing around here. Then, once we've graduated, Ken, the four of us can high-tail it the hell out of here. We can start our lives together, helping the wolf-people without this threat from The Bear hanging over our heads."

We were defeated. Her plan was perfect, except for the part where her absence would leave holes blasted in our hearts.

I articulated a very eloquent speech, and said, "Nae." Already the blood was oozing from the gashes her words flayed across my heart. I folded onto the couch before my ass hit the floor.

Like some distorted nightmare, I watched as she walked over to her purse to pull out her cell phone. I heard her order a taxi, but my brain was numb and refused to send messages to the rest of me.

I wasn't alone in my paralysis. Eaen and Armand joined me on the couch, and we sat as if awaiting our executions. Long minutes stretched as our brains slogged through less rational arguments that couldn't counter Naomi's. Plus, my thoughts kept circling back to Nae's leaving, and each succeeding revolution stabbed deeper into my heart, until only one word surfaced in my brain.

No.

Headlights, diffused by the blanket covering the living room window, spread across the walls. Naomi gathered her purse and jacket and headed out the front door without even looking back.

No, no, no.

Armand's deep growl rippled through my body.

The chunk of a car door blasted like a bullet in my guts.

No, no, no, no no… "No!"

Finally, I found my fucking spine, my legs, and bolted for the front door that Nae, sniffling back tears, had just passed through.

"Naomi!" I shrieked at the empty doorway and burst through it, my soul sucking me toward the taillights of the taxi. The searing bodies of the wolf-men shoved me forward because my body was nothing, powerless as it fell into the chasm of utter loss.

"Naomi!" I dropped onto the driveway, and couldn't get up off the fucking dirt. I couldn't even fucking breathe.

"Nae!" My shrieks turned to howls I vomited to the night sky, but the guardian of my soul, my snowy day, didn't come back.

Chapter Eleven

I woke up because it hurt to breathe, and stared up at the stars as if my eyes were disconnected from my spirit. I gazed up at the Milky Way, as if the strings connecting me to life had been amputated, and I floated disjointedly. I did not feel the damp earth beneath my bare skin, as I knew I should.

"Porcupine."

Go away.

Ken. Tongue roll on the n with a full pause before the Rickey.

"Ooh, shit."

"Porcupine?"

I barely heard Eaen call my name over the thrum inside my skull.

Luna.

"I'm here."

"Kenrickey?" Eaen's dark head blocked the night sky from my view. "You are here," he said in answer to my mumblings to Luna. Which was what she'd wanted, I figured. To bring me back to the living. I felt warm hands encase my shoulders and then my body shook gently against the ground.

"Eaen."

"Yes, Porcupine?"

"Stop shaking me. I'm all right."

He crouched back onto his haunches, and once I'd turned my head away from the stars, I saw he wasn't alone. Armand crouched on his thickly muscled legs beside him. I grinned pathetically. "Hi, guys."

"Porcupine," they gushed in unison. "We worried, we did not know if you were going to live through—"

Eaen's face darkened as he cut off his words.

It was then the physical pain emerged, and grew as though my consciousness had awakened it. I had a spear in my chest skewering me to the ground, and it really did hurt to breathe. I hadn't been imagining it.

"Naomi?"

"She is gone, Brother." And the sorrow they conveyed from their lowered heads and sagging shoulders told me it was true. The agony I was feeling was loss.

I lay in pained silence a while longer, then finally took a shallow breath and spoke. "Where are we?"

"In the forest by the river," Armand answered solemnly. He, too, nursed a broken heart. Twice-fold he'd lost his sisters.

I sat up and crawled to him, and hugged him to me, my brother in life and grief. But, I couldn't even say I was sorry because I wasn't. I didn't regret bringing Nae into our lives. She was our sun and we orbited around her.

Oh, Christ-Jesus, how was I going to bear seeing her with him?

I crumpled around Armand and keened like an orphan. Eaen's taut stomach blanketed my back and we three huddled there in the forest by the river, until daylight came and pushed away the shadows.

* * * *

The day following Nae's departure, I drove the Subaru toward campus, yet couldn't say how. I had no recollection of the drive, other than the memory of blurry scenery in my peripheral vision.

Out of habit I looked for her in the parking lot as I pulled in, but she wasn't there. I stumbled to Hersey's class alone and occupied a chair. Naomi and The Bear never showed, and for that I was grateful, because I could no more wrest her from his arms than I could have forced her to stay with her pack the night before.

I shuffled to Hersey's office at his request when class was over.

"God, Ken, you look like hell."

I stared at him.

"Er," Hersey cleared his throat. "Well, then." He rubbed his hands together like he was cold, or nervous. "The reason I wanted to see you—"

"Stay the fuck away from my house."

He shut up, his guilt blooming on his cheeks.

The rush of blood to his face stirred me, awakened the predator within and I crept forward, my muscles shivering tensely, aching to hurt him. I stopped when our toes nearly touched, then followed my nose toward his neck, where his fear puffed in whiffs from his quickening pulse. I leaned back to lock his eyes with mine. "Come near my property again, I will personally cut your legs off and throw them in the river."

"I didn't—I wasn't—"

I arched an eyebrow at his stuttering lies.

"Ken?"

I raised my hand to point at his chest and the pussy flinched. "Don't ever beckon me to your office again, *Mark*. I'll come when I think it's necessary, and not before."

I turned my back on the pathetic crumb, and left the building without waiting for his reply.

* * * *

The days passed like an automated assembly line. I went to class, endured the crater that opened to swallow me whenever Nae walked in the room, and tuned out the constant static that had now taken up permanent residence at the base of my skull. Yet, it wasn't my only plague. I nursed a low grade fever, as if Naomi's leaving left me permanently ill.

Some nights I lay awake wondering why, now that Jeff was basically out of the picture, the buzzing hadn't diminished or gone away completely. Eaen and Armand could offer little insight or help, but agreed something wasn't right about the whole mess.

Why hadn't the fizzing erupted whenever I was in Hersey's office? Apparently, Luna hadn't been too worried about us succeeding at keeping the professor from their territory. She'd concentrated her powers on her little brothers' deaths.

Or, *our* deaths. Nae had most likely been right, that the reason for the buzzing had nothing to do with warning us. Perhaps, Luna had triggered my dormant wolf to life, and the buzzing was a symptom of my shifting. Looking back, I realized when it sparked to debilitating life, I was violently angry or would have been soon. So maybe my emotions were what triggered it.

Hell, it explained why the droning in my head continued even after Nae returned to The Bear. And now to stack more shit onto the heap, graduation was days away and my parents were due to arrive. Wonderful. I was sure they'd be thrilled to see me in my current state. I was an effing mess and I knew it. Christ, I was hunting with Eaen and Armand every night. And after we filled our stomachs, we went in search of coyotes with a vengeance, meting out our wrath and anguish on those poor, unsuspecting beasts.

We were merciless, and I was oblivious to the successful snaps of their flesh-ripping teeth as I tore their writhing bodies apart. Because I was desperate to hear their screams. They slaked my own terror at being without Nae.

Like I said, I was a mess, and relied heavily on my brothers to pull me through my days.

I couldn't have asked for better care. In return, I got them more books and maps, and showed them how to navigate the internet so they would have a better understanding of their enemy. We also went on drives, and made several successful attempts at getting Eaen and Armand near people. All the while, I'd managed to answer enough questions correctly on my finals, and to get a passing grade on my thesis. I would graduate.

Hurrah.

The three of us, in our grief-driven lifestyle, bonded to the point where I couldn't tell myself apart from them, even when they were wolves. I was seeing less of myself in the humans around me, which I guess had been inevitable from the get-go.

It had only been two weeks since Nae left us, and it felt like two years.

Yet, I had to get my shit together and do some serious re-wiring of my brain, even though the freakin' thing continued to hum like a beehive. Armand and Eaen were touchingly vigilant whenever it intensified, sticking close until the jolts subsided, and often enough I caught them exchanging worried glances.

Regardless my condition, graduation still loomed, and my folks would be arriving soon. Which meant the house needed cleaning and the blankets had to come down. No more den living while my parents were in town.

I hauled our clothes to the Laundromat, and had company while I went. Armand and Eaen paced the parking lot on their two legs as people came and went with their own baskets of laundry. Their success was a momentous milestone, and flush with our victory we decided they should stick around while my parents stayed for graduation.

We'd just have to be supremely careful. But if they could stay on two legs around strange humans outside, and within the confines of a house with people they knew wouldn't harm them, then they could do it anywhere. Almost. We weren't quite ready to test them in crowded areas, but already they'd made extraordinary progress.

But testing the wolf-men's ability to remain in human form wasn't the only reason we agreed they should stick around when my folks arrived. We had questions. Top of the list being *Who is my real mother?* Because, somewhere along the line, I'd lost that young man who had stumbled his sloppy ass through the north woods. I had to know the truth, God forgive me the pain I would cause my parents who loved me, but I had to know.

So did Eaen and Armand. We owed the truth to Rand, too, who had followed through on his promise to stringhalt Hersey and his trip north. If the Rickeys weren't my original parents, then maybe they knew who my real mother was. Maybe they knew where she was headed after stowing me away in the safety of humans.

In the safety of humans. Man-oh-man, but my thinking had done a one-eighty in the months I'd been with my brothers. Nae's leaving, too, seemed to have fast-forwarded my metamorphosis. No fangs or fur had sprouted yet, but by now, none of us could rule out that it would eventually happen.

For all my wanting it before, the reality of it frightened me almost witless, and the *what-ifs* badgered my thoughts in the dead of night, while Eaen and Armand slept beside me.

For my parents' sake, though, I fought it. I didn't want them to see me changing, for criminy's sake, because I wasn't sure I would be able to control when, or where, or even how it would happen. I didn't need fangs sliding forth as I smiled for the camera at my graduation.

The days passed until I stocked the fridge as the final chore to be done, and then the three of us sat around on the front porch waiting for my folks to arrive.

"How do I look, guys?" I had on clean jeans and a long-sleeved t-shirt to hide the multitude of injuries marring my skin. Eaen and Armand wore shorts to help keep them cool.

"Like a wolf in human clothing," Eaen replied seriously.

"What? No, come on. I look okay, right?"

The two wolf-men exchanged perceptive glances, and then Eaen grabbed my arm to pull me over to the living room window so we could see our reflections in the glass. Armand stepped up to my other side.

And my heart fluttered madly until I took a deep breath.

Eaen was right. It was hard to tell me apart from them.

"You have the forest-born look in your eye, Porcupine."

"Yeah?" Despite my fear, I was proud. I'd earned it.

"Yeah," Eaen mocked, but winked. His smile told me he was proud, too.

"We will *all* have to be careful around your parents, Kenrickey," Armand warned, and after seeing my reflection in the window, I took him seriously. My change couldn't be far off.

"Ah, crap. My mother's going to see right through me."

"They usually do," Eaen laughed, as he clapped my shoulder. "But you will be fine."

We didn't have time to worry about it. My parents' Lincoln pulled into the drive, and all three of us took simultaneous deep breaths. I pressed my fingers to the base of my skull, which was becoming as much of a habit as running my hands through my hair.

As soon as the car crunched to a stop, my parents stepped out into the afternoon sunshine and beamed their welcome. They looked as I'd last seen them; they hadn't changed a bit. I went right over to my mother and gave her a tight hug, lifting her off her feet.

"Put me down, Kenny," she giggled, like a mom happy to see her son. Shit raindrops, I didn't want to hurt her with my questions. I set her down, and she stepped back a few paces. "Now, let me get a good look at you."

I stood up straight and cocked my head like she was a nuisance and I was twelve.

"Heavens to Betsy!"

My mother actually used that phrase when she was shocked.

"Donnie, would you take a look at our Kenny."

I didn't give her any more time to investigate closer, and hugged my father, who had made it around the nose of their Town Car.

We exchanged wholesome, back-slapping father-son hugs. Man, I had great parents, I really did. I hurried to introduce them to Eaen and Armand before my thoughts turned to Nae, who should have been with us.

"Mom, Dad. These are my two br—friends, Eaen and Armand."

"Well, how do you do?" My father said, as he and my Mom stuck out their hands. For a brief instant, both wolf-men froze with uncertainty. Then Eaen, our courageous pack leader, stuck out his long hand to clasp my mother's in his own.

"It is a pleasure to meet you, Kenrickey's Mom and Dad."

I scrunched my eyes shut and clapped my hands to my scalp.

My mother laughed as she turned to me. "Now, isn't that funny, Kenny."

They gave their warm greetings to Armand, who was holding up surprisingly well considering he was our most reticent member of the pack, and I knew it helped tremendously that they didn't stare at his yellow eyes. Except my father held his hand for a nano-second longer than he should have.

Was I paranoid? Probably, but given our circumstances, I found myself on the alert for every clue, any trace my parents suspected something.

Introductions finished, my mother bustled around the car, clucking in her usual way about unpacking and getting settled, and the three of us heaved sighs of relief while we exchanged hopeful smiles. My parents had not recoiled from the wolf-men's unusually shaped hands, nor had they gaped like mesmerized mice at their luminescent teeth. Were they trying not to give themselves away?

Armand and Eaen were doing really great, and I almost howled about the success, but bit my tongue and weighed myself down with luggage instead.

Stay human, Ken. Remember to be human.

Eaen and Armand remained outdoors while I got my parents settled in the house, showed them around, and talked about how my semester at school had gone. In spite of the questions hovering like biting mosquitoes, my heart gladdened to have them meandering around our home, peering closely at things for clues to their son's well-being. They were a joyful reminder of my carefree childhood. My parents were comforts of my past, even though I was no longer the son they'd borne.

I embraced my mother, just because I loved her.

"Ooh, ooh, Kenny," she shushed, but hugged me to her breast and patted my back. "God knows I'm glad to see my little man, too," she sighed. "But you're too thin, you're all bones, for goodness' sake." My mother pulled away and pinched my arm, like she was testing my health based on the thickness of my flesh. Then like a little sparrow she fluttered to the kitchen to fix her fledgling something to eat.

"Now, Martie, leave the boy alone. He looks great, for pity's sake. Like a man ought to." My father, in spite of his bravado, emanated a blush of sadness, as though he knew, too, his little man was gone. He gripped my hand and pulled me to him for another hug.

"I love you, Dad. Thanks."

He held onto my hand as we pulled apart.

"You're fine son?" He lowered his voice and eyed me closely. "Need money? How's the car?"

He'd be a doting old Dad under normal circumstances. *But...*

"Yes, I'm good. Had a rough patch with a girl, but I'm good." I nodded my head and then pulled away. Loving Christ, why did I bring that up? I swallowed around the knot lodged in my throat, trying to loosen it.

"Yeah, well, son." He didn't say anything else. He was a married man who knew what it was to find the right girl. Or he suspected something was up. Christ, I had to shake this suspicion until we could talk.

He went to the kitchen to grab us some cold beers from the fridge, and as he did so he placed his arm across my mother's back and leaned down to kiss her. They smooched quickly, exchanging intimate smiles, and then went about their own business. I would remember that scene always.

"Let's check out the place from the outside, see about that foundation." My dad led us out of the house, and then divvied the beers between the four men.

Okay. This was another test for Armand and Eaen, who didn't drink beer. Hell, they drank nothing but water. I led the charge with a quick swallow for them to emulate, and then proceeded to distract my father with details about the house and the surrounding property. The wolf-men tagged along, feigning interest, and like the quick minded souls they were, asked logical questions and made intelligent points. Who knew they understood plumbing and pitch of ground for drainage?

I was busting with pride for them.

By the time the sun set, *Kenrickey's Mom and Dad*, as Eaen so wolfishly called them, were ready for bed. Their trip had been long and they were tired. Plus, they added boastfully, they had a graduation to attend the next day. I waited for them to go through the nightly rituals of brushing their teeth and so on, and waited for them to settle into the spare bedroom.

I snuck outside as soon as their breathing evened and I knew they slept.

The wolves came out of the bushes when I rounded the corner of the house. As a ruse to skip an agonizing dinner scene, I'd told my parents Eaen and Armand had night jobs I drove them to. We loaded into the Subaru, drove a short ways, and then I let them out. It would've been pushing it too far for the wolf-men to stay while my parents ate, although my roommates' refusal to eat cooked food would have been a great segue to the conversation we needed to have.

"Come into our room when you get back, and don't forget to put your clothes on before you do. Just in case." I didn't need to tell them I was stalling them. Every cell in my body screamed for me to shed my own clothes and join in the hunt, to leave the sleeping humans behind. I took a deep breath to quell the urge.

"Have fun," I added wistfully, and then the black wolf swung his flank around hard enough to body slam me to the ground.

My lungs released an *oof* as my back struck the dirt, but I recoiled within half a breath and lunged for a body tackle with my arms clamped around his chest like a vice. He squirmed and kicked his legs, and then the blonde wolf drove his broad head between us to peel my grip from Eaen, and as I fell backward he plopped his blonde, furry rump on my chest, pinning me to the ground.

"I give," I cried in a hoarse whisper, spreading my arms flat. As soon as he got up, though, I snagged his front leg and tried to flip him. The black wolf didn't waste a second to repeat the maneuver Armand had just executed. I found myself flat on my back again, only this time I bore the weight of two furry asses, complete with bushy tails fluffing under my nose.

My laughter, too long absent, dribbled forth, and my tears fell as my laughter rippled, but the release felt good. Eaen and Armand lifted their rumps and nudged their noses against my prone body.

"Thanks, guys. I needed that."

Armand shuffled backwards, fanning his expressive tail.

"Yeah, I'll be fine now." I sat up and wiped my face. "Thanks again, you two. Now, seriously, go and have some fun. I'll be okay."

I watched until they slid completely out of sight into the shadow of the trees. The yearning to follow still pressed on my guts, but our little wrestling session had released some of the pressure. I lay back against the ground to stare up at the night sky, and let my heart gorge itself on memories of Nae, who was never far from my thoughts.

She would receive her degree the next day, too, and I knew how special that would be for her, what it had cost her. She would have no family to cheer when she walked to the stage, no one to truly appreciate her success. Except for me, and I wouldn't even be able to offer her a congratulatory handshake.

But I had to sever those thoughts with a scalpel, because it did nothing but eat at me like a cancer, and I was finally fitting pieces of myself back into something that would, at least, appear whole. My mate was with another, and if I dwelt on that, I'd ruin our plan for protecting the wolf-people, and completely annihilate the honor in our woman's sacrifice.

I was still outside licking my emotional wounds when the wolves

214

returned, panting, and smelling of fresh blood. I got up onto all fours to greet them, and plucked a feather from Armand's chin. Tails wagged in sweeping arcs and we rubbed our bodies in greeting, then walked to the house and went to bed, where the three of us knotted together in a warm, consoling coil.

* * * *

"Kenny, where's your tie?" My mother fussed at the buttons of my shirt and tugged at the collar, while I pulled the noose out of my back pocket and handed it to her. As soon as she snugged it around my neck I stiffened to fight the reflex to slip out of it.

It was just a tie, not a collar, and I gained a new appreciation for Grane's desperation, who had never had anything around his neck except reprimanding jaws.

My mother pretended her son hadn't lost it for a second. "There," she smoothed the tie along my chest before stepping back to admire her handiwork. "You look wonderful, baby."

I lowered my head so she could smooch my cheek. My father stood behind her and beamed proudly at his boy.

I probably should have been embarrassed by their doting, but I wasn't. I'd grown accustomed to shameless displays of affection to such a degree that to act without forthright honesty had become awkward and unnatural. It had been that candidness which had drawn me irretrievably to the wolf-people. I'd never felt so accepted by anyone in my life, barring my parents, of course. And Naomi.

Well, there she was again, along with a revving up of the constant hum in my skull. *Oh, shit. Not today. Not in front of the folks.* I jabbed my fingers into the spot where my spine joined my head and willed the buzzing to ease off, even as my guts sank with its warning. I was dripping sweat in my dress clothes.

I slipped into the bedroom to tell Eaen and Armand, who had opted to stay out of the way under the pretense of being tired from working all night. Which was true, if we didn't split hairs.

"Kenrickey, how bad is it?" Eaen searched my face as his brown eyes layered.

"Manageable, right now. But if I can't stop it from tingling down my spine, I'm going to scare my folks." Which was exactly what I didn't need. They needed to see me graduate, celebrate over a normal dinner. *Then* we could hit them with the truth. *Gradually.* Hell, if my mother saw me wadded into a helpless ball on campus grounds, she'd freak and call an ambulance. And if my first-ever shift into a wolf happened in front of human witnesses? Yeah, I needed to fight this, just for a few more hours.

"Just keep a sharp eye out while I'm gone okay? Maybe head for the woods?" My chest tightened. Why did I have to pretend my graduation even mattered? My heart was here, with my two brothers, and just maybe we were being warned by Luna that something was brewing other than the annihilation of who I used to be. The buzzing weighed with a ferocity it hadn't shown since Nae left us, and I was reluctant to leave my brothers' sides.

"Of course, Kenrickey." Armand's concern shined in his yellow eyes as he held my arm. I knew I wasn't the only one he worried about just then, which was why I had to leave them.

"I'll keep my eye on Nae, Arms," I promised easily. I would have been staring at her through the entire ceremony anyway. If I could stay upright.

I shuddered and dragged my hand across my scalp as the tingling crept lower along my spine. "You have my phone, right?"

Both brothers nodded as their lithe bodies heated.

"Good. Wish me luck, huh?" I slapped on a brave face and winked.

"Luck," the wolf-men said in unison.

"Right." I stood up, took a deep breath, and stepped out of the bedroom, shutting the door softly behind me.

"Are you ready, Kenny," my mother stood in the living room with her purse hooked over her arm and looking smart in her new dress.

"You look beautiful, Mom, and yes, I'm ready."

"Where's your cap and gown? Donnie, did you remember the camera?" My mother babbled with last-minute haste as we shuffled out the front door.

I tried my damnedest to ignore the sizzling that mushroomed to stuff my head as my father drove us to town, and had to concentrate on what they were saying because the noise in my skull muted other sounds.

216

Shit, shit, shit, this wasn't going to be good. Sweat trickled between my shoulder blades, my body's warning of things about to go down. Like itself, I thought ruefully, and focused on steadying my breathing, because this time I was scared. I was shaking with the force of the vibrations burning down my spine.

"Are you okay back there, son?" My father peered into the rearview mirror.

No, I think I'm turning into a fucking wolf right now. "Ah, yeah. Just a little nervous."

My mother twisted in her seat as far as her seatbelt would allow. I concentrated on her moving lips. "It will all be over too fast, Kenny. You'll look back on this day as one of your best."

Not at this rate. "I know, Mom." If I could just focus, settle myself down, maybe I could at least maintain.

To distract myself, I stared out the window at the passing trees. The forest seemed to creep by as the car rolled forward at what my father considered to be a comfortable speed limit. The guy had no idea how the slow pace tortured me. I cranked the window down and stuck my head out the way Eaen liked to do.

When we finally pulled into the campus parking lot and cruised around to find an open space, I scanned the crowds in search of Nae and The Bear. There were little groups of people everywhere, some obviously family of the graduates, some collections of friends, and some were extra campus security and Machias police officers, enlisted to keep the growing crowd safe and moving along in the proper directions. But there was no sign of the two I was searching for.

I fell out of the car before my father put it in park because the frizzing had coalesced to encompass my entire spine, and its fingers were spreading beyond that to my arms and legs.

I mumbled to my parents that I had to go get my cap and gown, and then strode toward the Science building without waiting to see if my folks heard me. I needed to find a bathroom where I could splash cold water on my face. Hell, I needed to splash cold water over the whole of me. At least the Science building sat near the edge of the woods. If I had to escape at the last minute, I could probably make it to the protective covering of the trees.

Hallelujah for small, out-of-the-way campuses.

As I bee-lined for a bathroom, I kept my eye out for Nae, since she and Jeff would have to claim their graduation garb if they hadn't already. The sun melted itself to my head as I walked, blinding me so I had to squint through the sweat burning my eyes.

Please, Luna, let me function long enough to graduate in front of my folks. Let me pass as human just a little longer.

I raked a shaking palm across my head as the buzzing gained weight with its volume. I scoured the area, but all I could see were students milling in and out, all in various stages of dress. Some were completely regaled in their caps and gowns, while others merely shouldered their robes without zipping them, and some posed for photos. All were carefree and laughing.

I took a couple of wobbly steps toward the building, hoping I might find Naomi inside, because the buzzing was fast consuming my entire body. It wouldn't be long before my body rebelled and curled into itself. And if my parents hadn't gone straight to the gymnasium and followed me for last minute pictures? I forced my concentration away from that looming possibility and struck my arm out like a drunk to steady my teetering body as I willed myself forward.

Aw, fuck, I wasn't good. Forget the bathroom and the ceremony. I needed to get to the woods.

"Ken!"

I rolled my eyes toward the trill of my salvation.

Nae.

She was running toward me, her black graduation gown flowing around her like a magnificent raven. I swayed unsteadily as the world around me muted, as though I was underwater, but instinctively held my arms out for my mate. She slammed right into them, clutching herself to me with a desperation I could share.

"Oh, Nae, sweet Jesus." I cupped her head in my palms, pressed my face to her cheek, and sucked in the glorious scent of her. She indulged me for a few seconds, then pulled back to look at me.

"Holy shit, Ken. You've got to get out of here."

"Yeah." But I started looking around for The Bear instead of an escape route. "Where's The—"

"That's why I came running when I finally saw you. He's gone. He said he had to get his tie out of the car while we were standing around talking to some friends. God, Ken, I'm so sorry. I could see the car from where I was, I didn't think he'd pull something *right now*. He drove off, Ken. He drove off."

I crammed her to me again, as much to calm her as to feel her weight in my arms like ballast. "It's okay, Nae. I'll find my folks and get their car. Did you think to call my cell?"

Her scent wafted as she nodded yes, and I couldn't resist breathing it in, even as my skin started to itch. "Good. Did Eaen answer?"

"No. No one did. We've got to get home."

Home. Was there a sweeter word in any language? I gloried in its utterance, but then my guts rebelled.

"Aw, shit." I drew away from Nae to crouch on the ground, my fist balled into my abdomen, my body flaring like a struck match. "Have you seen Rand? Christ, is he here, Nae? You've got to find him."

I couldn't look at her. Hell, I could barely focus on the ground in front of me. Then a polished pair of leather dress shoes entered my line of vision.

"Kenny?"

"Dad?" I peered up at the man I'd called father my whole life. He was obscured in shadow, the bright sun glaring behind him. He crouched into view. "Kenny, your mom's bringing the car around to get us." He reached to help me up, but I faltered away, sticking my arm up to halt him.

"God, no, Dad. Nae?" *Get him out of here.* "I'm all right. I just—" I staggered upright, my muscles singing as I struggled against their will.

"Ken?"

This was turning into a goddamned intervention, because there was no way Naomi had found him that fast. "Rand?" But, shit, I sure was glad to see him. I smiled, but wasn't sure if that's what he saw, or not.

"Oh, man." I couldn't miss the worry. But I didn't smell fear, like maybe he wasn't that anxious, or he was masking it.

"Not me," I sputtered with a tongue that wasn't cooperating. Thank God for Nae, who once again came to my rescue. Too much was happening at once, and I wasn't in any shape to keep it straight. Hell, I was one of the things happening to confuse things. But we hadn't told Rand about The Bear. We'd put him on Hersey's trail while we dealt with the jealous ex-boyfriend. The wolf-man didn't have a clue about the danger Eaen and Armand were in right now.

"It's Eaen and Armand." She was brilliant, a magnificent empath, a mind-reader. Along with the burning churn of my guts, I felt the twinges of pride that she was my mate, that she was right here with me, standing knee-deep and brave in this mess.

My dad interrupted her explanation. "Your mother's pulled the car up, Kenny. And I don't know what's going on, but I'm getting you out of here."

"Mr. Rickey." Rand's authoritative growl wasn't to be brooked, no matter what the species. My father halted, and turned to face the man who was interfering with his helping his son. He actually braced up to Rand.

"I don't know who you are, mister. But my boy is sick and I've got to get him out of here." His cool hands clasped my shoulders.

"He's not sick," Rand challenged. He and my father faced off, each of them daring the other to tell the truth. It was Rand who caved, but his gray eyes were sharp. He was in hunting mode, and my father had become his prey in this game of words. "He's turning into wolf."

I glanced at my dad to see if he thought Rand was bluffing, or downright insane. But he nodded, his lips pursed tight in determined bewilderment. He wasn't denying what Rand admitted. If my body wasn't currently writhing under my skin, I might have appreciated the situation. There was a lot at stake here.

But my brothers' lives were at stake, too, and I didn't give a shit about my turning into a wild animal while they were in danger. I had to get to them, had to help them with The Bear.

"Christ," *I think I just growled.* "If mom knows too, let's get the fuck out of here." Well, that's what I thought I said, but my ears and everyone else's heard something a lot more garbled. I figured this because Rand got wicked tense as he took my arm.

"Get him in the car."

Nae and my dad jumped into action, and I tried my hardest to keep my legs from coiling under me, I really did. My dad and Rand slid me across the back seat, and I pressed my burning face to the cool leather. Then Nae's scent blotted everything out as she squished in next to me, with Rand on the other side. My father jumped in front.

"Drive, Martie. It's happening." He didn't need to elaborate. Their years together must have allowed them to communicate in code, because my mother laid rubber leaving the parking lot. She'd never been one to drive conservatively like my father did. We'd always joked she'd been a race car driver in another life.

So. My parents knew; had kept their secrets. I'd have to deal with that later, because my head suddenly exploded and everything happened fast. A strange yowling filled the car as my spine curled, pushing my limbs to my core as I threw my face back to gulp air.

I flailed. Couldn't fit on the back seat. And felt Rand steadying me, pushing me back up off the carpeted floor. The roof of the car with its trendy dome light circled in my line of vision as my torso twisted backward. I pushed my paws *oh fuck* into the seat in front of me.

My heart, already ramming itself against my collapsing ribcage, fluttered madly. I tried to say *paws,* but I whined instead, my lips drawn too tight around the creeping forth of one hellacious mouthful of teeth.

"You're doing great, Ken."

I rolled my eyes toward Nae, whose reassuring tone stroked like butter across my frantic heart, and the sight of her, the wondrous vision of my mate in my wolf's eyes, stilled me like I'd just been submerged in a warm bath, the weight of the water against my body pressing with soothing force. That's what it was to behold my Nae, who crunched herself against the door to give me room to shift.

She was crying, but her tears shimmered like prisms on her flushed cheeks. And her blonde hair had turned to golden tresses framing her radiant face. Hell, the whole of her glowed radiant, her scent as crisp as if I stood up to my belly in a heavy snowstorm.

I tried to kiss her. But instead of my arm reaching up to cup her chin, a hairy leg with a paw swiped up toward her face, just as my tongue slipped out from behind my long, sharp teeth to lick her.

Holy fuck! I shrank back, then had to push my butt in the air because my backsides fetched up on Rand and twisted my tail so it hurt. *My goddamned tail, for criminy's sake.*

"Easy, Ken, okay? You hear me? Go easy, and turn your head to look at me." *Look at me.* His silent command cut through my panic, slicing itself straight into my brain so I heeded it instinctively, obeyed it far quicker than his spoken words.

"Good." He leveled his gray eyes on my face, held my gaze with his own so I concentrated on staring him down. "That's good, Ken." *Yawn.*

What?

Yawn. He feigned his own inhalation so I'd follow suit, like the things were truly contagious.

I spread my jaws, felt the muscles in my face contract and stretch. Immediately, my heart simmered down, steadying itself into a temperate pace, and my head cleared so I could think straight, not simply react to what was happening to me.

"Yawn again," he commanded.

I did his bidding without second guessing. The guy was talking me through the most extraordinary and terrifying thing that had ever happened to me. Given the moment, I focused on him like he was a god.

Rand's gray eyes softened and his lips hinted at the trace of a smile. "You're taking it better than most, Ken. You're coming through like a champ."

A champ. I felt eight years old again, hanging on the praise of my dad, and the idea of it struck me as funny. Movement behind me snagged my attention from Rand. I twirled to face it, but it slid from view, only to reappear again behind me.

Rand's laughter rippled across my fur like a living thing. "It's your tail, Ken. You're chasing your tail."

No shit. Not five minutes as a noble wolf and I was chasing my goddamned tail. How's that for dropping me back to earth. But it was funny, and happiness built up inside me to the point I thought I'd burst. The car suddenly shrunk, closing me in too tight for the energy whipping through my muscles, zipping my blood through my veins, under my skin. I had to run. Holy mother, I needed to run.

I pushed my muzzle along the back window, tried leaping out of it, my claws digging into the leather, rupturing it. The scenery bobbed and slashed by.

Then it hit me. The car was speeding down the road, my mother driving so fast the Lincoln floated as we crested hills. She meant business in getting me home. Back to Eaen and Armand, who hadn't been given the heads up The Bear was on his way to kill them.

I almost hopped into the front seat to hurry things up, but as soon as I noticed how focused on the road both of my parents were, I decided to remain behind them. My mom flicked her eyes up to the rearview. "Heavens to Betsy," she murmured. The fear shining in her blue eyes physically hurt my heart.

"Keep your eyes on the road, Martie." My dad kept staring straight ahead, but he knew what distracted her without even looking. After so many years together, I figured they could guess a lot of things about each other. My mom turned her focus back to the ribbon of tar the car was swallowing, and didn't look back again.

Frustrated, I licked at Nae's beautiful face, trying to communicate my anxiety about reaching my brothers in time. She wrapped her arms around my neck and buried her face into my ruff. Her breath felt warm and steam trapped in my fur.

One second my heart was breaking for my mother, and the next it was soaring, pounding so hard I could feel it hammering against my ribs. My Naomi was back with me. With us. I wanted to hug her back, run my hands along her body to feel her again, to touch how real she was.

It didn't take long to learn being a wolf had its down sides. Not only could I not hold the woman I loved, but I couldn't talk to her, either. How could I ask her about Jeff, how could I get any information about what we were speeding toward?

Rand.

"Yeah?"

Jesus Christ, he heard that? I whined. I couldn't freaking help it. Here I'd been getting frustrated when the answer was sitting right next to me.

Ask.

"Ask?"

My tongue involuntarily ran a course around my lips, across my nose. My nose. My tongue was so long it could run across my nose. I shook my head, felt my ears wobble. Dear God, this was going to take some getting used to.

Naomi.

Rand's eyebrows furrowed together. "Ask Naomi?"

My tail wagged. Yes. Ask Nae about Armand and Eaen. But I forgot to concentrate, made my sentence too long for the intention to transmit, so he didn't get the last part.

I tried again, piercing my eyes on his.

"Eaen and Armand. You want me to ask Naomi about Eaen and Armand?"

Yes! Holy Christ, it was like playing charades with chimpanzees. But Rand didn't get the chance to ask Nae anything because we were barreling down on the turn to our driveway. My mother hit the brakes hard and slewed the car in so it skidded sideways.

"Mother of pearls, woman." It was as close to swearing as I'd ever heard from my father's lips. He was rattled, understandably.

The Bear's car was nowhere to be seen, but Nae was out of the Lincoln before my mother could jam the car in park. I leapt out behind her, and almost drove my face into the dirt. I'd overshot my hind end so the front end of me had to scramble to catch up. I was Bambi on the frozen pond. Real menacing.

Yet, I didn't care. I just quit thinking and started acting, isolating the scents bombarding my sinuses as I galloped toward the house in search of Eaen and Armand. I was on the front porch within a few long bounds, exhilarated by the power in my new body.

And stood facing a closed door. *Damn.* No thumbs. The exhilaration took a nosedive. I smelled Nae before I felt her thighs against my butt. She leaned past me to open the front door.

"Find them, Ken. Please, God, find them." She was seriously frightened. What the hell had she been dealing with since going back to Jeff, anyway? She'd texted once to say she couldn't find the boots, but otherwise we'd heard nothing. I hadn't dared contact her, either. I didn't want her to get into trouble.

I pushed my body against her and whined, and she never hesitated to curl her cold fingers into the fur at my shoulders so I could pull her along with me as we entered the house. The scent of our brothers hung everywhere, but nothing fresh drifted around. They weren't there.

Neither was The Bear, so where the hell was everybody?

Chapter Twelve

I spun around and bolted back out into the yard, amazed that my wolf's body was so lightning quick and agile. A guy could definitely get used to this. Yet, I couldn't take the time out to fully savor the potential. I had to find Eaen and Armand, make sure they were all right, that they weren't dead because of Jeff.

I lowered my muzzle to the ground and copied what I'd seen the other wolves do a thousand times. I canvassed the yard, trotted in sweeping circles until I could find the freshest scents. What I wound up with stopped me dead, my heart jacking into my throat and boxing at my insides like Mohammed Ali, right along with the stinging and the butterflies dancing.

The Bear had been here.

I quit looking for my brothers to follow the human scent. It wasn't hard. He left a trail so obvious I probably could have found it without being a wolf. If he wasn't so freakin' dangerous, he'd be a blasted moron. He'd circled the house again, peering in the windows before returning to the ridge where he'd lay in waiting that first time.

So, where the hell were Armand and Eaen if The Bear hadn't gotten them? I backtracked, slowed my pace so I could concentrate, started back at the beginning from the front door.

Sure enough, a stronger scent trail curled a path around the corner of the house to the back, and led along the path we liked to use to the river. I circled the gnarled, wind-tilted witch-wood berry tree where we sometimes laid our clothes out before we hunted. Their scent clung heaviest here, as if they'd spent a considerable amount of time in this spot. They'd even gone so far as to rub themselves all over the trunk of the tree and the ground at its base.

But Jeff's scent lingered here, too. A little sniffing of the wind, and I could tell he'd traveled down from the ridge. But there were no signs of an attack. No blood, no scraped ground. I kept snuffling as I studied the ground, and then I found why Eaen and Armand had marked this spot. They'd left a note.

And The Bear must have been watching from his vantage point on the ridge.

The scroll of paper was wedged into one of the crevices where the roots of the tree had pulled loose from the earth. Armand, the martial strategist, had left me a note, and Jeff's heavy scent told me he'd most likely read it after my brothers stashed it and left the area. Automatically I reached for it, as if I had a hand, for shit's sake, but all I managed to do was flatten it with my paw and drive it deeper into the cleft.

Shit, crap, fuck. When this was over, I was going to quit swearing.

I bolted back to the house to get Nae, and almost ran her down. She'd seen where I'd gone and followed. Not smart. If Jeff had been around? Forget it. He wasn't, and she was here to help. I shoved my fear back down by rubbing my face against her thigh, surrounding myself with her goodness, let my tail swish as my body responded reflexively to the closeness of my mate.

Of course, she read my anxiety, was still anxious herself. "Ken, I love you, too, but what is it? Did you find Eaen and Armand?"

I nudged her with my head to push her toward the tree, then trotted out past her so she'd follow me. Within seconds she had the note in her hands, unrolling it. She read it aloud.

"Porcupine." She paused to grin at me, her hazel eyes dancing for a brief second. "That's cute."

Yeah, yeah. Just hurry up and read it.

She cleared her throat.

"Eaen and I worried for our brother. You did not seem all right to us, and we fear your change is too near. This is not a time for you to be alone. We have gone to your school to watch out for you—"

I didn't wait to hear more.

"Ken, wait!"

I didn't. I couldn't. I had to shift back to human to drive to campus. I didn't have time to play twenty questions with Rand so I could beg a ride.

But how to reclaim my human form, for God's sake? Sure, the wolf-people made it look easy, but they'd been born to it. What was I supposed to do to trigger the reverse in body chemistry?

I bee-lined it for Rand, who had remained outside by the car with my parents while I'd been searching. My parents were huddled together, looking down at him squatting on his knees in front of them, much as he had sat when he'd made himself submissive to our pack. He had things to say, to ask, and didn't need a confrontation to louse things up.

But whatever he and my parents were talking about could wait. I needed his help now. I galloped up to them, my legs demolishing the distance with breathtaking speed, and careened to a claw scrabbling halt before I bowled the other wolf-man over.

Rand, change.

He teetered sideways, caught himself, but readjusted to his hands and knees, obviously comfortable with it in spite of the incongruity of two people standing upright beside him.

"Change?" He looked over his shoulder at my parents.

Me. Change.

Dawning really does have an expression. So does relief. I don't think he wanted to shift right in front of my folks. "All right, Ken." Rand sat back on his heels, rubbed his hands down the tops of his thighs. "Sit down and yawn. Take some deep breaths and let them out slow." He looked back over his shoulder again at my parents.

"Maybe you shouldn't watch—"

"No. He's our son." My mother was crying, but her blue eyes were hard and shiny, her jaw tight. "Go on. Whatever you're doing." My dad hugged her closer as he nodded.

"All right, then." Rand turned back to where I'd sat down. I was nervous as hell, but willing to wait a few seconds while he was intent on being nice to my parents. He leaned toward me to sniff the air. "You're wound up, but I think we can do this."

Nae came running up behind me, puffing like a steam engine. "To hell with that, we don't have time. Do it in the car. We've got to get back to campus."

* * * *

None of us questioned her. We arrived back at the graduation ceremony just as fast as we'd left it, but at least this time there wasn't an atmosphere of chaos in the car because of yours truly. Sure, I regained my human form, all naked and dripping sweat, in front of my mother. But she kept the car from shredding a new road into the woods. I never knew she had so much mettle.

The first thing I did when I had my arms back was clutch Nae to me, and smother her snowy smelling neck and face with kisses. She'd been so fucking amazing through all of this, and she clung right back despite how slick with sweat I was.

I cherished our reunion, could have formed my naked self to her curves all day, but there were things to say. Namely, I had to tell the other wolf-man what the hell was going on with our pack and The Bear. Right in front of my folks, like they hadn't already been dished out enough to deal with.

"You should have told me this before," Rand cursed, his gray eyes layering. "If he harms Gor's—" he clamped his jaw shut and stared out at the scenery whizzing by, his shoulders bunching with his fury. Even though I radiated enough heat to boil spaghetti, I felt his.

"Just find them, all right, while I go after The Bear." Effing right, I'd deal with him. I was going to kill the bastard, so Rand could just lose the anger. Besides, his getting all righteous didn't do squat for my control. My skull wasn't buzzing, but my spine had caught fire.

Rand dropped his gaze and pushed his shoulders down, as if he sensed how close I was to losing it. He probably did. It wasn't like I was a pro at handling my shifting yet.

But there wasn't more time to plan any kind of strategy. My mother bounced the Lincoln onto campus property, and Nae, Rand, and I leapt out of the back before the car came to a full stop.

Rand, speedy even in his human form, snagged my arm and twirled me to a standstill. "Ken, there are human witnesses." His gold-flecked gray eyes roved the length of me before he quirked one eyebrow to drive home his point. "You're naked."

Oh, yeah. I had so much on my mind I didn't even think about clothes. My father rummaged in the back seat for the pants I'd sloughed off during my change into wolf.

"Here, son. Be careful."

"Thanks, Dad." I hugged him. Through everything that had been happening in the last hour or so, he'd said nothing. Hadn't wigged out, didn't go postal at the sight of my naked body covered in scarring puncture wounds and contusions. Nor did he shun me. Jesus, I was one lucky son of a bitch.

His eyes filled with unshed tears. "Find your friends. We'll wait here for you."

I nodded so I wouldn't have to speak past the knot squeezing my throat, then tore off across the parking lot once I had my pants hauled up over my hips.

The campus, aside from a shit-ton of cars, was fairly devoid of people. Most everyone was still inside the gymnasium for the ceremony, so I was able to run headlong toward the eastern side of the property where I figured Jeff would have arrived. I sprinted past some parked police cars. A knot of campus security and cops were hanging out waiting for the throng of people to emerge so they could get back to work. I raced by without looking sideways at them. Maybe they'd think I was late for graduation.

I found The Bear's black Jetta haphazardly parked in a towing zone, like he hadn't bothered cruising the parking lots for an empty slot. He'd been in too much of a hurry was my guess. One peek in the windows and I knew he wasn't inside.

Where the Christ did he go?

I scanned what I could see of the campus, and cringed. The ceremony had just ended because a rushing queue of graduates snaked outside to cheer and greet their loved ones, who were following on their triumphant heels. The whole area ballooned with celebrants as more and more people spilled out of the gymnasium, their numbers running over the pavement onto the grass as still more people, like a swollen river, gushed forth from the building.

How was I going to find The Bear in that crowd?

My spine churned a slow, rising heat, radiating glowing embers to all four limbs. I was getting too emotional. I had to calm down, and started gulping breaths like a fish flopped from his bowl. But I kept scanning the crowds for Jeff. Every oversized person became him, and my eyes darted from one possible candidate to the next in a maddening, life-threatening version of Where's Waldo.

Where the hell would he be?

Then it hit me, just as I felt the quivering in my guts, then in my muscles, which trembled like hot, slick eels beneath my skin as the wolf inside me burned to release itself.

In a jolt of insight the details of Luna's image flashed across my brain. He would be hunting. And never mind if I turned wolf I would be fulfilling Nae's prediction that I was The Bear's third victim.

Except.

I would be turning into wolf in front of human witnesses, razing to ashes the very secret the wolf-people had spent centuries, and their lives, to safeguard. I would expose my loved ones, becoming the one true enemy of those I'd sworn on my own life to protect.

I had to calm down. Now.

Easier said, but doable.

I crouched and clutched my hands to my skull, willing the air into my lungs, trying my damnedest to envision the oxygen passing through my heated blood to cool it.

Out of the corner of my eye, I caught Nae running toward me, her graduation gown balled up in her arms as if she intended to shield me with it. Had she sensed, from so far away, how close I was to losing it?

Then I saw him, bearing down like the violent brute he was. My eyes riveted on the charging bulk, and I watched with hatred boiling as he caught up to Nae, and flicked her away like a bothersome pest. She fell hard to the concrete, but then abruptly swiveled her head toward the Quad. My gaze automatically synced with the path of hers, and my heart exploded in the confines of my ribcage.

Jesus living fuck, they're exposing themselves.

Eaen and Armand ran toward us, their muscles flexing powerfully against their sweat slicked skin, their nudity a potent contrast to the sea of people they were bulleting through. They were fantastically glorious in their strength of speed, and I stared in awe until they split as I'd seen them do countless times. Armand cut a broad arc to the right, and Eaen swept fluidly to the left.

They were hunting, too. To protect their pack.

The Bear! I heard my brothers' championed cry.

I jumped to my feet and shucked my pants. This was it. This was what we'd prepared for during our lethal forays for predatory coyotes, and it was now time to use our honed skills against the ursine human. I stepped in line to close the center of our pack's hunting circle.

* * * *

We chose to ignore the fact he lugged a shotgun in his beefy fists. We also overlooked his attire, right down to those damned boots of his. We simply concentrated on hemming him in, closing our snare to slow his charge toward me.

The closer he got the better the details of his features came into view, and the more maniacal he appeared. The guy was flipping insane, had lost more than one sandwich from his picnic basket. He hadn't just come off his rocker, he'd catapulted from it. What the fuck had our Nae been living with, for the love of Pete?

And now this mad rhinoceros was charging toward me, his gun riding his hip and aiming forward as his thick thighs pumped his bulk straight at me.

Bring it the fuck on. Because if he'd hurt even one strand of hair on our Naomi's head, I wanted him to feel all the pain of her boys ripping him apart with our bare hands.

Naomi screamed, and for a brief moment I turned my attention on her, saw the horror on her face as the very scenario she'd worked so hard to avoid unfolded before her. I wanted to reassure her, to tell her we weren't wolves, that we'd keep our human forms for this battle.

But The Bear was getting close, and the crowd dispersed in a screaming cloud, cleaving him a clear pathway and giving us plenty of room to maneuver him to where we wanted the lethal bastard.

His pace slowed as we closed in, herding him expertly toward the brick façade of the Science building, Armand nearing The Bear's right, Eaen to his left, and me in the center drawing the noose tight.

But Jeff didn't look cowed. He was enraged, and roared insults and

S. C. Dane

swatted his large arms as we drew closer, seeming to forget that the club he threatened us with could spit fire to kill us. But the guy wasn't thinking. There was no cold intelligence in his round eyes.

We corralled him, patiently pestering. Whenever Eaen leapt back from a feint, Armand or I dove in, ruthlessly tiring him as he swiped madly, while we three conserved our energy.

His lunges outward grew heavy, sloppy, until fear crept in to shadow the shine of mania in his eyes. Now he flinched when Armand, his fangs dropped menacingly in his human mouth, plunged closer, taunting him. The Bear grew unnerved, and ripe for the kill.

Yet, before Eaen leapt for the first crucial grab, I mentally checked him.

No.

Eaen halted as if I'd yanked an invisible chain, and he stabbed a retaliatory promise from his brown eyes toward me, his subordinate.

I softened my demeanor instinctively. "No, Brother. We'll have to hold him here. The cops are coming."

As if my words doomed his future and shot clarity into his skull, The Bear remembered he held a weapon, and he swung it round, aiming it straight for Eaen, who had been the one to charge first. I lunged sideways to knock my brother from the line of fire as Armand steamrolled like fury personified toward Jeff.

For as long as I live I will never erase the terror of hearing Nae shriek like a mother whose womb gushed blood. Nor will I ever expunge the image seared into my brain of her springing, seemingly from nowhere, onto the behemoth in front of us, just as The Bear pulled the trigger.

* * * *

My body spasmed when the blast rang out, and Eaen and I landed on the concrete in a bone-crushing heap. It took me a second to scan our bodies for the bullet wound, and as that second unfolded my heart flat-lined in my chest. I twisted myself around the stillness within to behold the cause of its death.

Naomi lay sprawled, face down on the Quad, and before I could manage my legs, shots rang out again and The Bear flipped spastically

232

like an upright fish before his bullet-riddled body slumped to the cement beneath him. He lay dead mere feet from our Nae.

The roar that escaped my lungs lifted me bodily toward my mate, who lay still upon the ground. Armand reached her first, hovered over her protectively, his bulging muscles shivering and his fangs unsheathed. I ran forward as if encased in glue.

No!

My blonde brother looked up as he straddled on his hands and knees over Nae's limp body. He wasn't going to let anyone near her even as he shifted to reveal himself to the human world.

"Brother, no!" Eaen flung his body across the distance, and the two of us fell on our pack-mates, smothering them both.

Nae groaned, the sound of it pinning our attention to the woman under us.

Jesus fucking Christ she's alive.

"Help us! Somebody fucking help her!" I screamed at the crowd hovering uselessly, yet saw nothing but my mate, the blood blooming outward from beneath her.

"Get out of here," Nae breathed. "Get out of here." She whispered, yet she strained as if she yelled her command, and her body lurched with the effort.

We'd been so focused on our dimming sun we had forgotten we had bodies, that it wasn't just Armand who was dangerously close to unfolding into wolf.

Jesus, she was right.

I flicked my eyes to the two faces that were mere inches from my own, spied their dropped fangs, Eaen's layered irises.

Get out of here.

"Run," I pleaded breathlessly, my tears flowing unchecked. "Run!"

My brothers faltered, torn between their hearts laying at their feet, and their loved ones up north who trusted we would keep them safe. Armand's face contorted into a tortured grimace as his yellow eyes sucked in the sight of Naomi lying in her pooling blood.

"Please, for the love of Luna!" I screamed, even as my own fangs slid forth. "RUN!"

They flinched like I'd burned them. And with a final, longing look they bolted, but not before Eaen clasped my wrist as hard as any handcuffs would have and dragged me behind him.

I ran even though my heart sat dead in my chest. But Eaen had been right to grab me, to haul my ass out of there. My body had started shifting right along with theirs. And I was the novice; I wouldn't have been able to abort the change and would have exposed them all. Already as we ran, I felt my muscles swimming along my bones, and we barely eluded the swarm of cops and security guards who descended into the chaos.

When I stole one last look back for Nae, she was being swarmed by paramedics, who were like ants building a nest as they scurried and scuttled purposefully. They ripped her clothes, jabbed at her delicate body, and plugged her with hoses. All in the struggle to save a life within a body that lay horribly still.

My mate's body. That drooped like the buck on the bank of the river.

I stumbled onto my contorting knees as we reached the safety of the woods, threw my face to the afternoon sky, and howled the grief as my human body lost itself to the wolf.

* * * *

We ran as wolves toward home, but didn't dare go into the house. The police would probably arrive to haul me in for questioning, and we couldn't risk my capture, not when I had so little control over the wolf that had finally emerged from within me.

So the interrogations, the shrapnel from The Bear's twisted obsession, would have to be dealt with by my folks, Rand, and Naomi, if she survived.

Holy living fuck. My Naomi. I lay with my belly to the ground, my body shivering under its thick fur, as a future without Nae loomed terrifyingly real. I pictured her body withstanding the attack of those intent on saving her, my heart physically wringing so hard it hurt. Then puked on the grass between my paws.

"Porcupine, we are sorry." Eaen, his body hot like an electric blanket on high, draped himself across my back, buried his tear streaked face into my ruff. Armand coiled himself around us, knotting us together as I pushed myself against my brothers, grateful for the weight of their sorrowful bodies, which helped to moor me, to keep me from running, running, running away from the grief.

Sometime later, when the spring moon grew stronger with the setting of the sun, my parents' Lincoln pulled down the drive with the front of Rand's SUV glowing red from its taillights. The immediate mess in the human world had been organized, and Eaen, Armand, and I emerged from the woods when we were given the signal all was clear.

Rand didn't wait for our question, he knew just by looking at us where our concerns lay. "She's going to live."

My breath exploded from my lungs in a relieved sob, and I fell to my knees right there in the driveway. Eaen and Armand went celebratory, howling and hopping around us, clapping their warm palms to my bare shoulders. I grinned. Like a goddamned redeemed fool, I grinned and cried.

Even Rand reluctantly smiled. "Yeah, the bullet missed her vital organs. They'll keep her at the hospital for a few days, but she should make a full recovery."

I got off my knees to hug the wolf-man who had stayed to clean up our mess, and hugged him so exuberantly I lifted him off the ground. "Thank you, Rand."

"Hey, kid, take it easy. It was no big deal," he gruffed. But I knew it had been, that his job had expanded way beyond the mere following up on the possibility of a cached wolf-man. Our pack had heaped a shit-load on his shoulders, yet he'd never flinched. No matter that he didn't look like a true descendent of Gor, his heart was just as pure.

"We've got a safe house in Vermont I'm taking the four of you to, and you can hang out there until everything's cleared up. We'll go as soon as they release Naomi from the hospital."

"Rand—"

He held his hand up. "Forget it. This is standard procedure when we bring in a new wolf." Never mind that he wasn't just bringing in a new wolf. He was offering shelter to a small pack, and giving us a future dedicated to helping the wolf-people to boot.

"You guys must really be desperate for new recruits," I kidded him.

"You haven't seen the mess you're getting into. Don't thank me yet." But he smirked, his gray wolf eyes shining with mischief. He lowered his guard with his teasing, allowing us to see a side of him we hadn't known. I took it as a sign of trust, in spite of what had happened earlier that day.

"My family would be honored to know a wolf such as yourself, Rand." Eaen's compliment flustered the older wolf-man, and Rand pursed his lips and nodded his head as he lowered his gaze toward the ground.

"Yeah, well, speaking of families. I've talked a bit with your parents, Ken. They're shaken, understandably, but they've agreed to tell us what they knew of the young woman who gave birth to you."

"My real mother? They knew her?"

"She stayed with them for a while until she was sure they were going to take good care of you."

Which they had. I couldn't have asked for better. And I'd repaid their unconditional love with this mess. I left Rand, Eaen, and Armand, and went to hug my folks.

As they had done my entire life, they opened their arms to me. My mother seemed so small, fragile, as if she thought my knowing she wasn't my real mother reduced her in my eyes somehow.

"Mom—" I started crying again, like I was their little boy. Yet, I wasn't the least ashamed of my tears for them, nor were they. My father wept openly, then took a deep breath to pull us up by our proverbial bootstraps.

"Kenny, son. Your mother and I, we wanted to tell you, but we'd hoped. And as the years went by, you were just a regular kid. We'd thought…well…" My Dad's cheeks flushed. "We didn't think you were like your real mother."

I didn't push him to say what I was; that the son they'd raised wasn't a boy at all, but a wolf. It was enough they still loved me. Hell, it was enough they were still standing upright and not keeling over with shock. They'd been through a lot in the last twelve hours, and they were holding up pretty well.

"Don't you worry about your things, Kenny. We'll take care of it." My mother cupped my cheek in her palm, as she looked up at me, her blue eyes watery but shining with pride. "So, when you're ready, you come home to get what you need."

She almost had me blubbering anew. "Thanks, Mom. I'd appreciate that." God, I owed them so much.

"I guess you weren't kidding when you said you had girl troubles," my father joked, lightening the mood so we could laugh, which did wonders for scattering the clouds threatening to gather. Instead of righteous anger and darkness, they stood fortified with love for their son, as they'd always done.

My brothers and Rand came over to join us then, spurring us to action. We'd be spending the next few nights in the forest while my folks cleaned up here and moved my things. Rand would be heading back to set things up for our induction into his world.

We parted our respective ways after more tears were shed with my folks. They'd come to see their son graduate, so I guess in a way they had. Although, I'm pretty positive they hadn't thought the future unfolding for their son was going to turn out the way it had.

Me? I couldn't have been happier, aside from Nae's close brush with death. I could have done without that. Yet, she would live to see us reunited, to see her boys, as she liked to call us. Our Nae had survived The Bear attack and would come home to us, to her pack.

I glanced back once as Armand, Eaen, and I wended our way down the path toward the river, and saw my folks standing at the corner of the house arm in arm, watching their only son begin his life anew.

With his four paws planted firmly to the earth, and his heart bound tight to those he loved, and those who loved him back.

Oh, and my fur didn't stick up haphazardly.

I guess I wasn't a real porcupine, after all.

The End?

About the Author

S.C. Dane lives anywhere in the United States that her wandering feet take her. A student of Life, she learns from the seemingly impossible, the improbable, and the bizarre, as well as the commonplace. She has yet to be disappointed.

www. pararnormalromancebyscdane.com

Other works by the author with Melange Books

Luna, Book 1 of the Luna Chronicles
Grane, Book 2 of the Luna Chronicles

www.ingramcontent.com/pod-product-compliance
Lightning Source LLC
Chambersburg PA
CBHW050511260626
47157CB00004B/1281